PRAISE FOR T
Ma̶ᴄ̶ᴀ̶ʟ̶ɪ̶s̶ᴛ̶ᴇ̶ʀ̶

Memoirs of a Dragon Hunter
"Bursting with the author's trademark zany humor and spicy romance...
this quick tale will delight paranormal romance fans."
—*Publishers Weekly*

Sparks Fly
"Balanced by a well-organized plot and MacAlister's trademark humor."
—*Publishers Weekly*

It's All Greek to Me
"A fun and sexy read."
—The Season for Romance
"A wonderful lighthearted romantic romp as a kick-butt American Amazon
and a hunky Greek find love. Filled with humor, fans will laugh with the
zaniness of Harry meets Yacky."
—*Midwest Book Review*

Much Ado About Vampires
"A humorous take on the dark and demonic."
—*USA Today*

"Once again this author has done a wonderful job. I was sucked into the
world of Dark Ones right from the start and was taken on a fantastic ride.
This book is full of witty dialogue and great romance, making it one that
should not be missed."
—Fresh Fiction

Also by Katie MacAlister

Fireborn
Starborn
Shadowborn

Shadowborn

A Born Prophecy

Katie MacAlister

REBEL BASE BOOKS
Kensington Publishing Corp.
www.kensingtonbooks.com

First Electronic Edition: June 2020
ISBN-13: 978-1-63573-077-7 (ebook)
ISBN-10: 1-63573-077-5 (ebook)

First Print Edition: June 2020
ISBN-13: 978-1-63573-078-4
ISBN-10: 1-63573-078-3

Printed in the United States of America

Chapter 1

"Now, that's what I like to see." Thorn smiled with mingled satisfaction and goodwill at the sight of the embracing couple before him. "I'm glad to know that you and the priest haven't been so grief-stricken over my loss that you parted ways. Did you miss me while I was in the spirit world? I have no doubt you've had endless trouble without me here to help, but there was little I could do about that. Oooh, is that land I see through the porthole?"

Despite the fact that he was unheard and incorporeal in his spirit form, he moved over to gaze out of the open window. "Hmm. Judging by the scrubby trees along the shoreline, I'd say that was Genora. Which means you've sailed all the way from Eris back home. Good work, lad. And I see by the carving next to the porthole that you've been hard at work making me a new physical form. That's not a swallow, though. Tail's all wrong, and the whole thing is bigger than my old form. I can't see the front of it, but you should consult a book of birds if you want to make a proper swallow for me. Er...lad? Should you be touching Allegria like that? In front of me, that is?"

It was at that point Thorn remembered that although Hallow was a talented arcanist, he hadn't yet perfected the art of talking to those who resided in the spirit world. Opting for discretion, Thorn took himself out of the small cabin...but not before getting rather too much an eyeful of the lad's hindquarters when he stooped to remove his boots.

The tang of salt air slapped Thorn full in the face as he emerged from the cabin—or it would have if there had been a physical face to slap. "Regardless," he said aloud, looking around him with pleasure—for he was a sociable being who counted conversation with his fellow kind as a treat—"it is a sensation nonetheless. Ah, this *is* Genora! Excellent! Now we shall see some action. My arcanists shall rise up and smite those who need smiting, and then Hallow and I will settle back to running Kelos the way it should be run. Greetings, Quinn. Who's that you're kissing? Ouch. That slap looked like it hurt."

Thorn watched with interest as a red-headed young woman, her dark eyes alight with indignation, stomped by him muttering things that he was prepared to wager were anatomically impossible. He remembered the girl from the village where he'd found Allegria after having lost both her and Hallow on the continent of Eris; he assumed she was a native Shadowborn. "One with a bit of fire in her blood, eh?" he said with a knowing wink to Quinn.

The captain, he was sorry to see, also did not possess the ability to notice those who, sadly, were confined to the spirit realm until their new physical forms were made. Instead Quinn rubbed his face with a rueful expression that turned into a grin when the large form of Deosin Langton marched past saying, "You'd better watch out. One of these days Ella's going to borrow Allegria's gelding knife."

"She loves me," Quinn called after Deo. "She just doesn't want to disappoint her master, so she pretends she doesn't like my attentions."

"What's this? Allegria is mentoring a Shadowborn?" Thorn drifted past a number of sailors working in fluid synchronicity to trim sails and paused before the figure of a small girl sitting cross-legged on a wooden crate. "Ah, it's you, the vanth. What's your name? Er…Dara. Demo. Disius?"

The girl looked up and gave him a good long appraisal before returning her attention to the small book in which she was writing with a pencil that left unpleasant rusty-red marks.

"Dexia, you didn't happen to see the blue tunic that Allegria gave me, did you?" The red-headed Shadowborn woman paused next to Thorn, glancing around the deck just as if she expected to see it hanging from the spar.

Thorn clicked his tongue at his bad memory. "Dexia, that's right. I remember now. You're with Quinn, or at least that's what Hallow told me. So much seems to have changed since that bastard Harborym destroyed my physical form. Here we are, almost to Genora, and a Shadowborn seems to have joined our company, not to mention the question of just where exactly are the queen and Lord Israel?"

"Not here," Dexia murmured.

"Frogsbane," Ella swore. "If Quinn stole it again just so he can pretend to find it and get me to kiss him in gratitude for returning it, I'll…I'll…

well, I don't know what I'll do, but it will be something." She marched off with a determined set to her mouth.

"So the queen and her swain aren't with us." Thorn thought on this a few minutes, absently moving with the ship as it rocked in the swells common to the west coast of Genora. He'd always been a good sailor, and didn't let the fact that he had no physical body stop him from enjoying the movement of the deck under his feet. "Are they on Aryia? Together? I expected Queen Dasa would have high-tailed it home to Starfall City as soon as she could in order to deal with that weakling Darius."

Deo's shadow fell through Thorn's incorporeal form when the latter turned at the bow and marched past Dexia, heading aft.

"You pace just like your mother when she's bored," Dexia told Deo, who paused long enough to shoot her an unreadable look. She met it with one of her own, tipping her head to the side to add, "Maybe you should have traveled north with her instead of accompanying us to Kelos."

"I can do more to help the queen retake her throne here than in the north," Deo said, the abrupt way he had of snapping off each word reminding Thorn of an ancient turtle who had lived in a fountain that sat in the center of Kelos back when it was a sight to behold. That turtle, like Deo, was known to be extremely cranky.

He reflected for a moment, a bit startled to realize that fountain had disappeared into rubble at least four hundred years before. Had it really been so long since he had been Master, leading his arcanists to glory with the Starborn against their most bitter enemies?

His gaze fell on Deo as the latter continued his path to the rear of the ship. "And there is the child who was supposed to bring peace to both the Starborn and Fireborn." He sighed, but brushed aside the regrets. "Too much introspection never did anyone any good," he told Dexia. "The queen is in the north, eh? She must be rallying the Starborn faithful to her before she routs that puling Darius from Starfall. Well, well, well. If Deo is going to Kelos, Hallow must have some grand plan in place. What of Jalas? Did Idril finally overthrow her father?"

"You had best heed the Shadowborn woman," Dexia said suddenly, tilting her head up to look at Quinn when he stopped to order a change to the rigging.

"No, no, we have to get past the shoals. Don't drop the handling sail until we're well by the Miser's Fingers and almost to Bellwether. What's that, Dex?"

The vanth grinned, her sharp, pointed teeth looking strangely at odds with her otherwise childlike countenance. "Ella. She's not like the white-haired witch you lusted after. She'll chew you up and spit you out."

"Who, Idril?"

"No, Ella. The witch would have gutted you where you stood had you tried to approach her."

Quinn made a face, then smiled. "Idril isn't a witch, although she was positively magical when the moon glinted on her silver hair..." His words trailed to a stop, and with a nervous glance back toward Deo, he gave a little cough and continued. "It doesn't matter what you and I think about Lady Idril. She is evidently promised to Deo, although why he let her go with Lord Israel to confront Jalas in Abet is beyond me. I don't trust her father further than I can throw a bumblepig. Does it matter that I think we should have descended on Abet as a group to take care of the whole Tribe of Jalas? No. I am but a humble servant to those who hold my talisman, and since Hallow hasn't seen fit to release us from my bond to him, we must do as we are ordered."

Dexia grimaced and returned to her journal. "I'm happy to be well away from the white-haired one, although I would have liked to taste the Tribe."

"I think we'll have our hands full here. And speaking of full hands..." Quinn waggled his eyebrows, brushed off his jerkin, and squared his shoulders. "I believe I shall go see if Ella wants me to tell her about Genora and the Starborn."

He moved off toward the cabins.

Thorn eyed Dexia. "What was Hallow thinking, letting Israel and Idril face Jalas alone? It's not like him to turn away from a battle. Far from it. He was always too quick to run to the aid of anyone who needed it. He is Master of Kelos now, leader of the arcanists, and not some mercenary soldier for hire."

"How long until we land?" Dexia asked one of the sailors who bustled by with a pail and scrub brush.

"Another two hours, possibly three if the wind continues as it is," the sailor answered.

"Has there been any sign of the Eidolon?" she asked, standing and tucking away her journal before stretching.

"Eidolon?" Thorn asked, astounded. "What is this? The Eidolon are confined in the crypts beneath Kelos. They do not roam Genora."

"None, thank the goddess," the sailor answered, using the hand holding the brush to sketch a sign made up of the moon and three stars. "Mayhap the captain is wrong about them roaming the land looking for men to prey on."

"Perhaps," Dexia allowed, watching while the sailor dumped the water overboard before disappearing into the hold. She turned and looked past Thorn to the shore. "Then again, perhaps they are waiting."

"For what?" Thorn demanded to know, his mind awhirl with all that had happened since his physical form had been destroyed. It seemed to him that everything that could possibly go wrong had done just that.

"Allegria and Hallow," Dexia said. Thorn turned to see them emerge from their cabin, their cheeks rosy, identical sated expressions plastered all over their faces. Hallow lifted a hand in acknowledgement of Dexia, and followed Allegria to where she stood at the rail, staring at the shoreline.

Thorn watched them with a growing sense of disquiet. Just what in the name of the moon and stars was going on?

Chapter 2

"Why aren't any spirits attacking us? Shouldn't there be spirits attacking us? I was told there were going to be spirits everywhere, blighting the land and slaying the living, and yet all I have seen that was even remotely threatening was a one-legged harlot who seemed to feel you owed her money for services rendered several years ago."

Hallow, riding next to Deo, looked first askance at his companion, then over his shoulder to where Allegria, the light of his life and fire in his loins, rode chatting with the red-headed Shadowborn woman she had taken under her wing. Allegria hadn't been all too pleased when the harlot had accused him of partaking of her wares and slipping out without paying—which Hallow had not done, since he had always been very scrupulous about such things—and now he sensed a bit of frostiness lingering in his wife's gaze when it rested on him. "Yes, well, I think the less mentioned about the lady in Bellwether, the better. As for the Eidolon…"

His words trailed away as a growing sense of unease prickled along his spine. He rubbed the back of his neck, eyeing again the thick copse of trees lining either side of the road that led eastward, toward Kelos. There was no sign that anything was amiss, but he felt as if his nerves were twitching a warning that danger lay all around them, ready to spring upon the unwary.

"They certainly aren't the threat I was promised," Deo grumbled, looking dissatisfied.

"You are the only man I know who gets snappish when someone isn't trying to kill him," Hallow commented with a wry sense of humor that he knew Deo would ignore. Allegria would have appreciated it, though. He glanced back to smile at her, hoping that her partiality to him would thaw any remaining coldness regarding their landing at Bellwether, but even as he caught her eye, a flicker of movement to the side had him suddenly filled with rage.

Arcany pricked his palms as he pulled on the light of the stars that sat behind the sun, but the chaos magic within him rode high, filling him with a red-hot anger that threatened to spill out at the potential threat to his beloved.

A man emerged from the woods with a basket of fallen branches strapped to his back. He watched the company ride by for a few seconds before lifting his hand in greeting and turning to march off to what was no doubt his home.

"Hallow?" Allegria pressed her heels into her mule, pushing between his horse, Penn, and Deo's massive black charger. "What's wrong? Why have your runes lit up like a lantern? Do you sense something? Is it the Eidolon? Ella," she turned in her saddle and called back to the Shadowborn woman, "tighten your bowstring, and make sure your quiver is at hand."

"At last!" Deo said, his voice full of satisfaction. He pulled his sword from his back scabbard, glancing around quickly. "Where are they, Hallow? I see naught. Are they visible only to your eyes? That will make it a bit more difficult to smite them, but if you tell me where they are, I will take care of them."

"There's nothing," Hallow said quickly, subduing the various magics that twisted inside him in what seemed to be an endless dance. The arcane power that he pulled easily from the sky even when Bellias Starsong was hidden, as she was now, was as natural to him as breathing. The blood magic that he'd gained during his visit to Eris was a little less natural, its complexity shifting and changing even as the chaos magic roared to life, drenching him with a hot, burning need. The runes etched in silver and bound to his wrists and ankles kept the chaos from overwhelming him, but lately, as his body learned to cope with the three different types of magic dwelling within, the chaos magic's rush of red power had shifted from the urge to destroy to one much less lethal.

Although certainly more embarrassing.

"Allegria," he said, his voice husky with desire. The need to slake suddenly overwhelming urges on her body rode high when the chaos magic chose that outlet for its power. There was a plea in his voice for her to move away from him, to give him the space he needed whenever the chaos took over his emotions.

Not that he often had been successful in quelling its demands by such means. Usually, he just hustled her off to whatever bedchamber had been assigned to them and indulged his desires, leaving them both boneless and sated. And although Allegria had said she understood the situation, and never blamed him when he interrupted her with one of the chaos times (as he'd come to think of them), of late she had started to bandy about the phrase, "my lusty stallion"— not at all a nickname he relished.

He'd always been in control of the magic he wielded, dammit, and he wasn't about to be known as a man who couldn't so much as glance at his wife without being driven to bed her. Vigorously. Sometimes multiple times a day.

"I don't see anything," Allegria was telling Deo, scanning both the tree line and the road ahead. "And the Eidolon I met were quite visible. I don't think they could be in a corporeal state if they weren't visible, could they? Hallow, do you know if—" Her eyes widened, accurately reading the mingled desperation, apology, and sexual desire in his eyes. She blinked for a moment, then gave a little chirrup of laughter that she hid with a hand placed over her mouth. "Oh. I see. It's…uh…no, Deo, get back on your horse. There are no Eidolon here. Hallow was…mistaken."

It was too much for him. He pulled Penn aside, dismounting and dropping the reins with an order for the horse to stay put. "I believe I need to…er…" He gestured toward the woods, unable to drag his mind from the struggle to control the chaos magic's lustful demands.

"Ah?" Deo made a face, then nodded. "Yes, I need to make water as well. Too much ale from the one-legged harlot that you refused to pay."

Hallow would have liked to dispute that comment, but the sooner he removed his body from the temptation of his delectable wife, the sooner he would regain the upper hand with the chaos magic. He stumbled off to the copse, swearing under his breath at the loss of control, promising himself that just as soon as they took care of the Eidolon threat, he would focus his attention on mastering the magic that had been forced upon him. Perhaps new runes? He'd never heard of protection against lustful urges, but he would simply have to search the library of the former master of Kelos for what aids he could find.

Everyone had evidently decided that this was indeed the perfect moment for a nature break, because the sounds of their small company dismounting reached his ears as he pushed deeper into the woods, his hands fisted as he struggled to control the arousal that gripped his entire body. If he could just have a few minutes to himself, he knew he could best it. At least until the next time he felt threatened.

"Hallow?" Allegria's voice wrapped around him like silken threads. Rustling sounds accompanied his name, along with the snapping of twigs. "Are you all right?"

"Don't," he warned, doubled over. His fists pressed hard into thighs while he struggled to leash the chaos that threatened to overwhelm him. One abstracted side of his mind mused over the fact that in recent days, the chaos power was gaining strength. Where once it had lain simmering inside him, controlled by the runes on his wrists and ankles, now it fought him whenever a strong emotion was triggered. "I can't...don't come any closer, else...else..."

"Else you'll make incredibly hot, fast love to me?" Her voice was filled with amusement, even as it stroked over his skin like the softest of silks, making him shudder with want and need and desire, all tangled up with the soul-deep love he felt for her.

He moaned, and suddenly, she was there, her summery scent of flowers in the afternoon sun filling his senses, her hands on his back, stroking him, no doubt intending to convey comfort, but it was too much, all too much.

"Allegria," he snarled, whirling around, his gaze scorching over her body despite the faded and worn Bane of Eris tunic that obscured it. "If you don't want me to pin you up against the tree behind you, and impale you on a penis so hard it could probably be used to take down the tree itself, then you had best run. *Now.*"

She eyed him for a moment, concern making the gold flecks in her ebony eyes glitter. Then suddenly she smiled, and without a word, peeled off both the tunic and leggings that covered her lush, long legs, legs that he knew wrapped around his hips perfectly, as if she had been created just for him.

A wordless moan of need escaped his lips. Unable to bear it any longer, he almost ripped off his own tunic and breeches, then lunged, the chaos driving him into action. But his love, his need to give her the pleasure she brought him just by existing, tempered his movements, gentling his actions so that when he suited deeds to words and pinned her against the tree, she was moaning into his mouth, her legs wrapped tightly around him as he plunged into her body.

They didn't last long, but that, too, was common in recent days. Before he'd been forced to consume chaos magic, he had preferred to pay lengthy homage to her body before allowing himself release; now it was simply a matter of trying to bring her pleasure before he lost all control.

"I have to say," Allegria noted a few minutes later, when he let her slide down his body until her feet were once again on the ground, "I really don't mind your chaos moments. I know you don't like them because you think it's the chaos controlling you, but really, Hallow, that was perfectly splendid. Fast, but splendid. Your hip flexibility is a wonder to behold. And that little twist you did—hoo! If such a thing were not unsavory, I'd say you should hold classes to teach other men how to do that thrusting twist. It was most effective."

He laughed even as he bent to retrieve the clothing that had been strewn on the branches and ground, one half of his mind filled with sated thoughts, the other worried that his need for her was growing stronger each day. "I appreciate your wishing to share the twist—which was inspired by the very same twist you used when you rode me last night—but I would have no idea what to charge for such a class, let alone where I would hold it. My heart, I didn't hurt you, did I?"

He asked the last when she grimaced while lifting a foot to pull on her leggings, making quick work of the cross ties. "Not at all, although if we have very many more of the false alarms that kick your chaos magic into a blaze, I will end up walking funny. I grimaced because I had a twinge in my posterior. All that time sailing has weakened my saddle muscles."

He gave her a quick leer as he finished dressing, calling out an answer when Deo bellowed impatiently for them before saying, "I will be happy to massage your abused parts later, but if I tried it now, we'll both be walking funny."

She took his hand as he led her through the woods back to the road, casting him a glance that turned from amusement to concern. "We'll figure out something, Hallow. I'll talk to Deo about adding more runes to the cuffs. Mayhap that is all that is needed."

"Mayhap," he said, but he had a feeling it was going to take more than a few extra containment runes to push the chaos back to its dormant state.

* * * *

It took them two days to ride to Kelos, but the rune that Deo recommended when they stopped the first night seemed to help cage the chaos beast that raged inside him, so that by the time the lone standing tower was visible in the distance, Hallow felt a bit more in control, and ready to face what lay ahead.

"I have to admit that I'm surprised we haven't encountered any Eidolon," he said quietly to Allegria where they rode at the rear of their company. Deo and Quinn, the lifebound captain who'd grudgingly allowed himself to be swept into their plan to subdue the Eidolon before turning their respective attentions to locating Nezu, argued over the best way to remove troublesome spirits from the mortal plane. "No one I spoke to in the three towns we've passed through has seen so much as a ghostly wisp, let alone a murderous thane and his soldiers."

Allegria gave a little shiver, rubbing her arms before deftly keeping her mule Buttercup from nipping the rump of the horse in front of them. "You don't know just how deadly that thane can be. If he's out of his crypt, and as angry as Sandor said, then I suspect he's laying plans that go beyond the mere slaughtering of people near Kelos."

"What sort of plans?" he asked, his curiosity getting the better of him. He had little knowledge of the Eidolon other than what Allegria had told him, and brief mentions in the journals of the former Master of Kelos. "Do you believe they wish to rule Kelos? There isn't much there but the spirits who are bound to the land, and they are mostly peaceful."

She raised an ebony eyebrow, silently reminding him that both the captain of the guard and the other spirits had attacked them when they'd first arrived at Kelos.

"Mostly," he repeated, smiling at her.

"I don't know what the thane is up to," she answered after letting her fingers trail over his hand where it rested on his thigh. The chaos magic threatened to wake up at her touch, but he clamped down hard on it. She hesitated, her brows pulling together for a few seconds. "I just have a feeling that he's up to something. When Sandor said that the Eidolon were running amok, I had the same sort of idea you had—that they were killing anything that lived. But no one seems to have heard of the Eidolon doing anything. It just seems odd, don't you think?"

"Yes," he said, absently capturing her hand when she would have withdrawn it, and twining his fingers through hers. "I think that Deo will have the opportunity he seeks to destroy spirits, although I have no idea how he expects to do that when chaos magic is powered by the act of death."

"I have the exact same worry. I might be able to do it, though." Allegria sighed and glanced upward, where a few fluffy clouds hid Kiriah Sunbringer from their view. "If Kiriah would remember that I exist, that is."

Hallow decided that the time was right to broach a subject he'd had some time to think over. If nothing else, it would focus his attention away from just how warm her hands were, and how much he loved their touch. "Does it not occur to you that perhaps Kiriah is withholding herself from you in order to protect you?"

She shot him a startled glance. "Protect me how? I'm a lightweaver, Hallow—wielding Kiriah's power is what I do. I shouldn't have to be protected from it."

"Not her power, no, but—" He hesitated, thinking of how best to put his thoughts into words that wouldn't insult her. "But perhaps she wishes to keep her power from you so that it cannot be used by another."

"Another? What other? Who could possibly be able to use the power of Kiriah other than a lightweaver, and possibly a priestess of her temple?" Her eyes narrowed in thought. "Sandor might, but I can't believe she would misuse such a blessing. Besides, one of the older priests once said that in her youth, Sandor had a sword made up of sunlight, and that she used it to banish the old ones. She has plenty of power of her own, so she need not poach mine."

"Old ones?" he asked, his mind quickly rifling through the various facts gleaned from his readings. "The stone giants?"

"Yes. But no one has ever seen this sword. Once, when I was a girl, I asked Sandor if it was like my light animals, and she told me it was not a subject fit for discussion, which really doesn't answer anything, does it?"

He chuckled at the expression of annoyance that crossed her face, wanting badly to kiss her, but knowing full well that although Buttercup tolerated Penn as she did no other horse, there were limits to what she considered her personal boundaries. Instead he squeezed Allegria's hand and said simply, "There is one who is strong enough to wield the power of Kiriah. Indeed, if what Queen Dasa said is true, he has long sought it."

"Who—oh." Allegria looked thoughtful. "But Nezu is a god, himself. Why would he covet Kiriah's power when he has his own?"

"A power that is limited in scope," he pointed out.

"Now that he's off Eris, you mean?" she asked.

"Being bound to Eris was what kept him from accessing power, not the reverse," he gently corrected her. "Did you not hear the queen discussing what she'd learned of her time with Racin?"

"Before we sailed, when you and Lord Israel were closeted with her? If you recall, that was the morning Quinn decided Ella's upper story was sufficient to be worthy of his notice, and she stabbed him in the thigh with a fork. I had to intervene before things got too out of hand, so I missed everything the queen said, although you told me it was nothing of great importance. Were you wrong?"

"No. Yes. Possibly," he said, first shaking his head, then shrugging. "The queen said Racin—or Nezu, as I suppose we should call him now—was banished to Eris by the twin goddesses. The fact that he was able to leave

Eris to travel to Genora proves he had greater mastery over the chaos magic than I suspect they realized."

Allegria seemed to chew that thought over. "That's why you think Kiriah has withheld her power from me, leaving me a lightweaver with no light? So that Nezu can't get it? I don't think I understand how he could take from me a magic granted by the goddess."

"He's a god," Hallow pointed out with another little shrug. "He managed to break his exile. I doubt stripping Kiriah's magic from you would be impossible for him."

She was silent, her fingers withdrawing from his. He wanted to take her into his arms, to breathe in the sun-warmed wildflower scent that seemed to cling to her no matter how long she spent in the saddle, and reassure her that all would be well, but he knew she had been greatly troubled by the loss of her connection to the goddess she served. She needed time to consider this new thought.

His concern for Allegria was shoved aside when the road curved and twisted its way to the ruins of the once brilliant Kelos. Hallow paused, hearing faint sounds lifted high on the air. He listened intently for a few moments, the entire company halting when Deo, in the lead, reined in his horse and lifted his hand in warning to the others.

Instantly, the chaos magic inside Hallow burned to life, but he was prepared for that, and pulled hard on the power of Bellias, filling his being with arcany. Its familiar sensation gave him the strength to harness—at least temporarily—the insidious red chaos that demanded so much.

The others—Ella, the little vanth Dexia, and Quinn—all halted, obviously catching the distant sound as well.

And then Hallow was flying forward, leaning low over Penn's neck, his hands drawing symbols even as he heard the sound of hoofbeats behind him, the shout of "Come on, Buttercup!" telling him that Allegria had gotten the jump on Deo.

Ahead, the crumbled outer wall spilled into the road with spiky fingers of stone that had once been smooth and white, but were now dusted with the gray grime that coated everything in Kelos. Half-standing walls dotted the area, with sharp remains of columns that had once been decorated with stars and moons, now stood as a sad reminder that even a place as venerated as Kelos could fall. Penn leaped one of the fallen columns when Hallow, with his eyes on the figure that flickered back and forth just beyond a pile of rubble, started murmuring spells. He was off Penn, and flinging arcany at the figure. At the same moment he heard a twang, and felt the air next to him ripple as an arrow sailed past and hit the figure just as his arcany peppered it with a dozen little holes of purest starlight.

The Eidolon—and Hallow had no doubt that the now-corporeal being with white, wispy hair flowing around his head like water was indeed one of the warrior race that had inhabited Alba before the coming of the Starborn and Fireborn—shrieked. It turned toward them, but its form melted into nothing, the strain of retaining a wounded corporeal form too much.

The spirit who had been fighting the Eidolon was one of the members of the guard that kept the other spirits in line. He turned a grateful look on Hallow, panting as he made a bow, his voice breathless when he spoke. "Master of Kelos, you are a sight most welcome to my eyes. The captain has been awaiting your—"

The man stopped when a sword was thrust through his chest. He stared down at it in surprise for a moment, then looked up to Hallow, his face filled with regret even as his form dissolved into nothing.

Another arrow split the air, catching the Eidolon who had impaled the guard in the throat. He snarled and yanked it out, stalking forward, a massive sword held in one hand, obviously prepared to cleave his enemies in two.

A roar sounded behind him even as Hallow rained down arcany on the Eidolon, melting him where he stood.

"Eidolon!" Deo bellowed, jumping onto the fallen column to quickly assess the situation before leaping off it with a cry that Hallow knew full well expressed unbridled joy.

There was nothing Deo liked more than a reason to fight.

"To the left," Allegria said, firing two more arrows before following Deo.

Kelos was originally laid out in a series of concentric rings, the center of which was the sole intact structure, the Master's Tower, where he and Allegria resided. Normally, a hush lay over the ruins, the grey ground muffling all but the sharpest of sounds. Now, however, the entire north side was filled with bodies as the spirits who resided there, once arcanists and learned men and women, fought two dozen of the biggest men Hallow had ever seen. They weren't huge, like the Harborym, but tall and thin, and all of them wore the armor of an age long past, their long white hair whipping around them as they spun, slashed, and stabbed.

Hallow didn't pause to consider the irony of spirits fighting other spirits—he simply ran when Allegria slid off Buttercup, nocking another arrow. "Hallow! That's the thane over by the armory."

He ran, gathering up arcany from the skies above and the ground below, the power of life from all living things surrounding him.

Allegria paused long enough to yell back instructions to her apprentice. "Ella, keep to the fringes and watch Quinn's back. Quinn?"

Quinn nodded, gripping the scimitars he favored. "I'll keep an eye on her."

Dexia, the being of dark origins who appeared to be nothing more than a girl child of approximately ten summers, dashed past Hallow, showing a mouthful of extremely pointed teeth, and with a shriek, flung herself on a spirit that was about to cleave Deo's head from his body. Her hands and teeth shredded the form of the spirit before he even knew what was happening.

Reddish gold light flowed around Deo when he slammed magic into another Eidolon, causing the warrior to burst into a shower of silver rain. Hallow sighted the thane, one of the three kings who ruled the Eidolon, fighting a familiar ghostly form.

The captain of the Kelos guard was doing his best to keep up with the thane, but even as Hallow watched, the captain was cleaved in two, from his shoulder down to the opposite hip.

Anger roared to life in Hallow. Ever since Hallow had assumed his role as Master of Kelos, the captain of the guard had been nothing but a burr in his side, but the captain was *his* burr, and no one else had a right to smite him. He allowed the chaos magic to slip out of control just a little, sending out a wave of the sickly red energy that destroyed everything it touched. Unfortunately, the thane had seen Allegria and, obviously remembering her visit to his crypt, yelled an oath and charged toward her.

Hallow spun around to help Allegria, but another Eidolon leaped forward, slicing at his leg, cutting deep into his thigh and making him stagger to the side. "Allegria! Behind you!" he yelled, warning her of the oncoming thane. She turned from where she'd taken up a position on the fallen roof of a house, her long, narrow swords flashing silver and gold as she fought.

"Goddesses of day and night protect us all," Hallow swore, jerking the black staff from his back, aware that it wasn't as potent as it should be without Thorn atop it, but focusing his arcany into it even as one hand danced, drawing blood magic symbols that hung in the air before slowly forming into a chain. He flung the chain on the Eidolon who had crippled him at the same time he slammed down his staff, blasting the spirit with arcany.

"What the—" There was an answering explosion from the south that for a moment, had him turning in surprise. Had Deo suddenly mastered the magic of the Starborn? He'd been threatening as much during the entire trip from Eris, but Hallow had no time to ascertain what had happened. "Stay strong, my heart! I'm coming to help you." He ran as fast as he could with his injured leg, his eyes on Allegria while she fought the Eidolon who had climbed onto the roof with her. Over the heads of other Eidolon,

Hallow could see the crowned head of the thane, indicating the king was working his way toward Allegria.

Hallow gritted his teeth against the pain and weakness in his leg, slashing out with the staff at the same time he alternated between sending balls of pure arcany into the mass of Eidolon and drawing the blood symbols that formed into chains taking down every Eidolon within range.

Another blast sounded from the south, this one closer, strong enough to rock the buildings.

"That was not from Deo," he growled to himself. He wanted desperately to see whether it was friend or foe who was wielding arcany, but greater still was the need to protect his love. A half dozen Eidolon stood between him and the thane, who was even now starting to climb the crumbled wall that gave access to the collapsed roof. With effort, Hallow stood still, gathered up every last morsel of arcany he could, and released it in a blast that not only sent the spirits around him flying, but knocked the thane down the wall at the same time. Rock and dust exploded around them, showering down in a painful rain. Hallow ignored the debris as he stumbled forward, slamming bolts of magic into the fallen Eidolon attempting to rise.

The thane snarled something in a language foreign to Hallow, leaping up the wall and lunging toward Allegria at the same time she sliced off the head of the Eidolon nearest her.

"Allegria!" Hallow yelled again, but she had seen the approach of the thane, and spun around to face him. He noted quickly that although she held both swords in her hands, her chest rose and fell rapidly, and her face was dirty with dust and sweat. She'd told him that she had barely escaped with her life the last time she'd met the thane, and now here she was facing him when she was clearly tired from fighting what seemed like a never-ending wave of spirit warriors.

Hallow started chanting as he climbed after the thane, his injured leg buckling under the strain, slipping out from under him and causing him to fall forward. He swore profanely, calling on Bellias to give him the strength needed to wield her magic as he tried to rise. To his surprise, strong hands grabbed him by his arms, jerking him upward.

"Master Hallow, I assume?" one of the two men grasping him asked. He was a short, stocky man with a close-trimmed beard, and the blue eyes of an arcanist. "I'm Tygo. That's Aarav. You called for us, and here we are. Just in time, it would appear."

"The thane," Hallow said, struggling to get up the fallen wall. "That's my wife up there with him. Help her!"

Aarav, a tall, thin man who was one of the arcanists Hallow had summoned upon leaving Eris, leaped forward, a blue-white ball of arcany in his hands. Allegria, with a cry that warmed Hallow's heart, leaped to the side, her swords slashing as she turned toward the thane, positioning him so that Hallow—and the other arcanists—could blast him back to his crypt.

Hallow stood at the top of the wall, his breath ragged and rasping while he summoned the last of his strength, holding the staff as arcany rippled down his arms onto the wooden shaft, little white and blue tendrils of magic snapping in the air, making the fine hairs on his arms stand on end. The thane, glancing toward them, hesitated a minute, giving Allegria the opening she was clearly waiting for. She lunged toward him, but just as her sword was about to pierce his throat, he turned, one hand grabbing her hair and yanking her up close to his body, using her as a shield even as Hallow and the other two arcanists prepared to destroy his corporeal form.

The thane's gaze met Hallow's even as his heart seemed to stop. "You will not succeed!" the thane snarled. "This time, I will have redemption!"

And then, in the length of time it takes for one moment to pass to another, the thane was gone, clearly having returned to the spirit realm.

And taken Allegria with him.

Chapter 3

"Any news, Lord Israel?"

Israel Langton, leader of the Fireborn, turned from where he had been staring out into the night, his eyes on the bonfires that dotted the town of Abet, and cocked an inquisitive eyebrow at the woman before him.

"I saw your headman return earlier," explained Sandorillan, head priestess at the temple of Kiriah Sunbringer. Although her brown eyes were downcast, and her demeanor was suitably placid and contemplative as befitted her profession, Israel was not deceived. He'd known Lady Sandor for several hundred years, and a fiercer protector of her people—short of Queen Dasa herself—he had yet to find.

"Marston traveled as far as the Neck," he answered, glancing back at Abet. He and his handful of men and women were all that remained of his company. They were camped on one of the three heavily forested hills ringing the east side of the capital city, ostensibly to await further members of his force, but in reality he feared it was more a matter of licking their wounds. The battle that his arrival at Abet had triggered had been quick and decisive, leaving him well aware that Jalas had not been idle during the time Israel had spent in Eris rescuing the queen and their son. "He found none but the infirm and elderly, those unable to raise a sword, or indeed, even to sit upon a horse. Crops lie untended, houses are abandoned, and the towns are empty of all but those who are least able to care for themselves."

"Jalas has taken them for what purpose?" Sandor asked, disbelief and horror in her eyes. "Do not say he has put to death all of the Fireborn?"

Israel returned to the small camp table at which he'd been sitting, writing messages. "Not slaughtered them, no. Marston said that great trains of

people, horses, oxen, and other such beasts were reported to have passed
through the Neck and onward north, to the High Lands."

Sandor's eyes widened. "Jalas has taken prisoner all of Aryia? How
can he do so? What does he intend to do with everyone?"

"Put them to work as slaves is my guess." Israel spilt the wax of a candle
onto one of the messages, sealing it with his signet ring. "Which makes it
much harder for us to retake Abet."

"Is it hopeless, then?" the priestess asked, her stillness making
Israel feel twitchy.

A veteran of many battles, most of them against the Fireborn's long-held
foes, the Starborn, Israel was well aware that times of inactivity were as
necessary as those when fighting exhausted his body and mind. And yet,
the fact that he had been denied entry into his own city, the one he had
built over the course of the last two hundred years, grated on him. He felt
restless, driven to action, but knew that until his small company received
reinforcements, it would be folly to try to drive Jalas from Abet.

The last such attempt had cost him two men and Idril.

"If it was hopeless, I would have withdrawn immediately," he answered
after giving one of the men-at-arms the sealed parchments to pass along to
the messengers. "Marston told me that it is rumored several towns along
the west coast escaped Jalas's tribesmen; the people hid in the caves that
dot the shoreline. If that is true, and Marston can convince them that Aryia
has need of their service, then all will not be lost."

"I will pray to the blessed goddess that is so," Sandor murmured, bowing
and withdrawing almost silently to her tent.

Israel's gaze flickered back to the dots of yellow and orange light that
were visible along the parapets of his beloved home. "Let us hope Kiriah
hears that prayer. We desperately need her help."

Sandor, pausing at the flap of her tent, turned and gave him an odd
look, opening her mouth to speak, then with a little shake of her head
entered her tent instead.

* * * *

The next two weeks passed with tedious slowness. Israel, driven by
the need to be doing something, *anything*, spent his days hunting, both for
game to feed the company of twenty-two who had followed him to Eris
and back, and for any survivors of Jalas's purge.

On the fourteenth day, he arrived back at camp with a handful of his men, hauling the carcass of a buck they'd taken down, only to discover a messenger just setting off to find him. Marston had returned at last, and with him another score of men and women.

"You are a most welcome sight," Israel said, clapping Marston on the shoulder and greeting the newcomers. "You all are, for we have sore need of strong sword arms."

"Lady Idril has not been released, I take it?" Marston asked when Israel ordered the newcomers be given food and places to sleep, and for the mounts to be fed and watered.

Israel frowned as he turned back to Marston, gesturing for his old friend and first in command to take a seat at his table, pouring them both goblets of wine. "She has not. Jalas might find his daughter's tongue sharper than an adder's bite, but I doubt if he would be foolish enough to simply turn her out. Holding her as a hostage guarantees Deo's good behavior."

Marston rubbed the whiskers on his chin, the lines of strain and exhaustion on his face revealing the speed at which he'd traveled from the other side of Aryia. "That is curious, most curious, my lord. One of the women I found upon the road was a handmaiden to Lady Idril. She said that she'd received a message a sennight ago that Lady Idril had need of her aid. I thought that meant she had escaped the hold her father had on her."

"A sennight ago?" Israel cast his mind back. "There was no action then that we witnessed. Yesterday there was a great coming and going of men. Mostly coming, but enough men patrolled outside the town that our scouts made note of it. That is the only sign we have seen of Jalas stirring."

"Surely Lady Idril would come here, to you, should she make her escape?" Marston asked.

Israel was slow to answer, his mind turning over the question. Though it was on the tip of his tongue to answer that Idril would naturally turn to her nearest allies, his familiarity with her stubbornness—rivaled only by that of his son—had him qualifying that statement. "She would if she had need of our protection. But it has been many years since I have understood the paths that Lady Idril's mind walks."

Marston shared a rare grin. "She is well matched with Lord Deo in that regard."

"Aye. And the less said about the sort of half-mad children they will have, the better. Tell me of what you found on your way to the coast."

The next hour was spent hearing of Marston's journey, of the fields left fallow and others filled with crops consumed by birds, of empty villages, and the old and infirm who were slowly starving.

Israel let his gaze wander over the people milling around the encampment, the men and women busily setting up pallets and tents, eating, tending their animals, or just lying on the ground, resting. A company of forty-two was not enough to challenge the Tribe of Jalas when he was protected by the strong walls of Abet.

"Take five of the Easterners you brought back, and give them supplies, a cart, and a horse. Send them to each region, and tell them they must travel from village to village, relocating those who are willing to do so, and making sure the others do not starve. They may draw on our reserves to feed those who were left behind, although I would prefer that local resources be used whenever possible."

It was evening before the logistics were taken care of, and Israel felt more anxious than ever to be doing something. Just as he was about to propose to Marston that a covert trip to Abet might be managed without rousing too many of Jalas's guards, he noticed something odd.

"Do you see what I see?" he asked, nodding toward the port side of Abet, and handing over his spyglass.

Marston took it, looked, then lowered the glass, his eyebrows raised. "Where are all the ships?"

"That is a very good question." He thought for a few moments. "I wonder... could Jalas be so foolish as to have sent his tribesmen away from Abet?"

"He might if he thought the sheer number of captives he drove north could turn on their captors and take over the High Lands," Marston answered, watching him closely.

"It is an interesting thought, and one that leads me to believe that a little exploration of Abet under the light of Bellias is in order."

"That is not needed if all you wish to know is how many members of the Tribe remain in town," a female voice called out of the darkness. There was a ripple in the company, from which emerged a woman with the lithe, elegant grace of a doe.

Idril, Jewel of the High Lands, strode forward with three handmaidens in her wake. She looked annoyed, Israel was amused to note, her gown torn and dirty, her face showing signs of mud that had washed off none too well, her hair poking out at odd angles—in fact, everything about her was unlike the coolly collected perfection that was the norm for Idril. But more unusual than the state of her clothing was her agitation. Israel had grown accustomed to seeing an invariably placid, unemotional expression on her face.

"Lady Idril," he said gravely, keeping the amusement from his voice at her unkempt appearance. He knew it must be costing her pride a great deal. "So the rumors were true, then? You escaped your father's grasp? Or did you make him see reason?"

"Reason," she said with a sound that in any other woman he would have called a snort. That, too, was unlike her. Idly, Israel wondered if the few weeks she'd spent in Deo's company had cracked her cool, calm exterior. "My father wouldn't know reason it if came up and bit him on his gigantic pink—"

"Lady Idril, you are with us again? Blessings upon you, child." Sandor's voice cut across her words without effort.

Marston choked, and bowing at Idril, murmured something about seeing to his duties.

Idril managed to get herself under control, her features smoothing out to an expression of blithe unconcern. "Greetings, Lady Sandor. I am, as you see, although no thanks to my father. To answer your question, Israel, my father has not been smitten upon the head with the reason stick. If such a thing existed, I would happily volunteer to be the one to beat him about the head and shoulders with it. I managed to get out via the Captain's Swain."

Israel blinked at the name of the seediest, rowdiest of all taverns in Abet, one frequented only by women who paid no mind to their reputation. "Via the trapdoor to the bay?" he asked, eyeing the wrinkled and filthy gown, one that bore all the signs of having been much abused.

"Yes." A fleeting grimace passed over her face as she lifted her chin. "My ladies were waiting for me, and assisted me ashore."

"Lady Idril fought us most strenuously," one of the handmaidens piped up in a high, bell-like voice. "She does not swim, and struggled so hard when she was in the water that we had to knock her insensible in order to drag her ashore, and then we had to hide in the swineherd's hut when Lord Jalas's men rode past."

"Yes, I don't think we need to go into all the details of my escape," Idril said swiftly, shooting a glare at the maid in question.

"And then she woke up just as the guard noticed Noellia outside the swineherd's hut, so we had to knock Lady Idril senseless again because she began to yell, and the guard came in to see, but luckily, we had just pushed Lady Idril out the window into the wallow, and the pigs hid her from view. Well," the second handmaiden added with a glance at her compatriots, "that and the mud, which was up to our knees."

Lady Idril looked as if she would happily murder her handmaidens, but after a moment's obvious struggle with such violent emotions, she lifted her chin again, and graced Israel with one of the cool, impersonal looks that were all too familiar. "My journey here was fraught with *many* trials, but I am at last free of my father, and able to help you take control of the city again."

"Indeed." Israel eyed her, his nose twitching with the scent of what must have been her time spent in the pig's wallow. "I will naturally welcome any assistance you can give me. Has your father called up more of his tribesmen? Is that where the ships have gone?"

"Just the opposite," Idril said, ignoring the soft, wet noise that followed when a bit of fern tangled with hay fell off her shoulder and hit the ground. Her chin rose, her eyes daring him to comment. "My father feels that you no longer pose a threat to him now that he's taken away your army and sent them north, to serve the tribes. There was evidently a skirmish that he felt boded ill—I admit to perhaps playing upon his paranoia—and thus, he sent the tribe north via the sea, so as to quell the insurrection that I hinted would be raging all over Poronne."

"That was astute thinking," Israel said, pretending not to notice when another clod of mud, straw, and leaf mould fell from a particularly spiky bit of her hair.

One of the handmaids giggled.

"Astute and prescient, perhaps," Lady Sandor murmured, her gaze on Israel.

Israel raised his eyebrows in an approximation of innocence. "If you are implying that I left behind a set of instructions for the people of Aryia to follow when I went to Eris, I have little to say except it would be most unlikely."

"Most," Sandor agreed, her mouth twitching.

Israel met her gaze with equanimity, knowing full well that although the priestess might adopt a staid and circumspect persona, she had a wicked sense of humor that she had once told him had led her into no end of trouble. That she'd been naked at the time and riding him like a rented mule had nothing to do with the assessment. If Dasa hadn't fought her way into his heart, making herself welcome in that inhospitable organ, he might have taken up the offer in Sandor's soft eyes.

He gave himself a little mental head shake. "So the city is empty? Then we shall retake it. Immediately. Marston!"

"It's not empty, no, but the five tribe leaders who were there sailed north yesterday," Idril answered. "Noellia, whatever that is on the back of my neck, remove it. No, don't show it to me. I would prefer not to know what it was that slid across my flesh. My lord, wait!"

Israel, who had started to move off to his tent to gather up his sword, and the roots and bones used to cast spells, paused at the imperious tone in Idril's voice. "If you are going to tell me it's folly to attack Abet again—"

"I am not. There is nothing I would like more than to see my father your prisoner, especially after he wed me to Parker, the most brutish of all the Northmen, in exchange for their support. I wished to ask you if there is news of Deo."

Israel couldn't help but raise his eyebrows at the woman who once, for a few weeks, had been his wife...in name only, he couldn't help but remember, fighting the urge to smile. Deo had yet to forgive him for the political marriage meant to calm Jalas and bring him into the Council of Four Armies, although he had resolved his differences with Idril during the voyage from Eris. "Your father wed you off for political reasons? *Again?*"

Idril's nostrils flared at the emphasis on the last word, but she waved away the question with an impatient gesture. "It is of no matter. I am betrothed to Deo, as my father well knows."

"You're going to have a hard time marrying him if your husband objects," Israel pointed out, feeling the corners of his mouth twitch. He steeled his lips into composure.

A martyred expression was visible on her face for a few seconds before it melted into her usual one of polite disinterest. "It is, as I said, of no account. Have you heard from Deo? Did he reach Genora? Has he found his missing Banesmen?"

"I have not heard from him directly, no, but Deo and the others should be in Genora by now. The Queen sent word that she was going straight to her kinfolk to seek the aid of the water talkers, and I expect she will communicate once she comes to an accord with them. Now, I must leave you. Since you just escaped from the city, perhaps you might prefer to stay here while I take advantage of your father's folly in leaving Abet so under-guarded. You could...er...avail yourself of my tub."

Idril's eyes narrowed into the meanest look he'd ever seen, aimed directly at him, and he had a suspicion that if she'd been given the ability to smite him where he stood, she would have done so. Instead, she inclined her head, causing a small snail to cascade off her hair, bounce off her left breast, and fly forward to land on the back of Israel's hand.

He removed it without a word.

Idril sent a scathing look at her three handmaidens, all of whom schooled their expressions into ones of humility when she marched into his tent to bathe.

It wasn't until dawn that Israel and his company, now armed with as many weapons as they could gather, approached the gate and demanded an audience with Jalas.

"Lord Jalas is not to be disturbed," the tribesman who guarded the gate called down from where he stood on the rampart. "Go back to the rotten log whence you slunk, Fireborn."

"My lord," Sandor said softly, touching Israel's arm. "There is something here…a sense of futility that disturbs me greatly. Perhaps this attack would be better left for another time, one when Kiriah is present to bless us."

Israel considered her for a moment. There were lines of strain around her mouth that he hadn't recalled being there before. "Futility regarding what, exactly?" he asked, loath to abandon the chance to take back the city that was by rights his. He respected Sandor and her ability to commune with the goddess, but he doubted if another opportunity so perfect as this would present itself again. He had to take advantage of it before more troops reinforced Jalas's contingent.

She hesitated a moment, one hand going to her throat. "I cannot see clearly the threat. I only know it is present. It leeches up from the ground like a poisonous vine, tainting everything around it."

Worry was evident in her eyes, and for a moment, Israel considered withdrawing. But just then, the guard on the rampart, evidently feeling himself in a position of power, shot an arrow that missed Israel's horse by a foot. "Stay to the rear," he ordered Sandor, pulling the splintered rocks, bones, and roots from a small leather pouch that was embossed with silver stars and moons at the same time he gestured to Marston.

The latter let loose with a war cry while Israel, focusing his attention on the Grace of Alba with which Kiriah had blessed all Fireborn, drew upon the living things around them. With his eyes on the guardsman, who had turned to call for reinforcements, he unleashed the power of the Fireborn, causing a flurry of feathers to swell up around the man, lifting him from the rampart and dropping him to the cobblestones below. Grappling hooks were thrown at the stone wall, and in a matter of two minutes, Israel and half his company had scaled the walls and swarmed the three guards who raced toward them.

A sense of rightness filled him as the company swept through the town, heading for the keep that towered over Abet proper. He was surprised for a moment at just how still the town was, for the residents of Abet were not known for their quiet lives. It occurred to him as he reached the central square, passing the well and a small fountain that had been put up to mark the birth of Deo, that Jalas had sent all the citizens north with their country relations.

It was just as he started up the steps to the keep that he realized why Lady Sandor had been so hesitant. He stopped midway up the steps when three men moved out of the shadows of the great double doors and stopped, their figures as black as the crows that wheeled overhead.

"Banes," Marston said in a gasp at the same time that Lady Sandor drew in a deep breath, the whisper of a prayer to Kiriah following immediately.

Israel held up his hand at the sight of the Banes of Eris, halting the company behind him. "Keep them back," he said quietly to Marston, knowing that the Banes would slaughter the men and women prepared to fight for him.

"Aye, my lord." Marston slipped away, herding the company back across the square with him.

Israel took a moment to study the face of each of the three Banesmen, not recognizing them. "You are part of my son's company?" he asked the three men, adding before they could answer, "You must be the men that Lord Hallow spirited away after the battle at Starfall. What do you here in Abet?"

"We seek revenge for our liege lord," the middle man snarled, his skin, a dusky blue, turning a darker hue while his eyes positively snapped with anger.

"For Deo?" Israel frowned. "Then you would do better to sail to Genora, for he is not on Aryia."

"We do not seek his grave, wherever you had him buried," the leftmost man said, making an abrupt gesture toward him. "But we will avenge his death, you may be sure of that."

"His death?" Israel shook his head, realizing that the men believed the scene that had played out in Starfall. He thought of explaining to them what had really happened, but knew instinctively that they would not believe him.

In their eyes, he was guilty of killing his own son, and little but Deo's presence before them would shake them of that conviction. No, the only way he'd get past them into the keep was by removing them from the picture. He wondered if he had the strength to defeat the three Banes on his own. One, perhaps, but three? He gave another little shake of the head.

"Jalas told us how you had planned to destroy Lord Deo the minute you realized that he had done what no one else could—he had mastered chaos power. Jalas said you feared the power Lord Deo held, that you wed the woman to whom he was betrothed, and that above all else, you sought a reason to have him removed from Alba, and when that chance presented itself, you took it. We are here to avenge Lord Deo's death upon you. We, who believed in him when you did not, will see to it that all know the truth."

A light touch on his arm had Israel turning his head to where Sandor stood, her gaze on the three men. No, he could not fight them alone, but he was not alone. Sandor stood in Kiriah Sunbringer's favor, and had magic of her own.

"Are you up for this?" His voice was soft, but he knew she could read the intention in his face.

"Always," she said with a little smile, and he had a suspicion she was remembering the time some three hundred years in the past when they had celebrated—in the most primal way a man and woman could—a hard-won victory over the Starborn. "Work our way from right to left?"

"Of course." He was making a mental note that sometime in the near future he would have to inform Sandor that Dasa, despite having been his enemy for centuries, held his heart, and nothing would change that. Those thoughts, along with the general sense of worry that had gripped him since their return from Eris, were pushed out of his mind, however, as his fingers clasped the bones, roots, and feathers, the old familiar words coming to his lips.

"Kiriah, bringer of life
surround me with the heat of your truth
touch my spirit with this place
and banish the energies that would act against me.
May the four forces heed my plea:
From the ground, I beg strength
From the rock, resilience
From the life around me, intention
And Kiriah above, power.
So it is, so it was, so it will be."

He released the power gathered in his talismans just as Sandor, who had been kneeling, her hands clasped together as she called upon the goddess to bless them, suddenly stood up and lunged forward in one smooth movement, a sword that had been strapped beneath her overdress flashing with the golden light of Kiriah Sunbringer. The rocks and stones that made up Alba answered Israel's call, the ground rumbling as cracks appeared beneath the three men's feet, the long lines turning black as they leached life from the Banes.

Sandor swung her sword, the runes on it glowing so brightly they left little trails of sparks on the air when she struck the rightmost Bane. His head bounced down the stairs before the other Banes realized what had happened.

The middle Bane roared, spilling red chaos outward in a wave that knocked Israel back several yards. Hastily, he scrambled to his feet, hampered by the long red tendrils that seeped out of the cracks in the rocks, twining around his legs and capturing him. He roared an oath, yelling for Marston to help Sandor when the two Banes turned their attention to her. Pain whipped through him with burning intensity, ripping breath from his lungs and causing the muscles in his legs to buckle from the strain. He felt as if he had been chained to anvils and tossed into an inferno—a sentient inferno, one that turned an eye to him and laughed in a mocking manner while he desperately summoned the Grace of Alba, throwing protective ward after ward onto the figure of Sandor. Despite the Banes' magic, her sword danced, flashing white against the dark wooden doors of the keep.

Before Israel could do more than send a fervent prayer to Kiriah Sunbringer to grant help to her priestess, the two Banes broke free of his magic and both turned to face Sandor. For a moment, Israel thought she was going to do the impossible and slay them, but in the space between heartbeats, the chaos magic they wielded snapped out. As it slammed into her, Sandor's screams rose high into the still morning air.

And then she was gone, a thick, wet puddle of chaos magic on the ground all that remained of the vibrant woman who had stood against legions of enemies for more centuries than Israel could remember.

Marston had reached him by that point. Israel stood stunned, refusing to accept that Sandor could be cut down so swiftly, just as if she was nothing more than a bit of ash ground underfoot.

"My lord," Marston said in a harsh, rushed voice, pulling on his arm. "We must retreat. The company will be slain by these monstrosities."

"She's gone," Israel said, his mind reeling for a few moments before he drew himself back from the brink of rage. The two Banes were now facing him, clearly gathering power to wipe out the rest of them. Israel threw a couple of hasty binding wards onto the men, pain pricking his palms when suddenly the bones and roots cracked under the strain of his spells. He threw them down, casting one last agonized glance at the spot where Sandor had stood, before giving in to Marston's demands.

They escaped while the Banes were still bound to the steps of the keep, allowing Israel and his company to retreat to their camp atop the southern hill. For a horrible few hours, Israel feared the Banes would pursue them, but to his relief, they remained in Abet. He stared absently at his hands, noting the scars of past battles, and the new, bloody lines caused by the breaking of his talismans. "I will have to get new ones," he said to himself, sorrow, guilt, and fury spinning around inside him in a complex knot of emotions that threatened to overwhelm him.

But he had not been a leader for most of his life without learning a few valuable lessons, one of which was that loss was inevitable.

"A senseless loss, though...no. That I will not stand for. She will be avenged," he swore under his breath. Idril, who stood next to him holding a wooden flagon, simply raised an eyebrow.

"The priestess will be in the spirit realm, waiting for Kiriah to call her to her side. Sandor is beyond such things as revenge," Idril said softly.

"I am not," he answered in a voice that was as bleak as the gray stones that formed the hill beneath their feet. He turned away from Idril, spurning her offers of attention to his wounds.

"What will you do now?" she called after him, her normally placid voice scraping sharp as a razor on his flesh.

He hesitated at the entrance of his tent, his eyes on the one next door. It belonged to Sandor. He closed his eyes for a moment, breathing deeply of the scents of pine, sun-warmed earth, and green, growing things. It was poor balm to the deep well of sorrow that filled his soul. "We can't defeat Jalas and the Banes that now serve him. We must have an army...and Deo. We will sail for Genora as soon as we locate a ship. The queen will have raised her army by now; we will join forces with her. Then with Deo, we will return and destroy the rot that has taken hold in Abet."

Chapter 4

It was the noise that made me want to scream in frustration.

A slight squeaking noise, followed by the whisper of tiny nails on stone had me opening one eye, the one that wasn't pressed into the rocky ground.

A squat butter-and-cream-colored bumblepig paused in the act of digging through my hair, obviously looking for things to eat. Its little whiskers twitched while it gazed at me with confusion.

"You're a bumblepig," I told the round, furry little creature the approximate size and shape of a loaf of bread. "You eat plants, not hair. What are you doing in the spirit world? Do bumblepigs who have died come here, too? I'm new, so you'll have to take pity on my ignorance."

It ignored my questions, instead shuffling forward on legs that were comically short when compared to its rotund body. After taking a delicate nibble on one of my curls, it continued across the rest of my hair to the greener pastures of an area outside my cage.

"My cage," I growled, pushing myself up from the rock floor to glare through the wooden slats, grasping and rattling them for what seemed like the hundredth time. They didn't give, no matter how hard I struggled with them. "Damn those Eidolon and their cage-making skills. Hello? Is anyone there? I need to use the privy!"

Stuck where I was behind a large stone slab that had been propped up on a couple of plinths, I couldn't see anything but the wall of the cave into which the thane had dragged me. I gathered that the Eidolon, so long asleep in their stony crypt beneath Kelos, were more comfortable in dolmens than the usual tents or hide shelters used by those in the mortal realm, but that didn't give them the right to throw me into their extremely well-made cage and forget about me. "Hey! I am not dead, thus, I have bodily needs, and one of those is about to get very unpleasant if someone doesn't let me out! Not to mention the fact that I'm hungry."

I cocked an ear to listen. Beyond the massive stone tomb that the thane had chosen as his domicile, I could hear some signs that others were nearby. An occasional rhythmical grating sound was clearly someone using a whetstone on a blade, while a hushed murmur of voices came from a greater distance.

"Is this because of what happened earlier?" I yelled, shifting around in my cage to get my feet against the wooden bars. I grasped them, trying to simultaneously kick out at the bottom while pulling on the top, but the blasted things still wouldn't move. "Because I apologized for biting off the thane's nose. I don't think I should be punished for the fact that his body parts come off so easily. Really, the fault is his. If he hadn't dragged me into your realm, I wouldn't have been forced to attack. Not that it did much good, because he's faster in the spirit world than he is in mine, but still, if you were in my boots, you would have done the same. Wouldn't you?"

I held my breath, willing the unseen sword-sharpening spirit to answer me, but alas, he didn't rise to any of my conversational bait.

I sighed and leaned back against the walls of the cage, offering up several prayers to Kiriah. I might have tried to take off the head of the thane a few hours before, but I was still a priestess, and habit drove me to send several supplications to Kiriah for my actions of the last few days.

I didn't even bother to try to feel for her presence—Hallow had once told me that the influence of the twin goddesses was limited in this realm, and given that Kiriah hadn't been acknowledging my presence at all the last few months, it came as no surprise that I had no sense of her here.

"Nezu, now, *him* I can feel," I murmured, rubbing the goosebumps on my arms. The dim light and slightly damp feeling of the cave reminded me of Eris before we'd driven Nezu from it. And with that memory came sadness—what was Hallow doing right now? He must have seen the thane take me with him when he escaped into the spirit realm…was the love of my life worried? Was he trying to rescue me? Did he miss me, or was he perfectly happy to have me out of the way while he devoted himself to the problem of dealing with Nezu?

"Now you're just being maudlin," I told myself.

"That's understandable, given this place. You'd think the spirits would do something to make it a bit…well, nicer."

It was a woman's voice that had me sitting up straighter, peering through the gloom to catch a flicker of movement that drew closer. I gasped at the sight of the person who had come to a halt outside my cage. "What in the name of the twin goddesses are you doing here? Did Nezu tire of your treachery, and take your life?" I asked, wishing more than ever that I had the swords the thane had taken before imprisoning me. I squinted at her, not seeing what I expected. "Wait...you're not dead, either?"

"Of course I'm not dead," Mayam said, her brows lowering as she glared at me. "Lord Racin would never take my life. He knows I serve him most faithfully."

"Something you can't say about the man you professed to love," I pointed out, wishing that just for a minute, I was once again a Bane of Eris so I could deal with Mayam as she deserved. "Not to mention all the rest of us you betrayed when you gave the Queen's moonstones to Nezu. What are you doing here if you aren't a spirit? Are you here simply to mock me?"

She smiled. "Lord Racin wishes to see you."

That shocked me. "What? Why?" I asked, confused. That Mayam should be here in the spirit realm was odd, but odder still was the thought that Racin sought my company. I watched Mayam closely as she used a giant black key on the lock that closed the door of the cage, a spurt of panic filling me at the memory of Hallow's words about Kiriah withholding her favor from me in order to protect me from Nezu's attention. Had the latter seen the traits of a lightweaver in me even though I had not wielded Kiriah's power while I was on Eris?

Mayam grabbed my wrist and jerked me out of the cage, causing me to scrape my free hand painfully on the sharp rocks that littered the ground. "It is not for you to question the ways of gods, priestess. Stop dawdling. Lord Racin is annoyed at having to come to the spirit world to speak with the thane, and his mood will not be sweetened by waiting for you."

"I don't think exercising a little patience is going to kill him," I grumbled, stiffly getting to my feet. The cage hadn't been tall enough for me to do more than sit or crouch, and my back and legs made unpleasant cracking noises as I straightened up, but I ignored them as I mentally chewed over her comment. Nezu was here to talk to the thane? Why? What would a god, even a disgraced one who had been stripped of most of his power, have to say to a long dead warrior king? "Nezu must have something of great importance to discuss with the thane in order to come all this way. The living are not welcomed into the spirit world, not even those of Nezu's stature."

She shrugged, still holding me by the wrist, tugging me after her as she hurried down a narrow path that ran past the stone dolmen and wound its way around massive, jagged fingers of rock that thrust upward. "It wasn't that difficult to get here. You just need a spirit to guide you. Racin slew one of his Harborym and charged his shade to bring us."

The matter-of-fact manner in which she spoke left my insides feeling as cold and clammy as the cave itself. I had to admit I was more than a little surprised each time a bit more of her true nature was revealed. When I'd first met her she'd been my captor, but quickly became a compatriot…or so we'd all thought. "You've changed, Mayam, really changed. I'd like to blame the fact that you have sworn fealty to a vengeful, destructive god who wishes for nothing more than the total and complete annihilation of the Fireborn and Starborn, but I suspect that deep down, you're just mean."

Her fingers tightened around my wrist, the glare from her narrowed eyes no doubt intended to strike fear in my heart. But I hadn't gone through the events of the last year just to quail in front of a woman who had so little honor, let alone any real power. "I might return the compliment by saying that you are a know-it-all who thinks her shite doesn't stink, but my mother raised me to be better than that."

"Oh!" I said, outraged at the slander. "I am not a know-it-all! I'm the first person to admit that there are any number of things I don't know. I can't help it if the fact that I was a Bane of Eris, a priestess of Kiriah, and a lightweaver means I have more than a passing knowledge of things beyond your ken. And for the record, I know full well that my shite is just as stinky as—" I stopped, hearing just how ridiculous that sentence was. I took a deep, calming breath, and continued, "We have strayed from the topic of what Nezu has to discuss with the thane that is so important he must kill one of his own Harborym to come here."

"All will become clear in time," answered a deep voice that reminded me of rock grating on rock. The sound rolled out into the cave as we emerged around a bend into the entrance,where the thane's twelve remaining soldiers had set up a camp of sorts. Nezu stood next to the thane, his red skin glistening as if it had been oiled, the long black braids that hung alongside his face slithering across his shoulders and upper chest as he turned to look at me. "This is the priestess? She is…not what I expected."

I mused that after he had consumed chaos magic Deo was changed—like me, he'd lost the color of the Fireborn—but whereas the other Banes and I had undergone minor physical changes, Deo's body had reacted to the magic by growing in stature until he was a head taller than Hallow. I didn't know if Nezu ever had a lesser form, but now he stood a good two heads taller than Deo, towering over me in a manner that made me feel like a child in comparison. Beyond him, two Harborym stood at the cave entrance, their backs to us, clearly watching for any intruders.

Just who the god of shadows expected to attack him in the spirit world was beyond my understanding, but I had never claimed to follow the logic of gods, especially not Nezu. Mindful of the proper manner to greet someone of his stature, however, I made him the bow that Sandor said indicated humility without subservience, and murmured the traditional greeting. "Blessings of Kiriah upon…oh. Er…" I stopped, uncomfortable asking Kiriah for a blessing on her troublesome brother.

A grimace passed over his face before he turned back to the thane, who stood with arms crossed over his chest, his long, wispy white hair moving around his head as if it had a life of its own, shifting and moving on the slightest breeze. "*This* is the great prize? She is nothing more than a mouthpiece of the sun god. Of what use is she to me?"

"She is most powerful, blessed in Kiriah's eyes," the thane answered, and once again, I wondered how he'd known who I was when he was supposed to have been asleep deep in the crypts beneath Kelos.

"She doesn't have the scent of power about her." Nezu turned to run his gaze over me again. I had to steel myself to stand still. "There is no stink of Kiriah about her, only that of Bellias."

I wondered why I smelled of arcany, but figured it must be some residue from the intimate contact I'd had with Hallow a few hours before.

Beside me, Mayam rushed to say, "The priestess claims she is a lightweaver, my lord, although during the whole time I was with her on Eris, she never summoned up so much as one single ray of sunlight."

"As if anything could get through the perpetual twilight that fell on Eris when the twin goddesses bound—" I stopped the second my mind pointed out to whom I was speaking. The less I reminded Nezu of his exile, the better. I could almost hear Hallow's voice gently chiding me for trying to prove my abilities to a god who would not hesitate to crush me in order to strip from me Kiriah's power. I cleared my throat, and said simply, "All priestesses of Kiriah carry with them her blessing. I am no different."

Nezu studied me for a moment with a gaze that just about flayed the flesh off my bones. He turned back to the thane. "I don't see anything special about this priest, but I will grant your request. In exchange for her, I will summon the All-Father."

The thane, who had been regarding Nezu with half-closed eyes, smiled. His visage showed the number of long centuries he had lived before the Eidolon had left the mortal realm and retired to their crypts buried deep in Alba; his smile was both unnatural and disconcerting. "We are in agreement, then. I give you the priestess to do with as you will, and in return, the All-Father will be destroyed. I must raise the rest of the Eidolon to do so, however. They have been too long asleep, and it will take much to rouse them."

Nezu was silent for a few minutes before he gestured toward Mayam, who released her hold on my wrist, scurrying forward. "My servant will fetch one of Bellias' moonstones. Use it to waken your army, and do what you could not do before my coming."

The thane bowed his head in acknowledgement while all sorts of warning bells went off in my mind. Who was this All-Father of which they spoke? Why did the thane want him destroyed? And most importantly of all, how could I use this turn of events to rid us of Nezu? The moonstone… it might have the power to leash him, but I was not learned in its use, and doubted if I had the power to hold him, even if I was to get the stone away from the thane.

"Take the priest to my camp and bring back one of the moonstones," Nezu commanded Mayam before turning back to the thane. "Is this the extent of your company? I want a spirit found who is hiding in this realm—"

Mayam yanked me after her, hurrying toward the entrance of the cave, where two Harborym lurked. I tried to dig in my feet in order to hear what it was Nezu wanted of the thane, but Mayam was evidently desperate to please her master. "Stop fighting me," she hissed, giving me a vicious jerk forward when I tried to delay. "Or I'll have the Harborym knock you silly."

"Mean, just mean," I muttered under my breath. The thought that the moonstones must be nearby filled my head, causing my fingers to twitch with the need for action. I spied a familiar object poking out of a small open chest, and jerked sideways, snatching up my scabbard and crossed swords.

"Oh, no, you don't!" Mayam snarled, grabbing the scabbard from me before I could so much as extract one sword.

She looked as if she was about to throw the scabbard aside when I said quickly, "Do not cast them away. They belong to Deo. He's just letting me use them, and they have much value to him. He would be angry to know you tossed away his mother's swords."

"Huh," she snorted with a toss of her head, but she tucked the scabbard under her free arm. "What are Lord Deo's wishes to me? He is as weak as you are, a fact I soon realized. It is why when Lord Racin asked for my aid, I gave it to him willingly. Lord Deo was all talk and no action. Lord Racin says little, but his actions are unmistakable."

"Who is this All-Father he wants destroyed?" I asked, my mind turning over any number of plans. If I could pretend to stumble, I might take her down with me, and in the scuffle to get to our feet, I could get my swords. Or I could throw myself on her, taking her by surprise, and knock her out, retrieving my swords, after which I would go looking for the moonstones. On the other hand, I could simply wait until she took me to the stones, at which point I would either stumble or attack her, thus giving me both my weapons and the moonstones. Yes, that seemed the wisest plan.

The look she shot me was almost pitying in its smugness. "You are a priestess, educated and well-traveled, and yet you do not know who the All-Father is?" She shook her head. "Your ignorance is breathtaking."

I was about to tell her what I thought of her, too, but at that moment we approached the Harborym. They both stared at us until Mayam gestured for one to move aside. "The master commands me to his tent. Move, so that I might take his prisoner to the gaoler."

I thought for a moment the massive abomination might refuse her order, but after giving her a long look, he shifted just enough for us to squeeze between them out into the brighter light.

A small cluster of tents had been set up, and a few Shadowborn and Harborym moved in and around them. In the center was a large black and red structure that looked as if it was made up of a portcullis to which a tent had been attached. As we drew closer I realized the long iron bars set into thick wooden walls were a gaol of some sort, into which Mayam was no doubt about to cast me. I eyed the tent part of the structure, guessing that was Nezu's quarters. No doubt he enjoyed tormenting those whom he had captured, keeping them near him to witness their suffering.

"Take the prisoner," Mayam commanded one of the Shadowborn who stood guard outside the gaol. It was empty, I noted, but that didn't surprise me. I couldn't imagine how Nezu expected to confine an incorporeal spirit, but figured now was not the time to try to puzzle that out. "Lord Racin wishes her confined near him, where he might enjoy her screams."

Mayam released my wrist at the same time the man stepped forward. He grabbed me by the arm with a painful bite of his fingers into my flesh, drawing from me a gasp of pain. Mayam ignored it, and entered the tent, no doubt to complete her master's bidding, taking with her my swords and only hope of escape.

I stood for a moment, unmoving when the guard tried to push me forward, my heart sick at the idea of being Nezu's prisoner. The thane was bad enough, but I'd beaten him once—kind of—and I knew I could do so again. But Nezu was different.

"You come," the guard ordered, trying to give me a shove, but he was smaller than me, and I was tired of being pushed and pulled around.

If only Kiriah would hear my pleas. If she would allow me to tap into her power, then I could blast the guard, grab my swords and the moonstones, and be away before Nezu knew what happened. But it was no use even trying, my heart said in a sad little dirge. Kiriah, for whatever reason, had abandoned me when I most needed her strength. I bowed my head, about to give in to the inevitable when my brain prompted me with a mental image of Hallow shaking his head, his eyes glittering like topazes in a bubbling stream while he told me to have faith in myself.

"You will do as I order," the guard warned, giving me a hard shove toward the door. "Else it will go badly for you."

I closed my eyes, flexing my fingers, my mind working through the words of the invocation of Kiriah, calling for her grace and power to fill me.

Nothing happened. There was no sense of Kiriah, no familiar tingle of heat sweeping through me.

"What's going on out here?" Mayam asked, emerging from the tent with an object wrapped in a dirty bit of cloth. "Why haven't you put her in the gaol? For the love of the night, must I do everythi—"

Fury roared to life in me at her words, at the whole situation. "How dare the thane take me?" I almost yelled, jerking my arm from the guard's hold. "And your precious Nezu—who does he think he is that he can just order me to a gaol where he will subject me to the most heinous tortures imaginable? And for what?"

"I…you…you can't…" Mayam's eyes grew round when I snarled at her. Rage, hot and fiery, swept through me.

The guard lunged, but before he could touch me, he shrieked and leaped backwards, his hands singed with the strength of my anger.

The heat of Kiriah filled me, lighting up even the smallest part of my body, making my soul sing with the joy of it all as I spoke words of gratitude to the goddess, along with the promise that I would not repay her kindness with shame. The power of the sun roared in my ears, my body an inferno of intent. I glanced at Mayam, and knew without the slightest shred of doubt that I could destroy her where she stood.

But Kiriah's blessing was not that of vengeance, so instead of smiting her on the spot, I simply flung a net of light onto her that my fingers had automatically woven, and snatched from her hands the dirty bit of cloth that hid the moonstone.

"Blessed goddesses!" she yelped, and threw herself to her knees, words tumbling over each other while she sobbed out an apology, almost gibbering in her fear and anguish. "Blessed Kiriah and Bellias protect me. I meant no disrespect, for I am the humblest of all your servants. Show mercy to me, and I will become your devoted slave for the rest of my life…"

I flicked a glance toward the guard when he took a hesitant step toward me. His hair lit on fire. He screamed again, and ran off, disappearing into the gathering crowd of Shadowborn...and a couple of Harborym.

Two Harborym ran toward me, swords lifted high, their voices calling guttural oaths, but they were stopped in their tracks by a column of white-gold light that I called down upon them. Behind them, the remaining Shadowborn backed away slowly, their faces twisted with fear and disbelief.

I unwrapped the dirty bit of cloth and beheld a long greyish-green crystal about the width of my palm and twice as thick. "This ought to do the trick," I said, wrapping fingers that glowed golden around it. I spun around, intending to return to the cave where Nezu remained with the thane. It would have been the sheerest folly to face Nezu without Kiriah's blessing, but now that it flowed through me, I knew I had the power to wield the moonstone against him. I might not be able to destroy him outright, but I was willing to bet I could contain him in some manner, and force him back to the mortal realm, where Hallow and his arcanists could bind him.

I took one step before the light within me faded, leaving me feeling bereft and empty. "No!" I yelled, holding up my hands, watching as the glow slowly melted from my arms. "No, no, no! Not now! Kiriah, just two more minutes! That's all I need!"

Kiriah evidently didn't see things as I did, for she withdrew her power completely, leaving me as I was before: trapped in the spirit realm, the prisoner of a merciless god, weaponless, helpless, hopeless.

"Deo named me Hopebringer, and by the twin goddesses, I will not lose that, too," I growled to myself. Holding the moonstone firmly, I snatched up my scabbard from where Mayam had let it fall, quickly strapping it on, the familiar weight of the swords against my back giving me comfort.

Mayam remained on her knees, her body curled upon itself as she rocked back and forth, repeating a whispered prayer to Kiriah over and over.

"Right. I can't tackle Nezu without Kiriah's help, but I can take the other moonstones."

Just then a shout caught my attention. I whirled around and saw a veritable battalion of Harborym pouring around an outcropping of rock. A few Shadowborn had run to meet them, and were even now pointing back to the camp.

"Or not." I amended my plan. "One will do fine." I ran forward in the direction opposite from the Harborym, pausing when my conscience twisted painfully. I paused, swore to myself, then with a muttered curse that I really hoped Kiriah would never learn of, grabbed Mayam by the back of her tunic and hauled her to her feet. "Come on, you annoying woman, you."

To my surprise, she didn't fight back. She didn't even respond; she just followed meekly when I released the cloth and took to my heels, keeping up with me as we dashed around rocks, fallen trees, and large, dusty-looking shrubs, heading to the fringes of a forest that swayed in the light breeze.

"I can't believe I'm doing this. I should have left you where you were, but Sandor always said that Kiriah honors those who show mercy in her name, and since she's just blessed me—well, you can thank her for the fact that I didn't leave you where you were, that's all I can say. Not even going to tell me how bossy I'm being?"

We reached the edge of the forest as I spoke, the noise of the Harborym growing ever closer as they made up ground, but for some reason I believed the forest offered us a safe haven. It was a place of life, of growing things, of sanctuary for those who wished to hide.

Mayam gave a hiccupping half-sob, saying in a voice that had lost all its arrogance, "I'm not—I wasn't—Lord Racin said that you wish to destroy him. He is not as evil as you think. Once, I thought as you do, but then I learned that he has been betrayed, exiled from those he loves. Those who should have been closest to him drove him from all he held dear. It is for that reason that I plighted myself to his cause, but I see now that the goddesses viewed that as spurning them. Which I would never do! They are most beloved in my eyes."

"Mmhmm," I said, deciding that her mind must have become unhinged when I cast the light net on her. I wound my way around massive trees that caught at our hair and tunics, long streamers dripping from the upper branches, waving in the wind in a manner that reminded me of the thane's hair. "Stay close. It's getting thicker, and if I lose you, I am not going back to find you. Kiriah might not like it, but I will not risk being captured just because you can't make up your mind whose side you are on."

"I'm on no one's side," she protested, her voice still sounding thick. "That is, I want to help Lord Racin, but only because he has been so abused—"

"I think we're going to have to agree to disagree on that subject. Hold!" I raised a hand and held my breath a moment, listening intently. Mayam obediently stopped, glancing around. We had reached some sort of a game trail, the area thick with small shrubs and huge ferns that reached almost to my waist. Overhead, the branches of the trees whispered to each other in the language of the forest. I wished that I had Hallow with me, for I knew he'd made a study of such things, but limited as I was in my training as a priestess of Kiriah, I knew only enough to make out that there was no sound of large bodies crashing through the undergrowth.

I relaxed, lowering my hand. "I don't hear them. With the goddess's grace, we've lost them. Let's go find a high point, so we can see where we are, and then we can figure out how to get out of this blighted land."

Mayam followed me silently, but I felt her emotions leaching out, cloaking us both in a miasma of sorrow, regret, and despair.

Chapter 5

"I leave at dawn." Deo imparted the information to Hallow, then turned and headed for the stable to ensure his horse would be ready for travel.

"What?" Standing outside the single remaining tower of Kelos, his hands spread out over an intricately drawn field of stars that glittered silver in the lifeless grey dust coating everything, Hallow looked up in surprise. The two other arcanists he'd evidently summoned stood with him, the three of them forming a triangle. The air and ground in front of them were full of symbols.

Deo considered the center of the triangle, the focus of all the magic that flowed around the starfield. In the middle of it, a wooden staff had been stuck in the ground, with a wooden bird attached to the top. "I suppose you know what you're about, but I can't imagine anyone wishing to be bound to such a puny-looking eagle."

"It's not an eagle; it's a sparrow hawk, and Thorn will love it, assuming we ever finish this summoning spell. It takes three days if we all concentrate and don't die of exhaustion in the meantime. What do you mean you're leaving at dawn?"

"I mean that at dawn, I will leave," Deo said with more patience than was usual for him. He was in an exceptionally good mood, anticipating the battle waiting for him. Not to mention Idril. They'd only had a short time together after they'd driven Nezu from Eris, and he'd laid down the law about her running off and marrying whoever caught her eye when she was supposed to be waiting for him. But now that he'd made himself clear on that front—and she had finished blistering his ears with her thoughts regarding his quite reasonable commands—he missed her.

"I understand the basics of the sentence, Deo," Hallow said, snapping off each word at the same time he drew glittering symbols in the air. "What I want to know is why you feel compelled to leave right now. As it is, I've just sent Quinn and Ella to sneak into Starfall to keep an eye on what Darius is doing. Aarav and Tygo and I can't stop the summoning spell or we won't get Thorn back, and if we don't get Thorn back, he can't find Allegria and return her to me. Dammit, Deo, don't you dare walk away from me!"

"You have no need of me," Deo said, pausing to send a quick, potent glare to the arcanist. "I can't help you with Allegria's rescue, and you, yourself, saw the message I received this morning that my Banes have definitely sided with Jalas. I didn't believe it could be so, but now there is no doubt of their perfidy. I did not risk all for them to abandon me and join forces with a madman."

Hallow said something so softly that Deo couldn't catch it. "Regardless, we need you here in case the thane and his men return."

"The thane has been driven back to the spirit world. He will not return for some time," Deo said dismissively, his mind busy with the things he would have to say to his Banes when he saw them, alternating with the things he wished to do with Idril's fair body.

"You don't know that—Tygo, quickly, that spell in the lower right is unwinding. Ah. Good catch. You don't know that the thane won't return just as soon as he regains his power." Hallow pulled out a silver dagger and etched runes into the air above the staff. The runes glowed the same as the silver blue symbols on his wrists and ankles before sinking into the wood of the staff itself. "We have need of you here. If the thane were to come back now, we would be vulnerable. And since the whole reason you came to Kelos with us was to take care of the thane, I'd appreciate it if you could remain here to do just that."

Idril had never been one to be driven by the lusts of the flesh, but the most recent meeting with her had changed something inside Deo. His heart had always been hers, but now...now it was as if she was in his blood. He frowned to himself as that thought prickled along his flesh like a particularly spiky burr. How dare she make herself so needful in his life? He made a mental note to inform her that although her place was at his side, delighting him with her quick wits, barbed comments about those who spited him, and her nubile, lush body, he was a warrior first and foremost, the savior of the Fourth Age, and he could not always be stopping his duties to think of her silky thighs, and the weight of her breasts in his hands, and the way she tasted when he parted her legs and—

"Deo?"

With an effort, and an uncomfortably tight feeling in his breeches, Deo realized his mind had wandered to the point that he'd missed whatever it was Hallow was saying. "What?" he asked, mildly peeved that his contemplation of Idril's womanly parts had been disturbed.

"We need you here," Hallow said, his eyes narrowed, and his dagger glinting in the sunlight while he continued to cast runes onto the wooden stock of the staff.

"You have the spirits here to help you should the thane decide to ransom Allegria back to you," Deo said, dismissing the idea of remaining. The message his father had sent was most clear that his Banes had turned, and that, he would not tolerate. "The Banes must return to my side, after which, we will remove Jalas, and then deal with Darius and Nezu."

"You said you wanted to fight," Hallow called out when Deo resumed his path to the stable. "You have a far better opportunity to do so here, where the thane is likely to return, than with your own Banes!"

Deo ignored the comment, alternately focusing on his ire that his Banes, the men for whom he had sacrificed so much, would cast him aside, and the things he had to say to Idril.

The following morning, Deo mounted Crow, the big black stallion who had been his stalwart companion for many years, and rode to the west, leaving behind an angry Hallow who yelled some particularly inventive curses after him.

"—and I can only pray to both goddesses that your stones shrivel up until they are the approximate size and shape of runty raisins, leaving Lady Idril frustrated, and you childless to the end of your days for abandoning us in our time of need!" Hallow finished in a bellow that echoed off the broken walls of the ruined buildings. The three arcanists were still casting their spells upon the staff that would bear the spirit form of the former Master, all three men looking exhausted.

Deo lifted his hand in a rude gesture to indicate he appreciated the quality of Hallow's insult, but quickly dismissed the thoughts of the irate arcanist from his mind in order to better focus on the things he had to do. Hallow would move the stars and moon to rescue his beloved Allegria, and would be far more effective doing so without Deo there getting in the way.

"No," he said in what he thought his most reasonable tone of voice, "there is nothing for me to do in Kelos, and many things to do on Aryia, Crow. First, I must bring the Banes to heel. Then I will tell Idril to stop filling my mind with thoughts of her thighs and belly and breasts and the way her breath hitches when I rub my cheeks on the sensitive flesh of her woman's parts." He thought for a moment, shifting uncomfortably in the saddle. "Perhaps I will deal with Idril first. That would only be polite. Then the Banes, then Jalas, then a return to Genora to show my father how taking care of pesky gods is done. Yes. I like this plan."

Deo continued mulling over his plans for the next day, spending the night at the same inn where the company had rested on the way out to Kelos, and was on the road again as soon as Kiriah graced the morning sky. It was when he was about an hour outside of Bellwether, the sun warming him pleasantly despite the cool air of the coast, that a shout had him reaching for his sword and the chaos magic causing the runes on his harness to light up reddish gold.

Emerging from a curve in the road hidden by a jagged cliff, a small company of eight rode in tight formation. Deo narrowed his eyes as the men spurred their horses toward him. "Those are the queen's colors, but I don't see her. Besides, that's the Old South Road, and my mother went to the north coast, to the land of the water talkers. Who—ahhh. The goddesses are good to us, Crow. Very good."

Deo recognized the pale, pinched face of one of the men, the one who rode in the middle of the others, and joy sang in his blood. He waited until the men charged up to him, swords in hand, the lead-most calling out an order. "Halt! Stand down for King Darius of Starfall!"

"*King* Darius?" Deo dismounted slowly, giving Crow a pat on the neck that warned the horse to move out of the way of harm. "I was not aware that my mother had married, let alone raised her consort to the status of king. Darius, is that you hiding behind these sun-seekers?"

There was no worse slur for a Starborn than to be referred to as their once-most-hated enemy, and Deo took great enjoyment at the angry red face of Queen Dasa's former steward.

"The queen is dead. Long live the king," the headman said, dismounting and lifting his sword, aimed at Deo's heart. "You will kneel before him."

"I kneel before no man," Deo told the upstart soldier with a pitying glance, then brushed past him to where Darius was hiding himself.

"Lord Deo!" Darius looked alternately furious and worried. "What—what do you on Genora? We heard you had been banished to the land of shadows along with Lord Israel."

"You heard wrong. Stop that." He glanced over at the head soldier, who had been poking him in the chest with the sword, clearly trying to get his attention. "This is my only clean tunic, and if you make me get your blood on it, it will be itchy and unbearable all the way to Aryia."

The man sputtered in anger, saying—without taking his eyes off Deo—"Would you have me dispatch this uncouth cur so that you may proceed without vexation, my king?"

Deo stared at the man in wonder for a few seconds, then shook his head. Uncouth cur? Vexation? If that was the sort of man his mother had kept in her court, he'd have to have a few words with her. "I have no time to teach you how a proper soldier speaks, for I must deal with the one who has betrayed my mother. Darius! Come forth. You are now my prisoner, and I will take you with me to Abet, where we will address your perfidy."

"I am not perfidious!" Darius squeaked in his high voice, shoving the men in front of him forward. "Kill him! He wishes harm to me!"

The lead soldier swung his sword back at the same time the other six soldiers rushed forward to attack, but Deo had been carefully keeping the chaos leashed, and with a sigh and another shake of his head, he let the control slip.

It was over in a matter of seconds. "You have much to answer for," Deo told Darius while wiping his sword on the tunic of one of the now dead guards. "First you betray your fealty to the queen by taking her throne, and then you hide behind others rather than facing me yourself. No, do not struggle. If you fall off your horse again, I will simply allow it to drag you." Deo checked that the bonds holding Darius's hands behind his back were secure before tying the reins to his saddle.

"*Mmf frmfm hrn*," Darius said, the words muffled by the sleeve Deo had torn off of one of the dead soldiers and used as a gag to stop the man's unending curses.

"We are going to Abet," Deo answered to what he assumed was his question, and, mounting Crow, continued on the road to Bellwether. "Where you will answer for your crimes, and we will call to order a Council of the Four Armies. Well, we won't have Hallow, or the queen, and of course, Jalas is deranged and an enemy now, so there will really only be one of the four present, but I will represent the Starborn interests, and between my father and me, we will decide how best to deal with you."

Darius protested some more behind his sleeve gag, but eventually he stopped trying to kick Deo, and rode along glumly. They reached Bellwether just as Kiriah was taking her rest for the day.

"You, innkeeper! Do you have a secure gaol in this town? I wish for the usurper to be placed somewhere he cannot escape, since there are many charges for which he must answer," Deo told the rotund innkeeper when the man scurried out to greet him.

"Yes, yes, my lord, we have several rooms that we use for those transporting prisoners. Frog! *Frog!* Where is that boy? Never around when there's work…there you are. Take his lordship's horse, and see that he's rubbed down," the innkeeper instructed a gangly stable lad with a fond buffet to the head.

"No grain," Deo informed the boy, dismounting and handing over Crow's reins. "Not until morning. He's too heated."

A soft whooping noise had them all looking at where Darius lay face down on the ground, evidently having lost his balance and fallen off his horse in his struggle to make someone understand him.

"Send your brother to tend his lordship's prisoner," the innkeeper told the boy Frog as the latter led away a lathered Crow.

Deo hoisted Darius to his feet at the same time a man tottered toward him, calling his name. Deo ignored him, instead looking down the hill to the dock, pleased to see one of the ships that had made the trip between Genora and Aryia. "Evidently we've arrived just in time," Deo told Darius. "I will see to our passage just as soon as you are locked away."

"My lord Deo!" the tottering man said, plucking at his sleeve until Deo spun around to fix him with a glare.

"What is it?" he demanded, having little time to spend chatting with the local citizens.

"This is a fortunate day, despite the horrible trip here. It's a wonder I survived without heaving up all of my internal bits. How anyone can desire to sail anywhere is beyond me. If Lord Israel thinks I'm going to return to Aryia, he is well mistaken." The man's face was pale, gaunt, and unpleasantly moist. "But I must put my own suffering behind me. My lord, I come bearing a message."

"Another one? I just received a message yesterday." Deo took the letter that the messenger dug out of his jerkin. "Ah, this one is from my father, and the other few scribbled lines I had were from Idril. Here." He handed the man a few coins before grasping the back of Darius's jerkin, pulling him into the inn.

"I have cleared out one of the storerooms for your prisoner," the innkeeper said, bustling forward from a dark hallway. He paused as soon as the lantern he held cast its light on the face of Darius, who was moaning and making piteous noises behind his gag. "But…but that is Lord Darius, is it not? King Darius, I should say. Bellias bless us, whatever are you doing with him?"

"He is no king, and just as soon as my mother has gathered her kin, he will be lucky to have his life. As for what I am doing with him, I'm taking him to account for his crimes against Queen Dasa. Stop bleating at me, man. You are not about to perish. Did you act such a weakling in front of the queen? It's a wonder she didn't geld you and turn you into her handmaiden. No," Deo said after a moment's recollection of the sorts of things Idril asked of her maidens. It was almost frightening how cutthroat those handmaidens could be. "Not a handmaiden. Perhaps one of those male harlots who serve other men by dressing up as hairy shepherdesses. Although I doubt if the queen would keep a shepherdess harlot at her court. She'd be more likely to have the male harlots who pleasure women, a thought I must pass along to my father since it will be sure to make him grind his teeth. Innkeeper! Why are you standing here wringing your hands instead of placing Darius into your locked storeroom?"

It took some time, but at long last Deo was seated by the fire. Darius had been given food and wine, and locked away with a privy bucket and a pallet of somewhat smelly furs. Deo drank deeply of the ale provided him by a worried innkeeper before turning his attention to the bit of sealed parchment that the messenger had brought.

Deo, it read, written in his father's neat hand. *May the grace of both goddesses fall upon your unworthy head. By the time this reaches you, Idril and I will have sailed for the north of Genora, to aid the queen in the raising of an army. We leave Aryia because Abet is temporarily out of our reach. I am saddened—although in no way surprised—that your Banes have sided with Jalas against the Fireborn. You have much to answer for in creating those misbegotten creatures, who have now killed a valiant, brave woman.*

For a moment, Deo's heart seemed to cease beating. Had Idril been slain? By the goddesses, if anyone had harmed a hair on her head—he had risen out of the chair and was halfway to the door before he recalled the opening lines. He sat down again, quickly scanning the rest of the message.

Lady Sandorillan, the priestess of the Temple of Kiriah Sunbringer, died at the hands of your Banes. May the goddesses have mercy upon you, for right now, I feel none myself. If you were here, I'd strangle you with my bare hands, but it's just as well you are a continent away, where I cannot work out the grief of losing a stalwart friend and talented priestess to the monsters you created in your own image.

Deo frowned, guilt digging little needles into him before he told himself that he had not raised the Banes of Eris to attack the innocent. Their sole purpose was, and had always been, to free Alba of the Harborym. That they had indeed turned was driven home by the senseless death of Lady

Sandor, and he would have to think long about how he would respond when he again met them.

She did not die in vain, however, dispatching one of them before the other two finished her. Aryia has diminished with her passing, and I trust that you will make appropriate offerings for prayers to be held at the temple in her honor. This stains your soul most grievously, Deo, and although I am sure you are already trying to disclaim any responsibility for Sandor's death, you have much to atone for.

The censure fairly dripped off the parchment, but it wasn't his father's words that had Deo shifting uncomfortably in the chair. The goddesses knew that he had created the Banes to save Alba, but he accepted that by doing so, he was partially to blame for Lady Sandor's death. He *would* have to atone for that sin.

We sail with the coming of Kiriah on the morn. Since I have heard no word of the Eidolon running amok on Genora, I assume you, Hallow, and Allegria have things well under control there. Once I have met up with your mother and assisted her as is needful, we will head south to Starfall. I'm sure you will wish to join us there as your mother reclaims her throne, after which time we will address the issue of Nezu.

There was more to the message, warnings to be wary of dealing with Darius and some magister who served him, but guilt-laden as he was, Deo had had enough of his father lecturing him, and tossed the message onto the fire, thinking hard about his Banes, and what he must do.

The following morning he spent a good hour arguing with the captain of the ship that sat in the harbor, with the end result that his purse was lightened of quite a bit of silver, but by the time Kiriah had reached her zenith, the ship was sailing northwards, along the coast of Genora to the port town of Summit. Forty-six hours later, he rode down through the steep, winding streets of Deeptide, a town that perched on a cliffside like a mushroom on the trunk of a tree. He was mildly surprised that the port of Summit was located some five miles from the water talkers' capital, but as he looked down to the sparkling navy blue water, he realized that despite the name of Deeptide, the rocks continued down from the cliff, prohibiting portage. "Why, then, did the water talkers choose this location for their town?" he asked aloud. "It makes no sense."

"You are as ignorant as you are boorish," Darius snapped, his temper obviously frayed. But that was nothing compared to the whining Deo had been forced to listen to during the journey, both on ship and horseback. He didn't trust Darius, and kept him bound, although reluctantly he'd removed the gag on the voyage north. Somehow, Darius had spirited away the bit of cloth, leaving Deo without a suitable gag.

"I should have spent the time finding a replacement," he grumbled to himself.

"The water witches do not mingle with the Starborn, since they are not beloved of Bellias, as we are. I should have thought you would know this, since they are kin to your mother, but obviously, you never bothered to learn about them," Darius continued with a sniff that made Deo's fist itch to punch something. "They are children of Alba, placed here by the All-Father, keeping to themselves, which is right and proper."

Deo frowned while he dug through the dusty hallways of his mind. He had a vague memory of a tutor explaining to him the rise and fall of various races, but he'd had little time in his youth for such useless things. He made a note to consult his mother about it later, and ignored the pointed references Darius made as they rode down to the shore, where a temple sat at the tip of a long stone pier.

Idril was the first to greet him, moving out of the shadowed entrance of the temple when he halted before it, her lithe form bringing with it a deep sense of satisfaction as she glided toward him, a bevy of handmaidens trailing her.

"My lord Deo," she said, stopping before him and making an elegant curtsey. Her expression was as placid as ever, but he'd seen the flash of fire in her amber eyes. "You are most welcome, although we had no word that you were coming to Deeptide." Her gaze shifted to Darius, a momentary look of surprise on her face melting away almost immediately. "Darius, I did not know you sought to consult the water talkers."

"I don't wish to consult them," Darius snapped, wriggling on his saddle to try to free his hands from where they were bound behind his back. "I have been kidnapped, most brutally and heinously kidnapped by this monstrous behemoth."

"If you keep struggling like that—" Deo started to say, but stopped and gave a little sigh when Darius managed to throw himself off his horse. *Again.* "I'd think you would have better things to do than attempt to harm yourself in this manner. No, Idril, do not assist him up. He's taken to biting whoever is in range. He's worse than Allegria's bile-spawned mule."

Deo was tempted to leave Darius where he lay, but the sight of the queen and his father proceeding down the length of pier toward them had him jerking up the usurper, and even going so far as to brush off the front of the man's jerkin before turning to face his parents.

"Deo! What are you doing here? You are supposed to be at Kelos, assisting Hallow and Allegria," Israel growled. His father's scowl was a fearful thing to behold, but it paled in comparison to the look the queen was bending upon him.

"Once again you have intruded upon my plans in such a manner as to render them completely pointless," Dasa snapped, her nostrils flaring in a dramatic manner.

Stiffly, Deo made his mother a bow, one hand on Darius's back forcing him to do the same. "You must be confusing me with someone else. I have never made any plans pointless except those that aren't worthy of being undertaken, and I'm sure you would never make anything of that sort. Except, of course, for your plan to woo Racin into complacency, at which point you thought to kill him. That was the height of foolishness, as was proven when he escaped Eris."

Dasa's nostrils flared again. Deo wondered if he ought to point that out to her, since it wasn't a particularly flattering look, but upon second thought, he decided against it. Although she wore a becoming and delicate silver and blue gown, a sword was strapped to her hip. After becoming familiar with his mother's temper during the last eleven months, he decided there was no good to come of trying her when she was so armed.

"That plan would have worked but for your interference. Rather, that of both you and your father." Dasa transferred her glare to Israel, who ignored it.

Deo wondered whether or not his mother had dressed to entice his father. He wouldn't have thought so, since their relationship had ever been rocky, and the queen, while comely enough, didn't put much store in how she appeared to others. And yet the flowing garments she wore now were much fancier than he had seen her wear in the past.

"What exactly are you doing here? And why do you have *him*?" the queen asked, gesturing at Darius.

Another thought struck Deo. He turned to Idril. "Did you put that on just to please me?" he asked, gesturing toward the gold and white gauzy gown that fluttered around her hips and thighs in the breeze that rolled in from the water.

"No," she answered after a moment of narrowing her eyes at him. "I wore it because it is comfortable in this heat, and it is what my handmaidens packed. Also, it looks good on me."

There was no denying that fact. He smoothed his hand down his black tunic, which bore the mark of the Banes of Eris, a field of stars and a moon over a sun. He'd taken care to keep this tunic as clean as possible, since he knew Idril would likely be in the company of his mother by the time he arrived. "You look well."

"Thank you," she said with a little smile, patting one of the two long pale blond braids that hung to her waist. "I had a few trying days, but I believe that all of the snails have been relocated to a more suitable environment."

"Deo," his father said in a familiar long-suffering tone. "Your mother asked what you are doing here. You didn't come all this way just to gawk at Lady Idril like a boy whose stones have just dropped."

"I'm wearing my Bane tunic," Deo pointed out to Idril, in case she'd missed that fact. She liked him in black, or so she'd told him on their journey out from Eris. She had said it made him look darkly dangerous, and very sexy. She'd made it very clear that the only thing she liked better than him in black was him without any clothing.

"Yes, you are," she agreed.

"It's black," he said, gesturing toward his chest.

"You have an amazing grasp of colors," she said with slightly raised eyebrow. "I'm glad to know you aren't color blind."

"If I struck him on the head with the hilt of my sword, how long do you think he would be senseless?" the queen asked Israel.

The latter looked thoughtful, and pursed his lips. "Not long enough, I'm afraid. He has an exceptionally hard head. He gets that from you."

She narrowed her lips at him, her fingers twitching toward the hilt of the sword that hung at her waist. "As is usual whenever Deo is present, we have strayed from the point. Deo! Heed me!"

Deo had been on the verge of asking Idril what she thought of his tunic, but a warning note in his mother's voice drew his attention. He recalled himself to the questions his parents had asked, and waved a hand toward Darius. "I came to bring you the usurper."

"I am not a usurper!" Darius squawked, struggling to move forward. Deo held a hand on Darius's jerkin to keep the man from drawing too near the queen. "I was kidnapped by this monstrous—er—by your majesty's son. And may I say how thrilled and delighted I am to see you hale and hearty, Queen Dasa? We had heard the direst rumors, very dire rumors indeed, and everyone said that you had died on Eris, so, what was I to do? I have ever been devoted to you, and I knew I must take charge of the Starborn in a manner that you, yourself, would have done had you been in my shoes."

Israel shook his head, sliding a quick glance at Deo. "Why would you bring this puling mouthpiece to us?"

Deo frowned, not liking the anger visible on both his parents' faces. "I found him on the road on the way to Bellwether and knew you would want to punish him for declaring you dead so he could take your throne." He gathered his dignity around him. Would the day ever dawn when his actions would please his father? "Now that I have done so, I will return to Aryia and deal with my Banes."

Dasa shook her head, muttering to herself under her breath before announcing, "I must return to the negotiations that were so rudely disturbed. I will leave you to deal with our misguided son."

"Misguided!" Deo thought briefly of flaring his own nostrils, decided it was a look he didn't care to have Idril see, and contented himself with a frown at his mother's back when she stalked into the temple at the end of the pier. "This is the thanks I get for bringing her the usurper?"

"Thanks?" Israel took a deep breath, obviously trying to regain patience. "Unless you have Lyl stuffed into your saddlebags, there will be no thanks offered to you."

"Lyl? Who's Lyl?" Deo asked, little flicks of anger stirring the chaos inside him. "It is Darius who usurped the queen's throne."

"Not usurped, kept occupied for her return," the obsequious runt of a man said with an ingratiating smile at Israel.

"Did you not get the message I sent? No, you must have, else you would not have come up here to disturb your mother's delicate negotiations with her kinfolk. Thus, you must have seen the warning I gave you about watching the actions of Lyl, the arcanist who is stirring up the Starborn, and of the importance of your remaining at Kelos. With you, Hallow, and Allegria just two days ride from Starfall City, he will not cause trouble, knowing the threat you three pose him. And yet, you deposit *this* ill-begotten mongrel at our feet and expect praise. Perhaps you would like to explain this, Deo?"

If there was one thing Deo hated, it was being treated as if he was twelve years old, and had been caught doing something forbidden. He was a man grown, the prophesied savior of Alba, and yet here was his father demanding an accounting of his actions just as if he had been a heedless youth.

Guilt pricked at him again, remembering how weary he'd grown of the chastisements in his father's message. "I didn't read all of your missive," he admitted, holding his father's gaze. Deo might be many things, but he was no coward, and he owned up to his mistakes. "I was distraught at the knowledge that my Banes had turned and killed Lady Sandor, and I could read no further."

He assumed that Israel would continue to rail at him, but to Deo's surprise, a flash of pain twisted across his father's face, and he clapped a hand on Deo's shoulder. "I was overly hasty blaming you in that message. For that, I have my grief at losing a friend to blame. While it was your Banes who struck her down, I know full well that you would not condone such actions.

I have never doubted that your intentions are good...sometimes, however, the method you use to achieve them leaves me in doubt of your wisdom."

Deo started to relax, assuming that an accord of some sort had been made between his father and him, but that hope died immediately.

"The fact that you captured the wrong man, leaving a powerful enemy in charge of the Starborn, is another matter altogether," Israel ground out. "The goddesses alone know what Lyl will get up to once he finds out that you are no longer within striking distance of Starfall."

Deo swore to himself. There were days when he felt it simply was not worth the trouble of trying.

Chapter 6

"The All-Father and Life-Mother were childless and, desiring offspring, they created Alba and imbued it with many life forms: giants who later turned their faces from the skies and became one with the dirt and rock, trees and streams, thus blessing Aryia with their peculiar root magic known as the Grace of Alba."

"Mmhmm," I murmured, only half-listening to Mayam. I pushed aside long gray-green streamers from the massive tree in front of me, and paused, considering the village that lay before us. Spirits drifted around the small huts with the languid, almost elegant movements of those who chose to remain in the spirit realm. The spirits appeared in varying shades of grey, everything from the white of their hair down to the almost-black of the cloth that clad their incorporeal forms. This was the third such village we had encountered during our time in the spirit world, and like the others, the inhabitants here paid us little attention.

"Sylphs, ethereal beings who were a favorite of the Life-Mother, brought magic to the world, until they, too, faded away, this time into the stars that glittered in the night sky. Arcany, their magic is called."

"Fascinating," I said softly, narrowing my eyes at two shades who drifted past me. They bore familiar tunics, ones that I had seen on the shades who served the Harborym.

Mayam, who had insisted on educating me concerning the All-Father and the creation of the races of Alba, continued with her catechism. "The All-Father gave Alba the Eidolon."

That caught my interest. I stopped frowning at the spirits and turned back to where she was picking a bit of grey streamer frond from her shoulder. "Oh? Why?"

She shrugged. "They were said to have been fashioned in his own image, imbued with his strength, and for millennia, they ruled the five continents."

So this mysterious All-Father was responsible for the Eidolon being on Alba? And yet the thane—and by extension, Nezu—wanted to destroy him? I wished I could discuss the subject with Hallow. He knew so much more about the lore of Alba than I did, and he was sure to have insights that escaped me.

"Then the Life-Mother gave birth to twin daughters, Kiriah and Bellias, followed later by a son, Nezu."

I started to snort, but at a quick look from Mayam, converted it to a cough.

"For a time, the children watched over Alba with benevolent eyes, but soon...er...soon..." Her words trailed off. One hand fidgeted with a buckle on her belt, her expression an interesting mix of discomfort and confusion.

"Soon one of the children's gazes wasn't quite so benevolent?" I guessed, feeling a little sorry for her. During the day we'd been roaming the grey landscape of the spirit world together, Mayam had become more and more like the woman I remembered from Eris—less aggressive and antagonistic, more relaxed, and introspective, almost pleasant.

"Erm...yes." She cleared her throat and said so quickly the words were almost run together, "Nezu grew jealous of his sisters. The All-Father had made Kiriah the sun, her light touching everything that lived, blessing all growing things and providing warmth, while Bellias became the light that glowed from the stars and moons, piercing the darkness that was Nezu's own gift. Bellias brought to Alba the power of arcany, but Nezu was given no magic to bestow. It wasn't fair," she added, the last sentence spoken loudly.

"But life seldom is, don't you find?" I asked, and after giving one last glance at the spirits, walked through the village, headed in a direction that I hoped would lead us somewhere. *Anywhere.* I was growing tired of the cloying sense of being smothered. Everything in the spirit realm was muffled, from the sounds on down to the slow, methodical movements of its denizens. I felt isolated, and muzzy-headed at the same time, my brain slowing down to match the rhythm of life—or lack of it—around us.

"Life is what you make it. That's what my old master used to say," Mayam replied, trailing behind me.

"What master was that?" I asked, curious. I knew she'd been a handmaiden to a noblewoman on Eris, but had little idea of what her life had been like.

"My brother—you remember Jena?—he did not always belong to the brothership of the red hand."

"The blood priests?"

She nodded. "Before that, he studied with an abjuror, a most learned man, but one who had been cast from his order due to...irregularities. He allowed me to learn from him, as well, although he told me I would never make an abjuror since I lacked the focus my brother had."

"What sort of irregularities can an unmaker of magic perform?" I asked, pausing when I heard the sound of hoofbeats. Hoofbeats? Here? No one rode in the spirit realm. No one who belonged here.

With a finger to my lips to warn Mayam, I pulled her off the road and back into the tall grass that flourished around us. We lay down on our bellies, allowing the grass to cover us, although I parted a few strands to watch the road where it curved from the village we'd just left.

Three Harborym came into view, their relaxed poses signaling either a long time in the saddle, or a lack of interest in their surroundings. Or perhaps both—either way, it was all to our good, and I waited until they were well out of earshot before whispering, "They did not appear to be hunting for us."

"Not for us, no, but Lord Racin instructed several Harborym to survey the residents of this world, searching for those who might be useful to him."

"A scouting party, hmm? Interesting." I wondered how spirits would be useful to Nezu in the mortal world, where they were subjected to limitations, but decided that was a problem for another day. I'd have to ask...have to ask...for a moment, my mind went blank, and I couldn't draw forth the name I wanted. "Hallow!" I finally managed to say, accompanied by a shake of my head at my addled mind.

"What about him?"

"Nothing. I'm just tired, and my brain is filled with this damned pervasive dust. I think it's safe enough for us to cross. We'll go to the east for a bit, since the Harborym appear to be sticking to the west roads."

We walked in silence for a half hour before Mayam said, "Did you want to hear the rest of the history?"

"Please," I said, tired of my own glum thoughts. "Although I didn't know there was more."

"Some, not a lot. Jealousy begets jealousy, and so Nezu whispered into the ears of the three thanes, corrupting the Eidolon with his desire for what belonged to others."

I glanced at her, but to my surprise, her face was placid, not reflecting the discomfort that had been there earlier when she spoke of Nezu's actions. Still, it was interesting to know that he had a history with the thanes.

"The Eidolon, beloved of the All-Father, felt that they, too, were worthy of such power as was granted to the twin goddesses, and when the All-Father, angered by their greed, swore that he would destroy Alba before he gave in to their demands, they—the thanes—allowed desire to cloud reason."

"Blessed Kiriah's toes!" I gasped, shocked at the idea that the creator of Alba should be so willing to destroy his creation rather than allow the Eidolon to live. "What sort of a god was this All-Father? No, never mind, I can guess. I see that Nezu is much like his father."

"In a battle that resulted in the fall of the Eidolon, the All-Father attempted to destroy that which he and the Life-Mother had created," she said in a voice that was weary beyond words.

I glanced in concern at her as we struggled along a path that twisted around massive boulders up a rocky hill, but she seemed to be managing well enough. I noted absently that here and there, little spots of color dotted the landscape—the dirty yellow of a weedy flower, the bright green of scrubby little flowers that sprouted between the boulders—and for some reason, it gave me a bit of hope. If life—of some sort—could cling to existence here, then we were not doomed, as Mayam was wont to say.

"Since we are here now—here on Alba, not the spirit realm—I assume that battle did not end well for either party?" I asked, intrigued despite myself. Sandor had confined our history lessons to those that most affected the Fireborn, with only a few mentions of other lands.

"It did not. Kiriah and Bellias could not stand to see their beloved Alba destroyed due to the All-Father's rage. Instead, with Nezu's aid, they imprisoned him in the Altar of Day and Night. Then, with the Eidolon fallen, the goddesses brought the Fireborn and Starborn forth on Alba. Nezu, nettled that they did not think of his own children while they divided the continents between them, quickly claimed Eris for us. For the Shadowborn." She fell silent again.

I had a feeling there was more to the tale, but since we were approaching another village, this one of moderate size, I didn't press her for more. We paused on the edge of the village, watching the spirits. As with others we had encountered, these spirits took no particular notice of us while they drifted about their daily business. I was about to move on when there was a disturbance at the far end of the village, where a gabled hall towered over the other structures, and a man in long, flowing robes with spiky hair and a prodigious beard strode forward, gesturing and talking as he approached. On his heels, a short, fat, ghostly dog trotted.

"—you always in my way? Can you not see I have important business to conduct? There are two people here whom I did not expect to see, certainly did not expect to see, and they must not be here! Do you hear me? Must not be here! You! Ghost slayer! What is her name? It was told to me, but I've forgotten it. The boy wed her, I heard, which is right and proper, but doesn't help me with her name. Still, she shouldn't be here, no, she shouldn't. You, ghost slayer! It's dangerous for you. Do you not know the Eidolon have risen again? Some of them have, not all, because there are legions of them, but enough to make things very uncomfortable around here, very uncomfortable indeed!"

I stopped and blinked at the man who stood in front of me. He was the last person I'd expected to see here. "Er...Exodius?"

"Yes, yes, it is I, but what are you doing here? Did my apprentice send you with a message for me? He shouldn't have done that. He could have had any number of the spirits in Kelos do the job, not that I want to be bothered by them, because I have my own work to do here, very important work," he answered, his hands fluttering as he spoke. He added in an aside, turning so he addressed himself to Mayam, "Technically the boy isn't really my apprentice, but he could well have been so had he been born a few hundred years before. You're Shadowborn."

"I am," Mayam agreed, her eyes round. She edged a little closer to me.

"It's nice to see you again, Exodius, although I don't think we've been formally introduced. I'm Allegria, and this is Mayam."

Mayam made a little bob at him.

"Exodius was the runeseeker who...er..." For a moment my mind went blank, the information I wanted sliding away just as I tried to grab it.

Exodius and Mayam both stared at me, obviously waiting for me to finish my sentence. I gave a little rub to my forehead, deciding I must be more tired than I thought if I couldn't pull up the name of the man who filled my life with such joy.

"Used to be the Master of Kelos?" Exodius finished for me after the several seconds of silence. "I was, and a right pain in the arse it was, but that master of mine insisted that he had other things to do, bigger and more important things than leading the arcanists, but I ask you, what could be more important than being the Master of Kelos? Thorn always was a few bulls short of a herd, but there, that's what comes from being born of the Koshan."

"What's a Koshan?" Mayam asked me in a whisper, her gaze firmly affixed to Exodius.

I racked my brain. "I think they mastered the old magic, before Kiriah and Bellias."

"They did, and good riddance to them," Exodius said, evidently having heard our whispered exchange. "Maddening lot, all of them. But what are you and this Shadowborn maiden doing here? Where is Hallow?"

Hallow. My mind sighed with relief at the word. Why all of a sudden was I having such trouble holding onto his name? Just the echo of it in my head made me feel his loss. I wished I was in his arms at that moment, kissing his face, and…and…once again, my mind stuttered to a halt when I tried to bring up a mental vision of his face. I knew it as well as I knew my own, and yet, other than a vague image of bright blue eyes and blond hair, I couldn't seem to pull it into focus.

Mayam shot me a quick questioning look before answering Exodius. "I came with Lord Racin."

"Racin?" Exodius asked.

"Nezu," I explained. "He went by the other name on Eris."

"Nezu is here?" Exodius froze for a moment, his face devoid of expression.

"Yes. He was forced to come here because he wished to consult with… er…" Mayam waved a hand in a vague gesture, her face screwed up as she obviously tried to remember something. An expression of relief filled her face as she hurriedly finished, "With…uh…oh, the thane. The Eidolon thane."

Panic flooded me while I tried to recall anything about Hallow. I knew his body almost as well as his face, and yet, the memories that came to mind were emotion-based, the swell of love that rose deep within me whenever I thought of him, along with the sorrow of being parted. I felt as if part of me was missing, and yet… "Blast his delectable hide, why can't I remember what his man parts look like?"

Both Mayam and Exodius stared in surprise at me.

"I don't know the answer to that question," Exodius said slowly, giving me a long, considering look. "More to the point, I don't want to know why you should have a familiarity with the thane's man parts, especially as you are said to be wedded to my apprentice."

"I *am* married to Hallow, not that he's your apprentice. We are most definitely happily married, and I do not know what the thane's man parts look like. My pronoun use is also obviously suffering from lack of sleep. What did you ask? Oh, what we're doing here? Mayam, as she said, is here with Nezu, while I was kidnapped by the thane, he of whose man parts I remain in absolute ignorance. There was a battle at Kelos with the thane and his Eidolon attacking our spirits. And Hallow and I were just about to take down the thane—or at least drain his energy enough that he'd have to retreat to this realm—when all of a sudden, he yanked me here."

Exodius was silent for a minute. I studied him, making mental notes on the conversation, so that later I could describe the scene accurately to... to... "Oh, for the love of the twin goddesses, I just thought his name! It can't slip away a few seconds later!"

Exodius gave me a glance full of pity, shaking his head and saying, "It can, and it will."

"What do you mean?" Mayam asked just as I was about to do the same.

"You are living," he answered with a little shrug. "What is a haven to the spirits of the dead is a place of isolation for you. The longer you remain here, isolated from the world to which you have ties, the weaker those ties grow. If you diminish to a point where the physical world has no hold on you, you will in effect be caught between life and death, confined to an endless existence without hope of escape."

Horror filled me, driving before it the panic that had just gripped me. "Hallow! His name is Hallow of Penhallow of the region of Hallow, so named because his parents were just as quirky as he is," I said quickly, fear giving my brain the push it needed. The image of the man I loved rose in my mind's eye, everything from his glittering topaz blue eyes to his eye crinkles and on down to the chest that still made my knees feel like they were made of nothing more substantial than porridge. With relief, I grasped those memories, and forced my brain to dredge up a handful more. "And he has a most prodigious man part, one that stands and waves at me when Hallow is feeling amorous."

"Yeees," Exodius drawled, his lips pursed. "Rather more information than I expected to have in a casual conversation with you, but still, it's good to know you appreciate the boy. However, I think it's best that you leave the sprit realm despite the fact that you are clearly even now recalling several adventures with Hallow's man bits, which means you are not as badly affected as I first feared. That is well and good, but still, you can't stay. And as for you..." He turned back to Mayam, who shot him a startled look in return. His eyes narrowed on her. "I want you to tell me everything that happened while you were with Nezu, most particularly what his plans are."

"Why?" I couldn't help but ask, reluctantly dismissing a particularly wonderful memory of the experience Hallow and I shared against a tree on our way out to Kelos. I had a horrible desire to relive as many memories as I could lest I risk losing them, but instead I promised myself that I would move Kiriah and Bellias themselves if I had to in order to get back to my love's side.

Exodius was silent, once again making me wonder if he was quite so chatty as Hallow claimed he had been during the short time they were together. "He is...dangerous."

"To Alba?" I made a face, a bit confused by the statement. "That goes without saying."

"He is dangerous to *you*," Exodius interrupted, then abruptly made shooing motions at us. "I've changed my mind. I have much work to do, a great deal of work to do, important work, but regardless of that, I will take the time to find out elsewhere what I need to know about Nezu's plans. You must leave now, priestling. It's not at all safe for you here. Take the Shadowborn with you, but get out."

"I would be happy to leave, but I have no idea how to get out of here, let alone where we are. I thought the spirit realm was a slightly altered version of our world, but this place—" I looked around at the small village, and its ghostly denizens who drifted around aimlessly. "This is unlike anywhere I've seen."

"It is a spirit version of the physical realm, yes, but there are differences," Exodius said, shooing me again, going so far as to give me a little shove forward. "You'll simply have to find one of the entrances yourself. I have no time, no time at all to help you, not if Nezu is here. If he has met with the thane, then he must be planning to..." He stopped talking and simply spun around on his heel and marched off toward the large hall, the little dog trotting after him.

"He's helping the thane kill someone called the All-Father," I yelled after him, frustration uppermost in my mind. In an odd way, I relished the sharp, uncomfortable emotion, since I realized now that ever since I'd entered the spirit realm, my emotions had been dampened, almost as if they, too, were being slowly smothered. "Do you know who that is?"

Exodius waved a hand in the air, his voice drifting back as he continued to walk away. "You must leave, else all will be lost. Thorn can't do it by himself, after all. Return to your arcanist, and bring that big friend, the one with the red death inside him. Only together will you succeed."

"I cannot tell you how annoying I find it when people drop mysterious comments like that, and then expect me to just go on my way as if I understand," I grumbled, glaring at Exodius when his figure disappeared into the hall. "It's irritating, and if I didn't want to stay annoyed so I don't forget Hallow again, I'd go right up to the old coot and smack him on the back of his head with the hilt of one of my swords."

"He's...odd," Mayam agreed, and followed when I spun around, my hands on my hips as I carefully nursed my anger. "Where to now, do you think?"

I hesitated a second, drawing a mental map in my head of our journey through the spirit realm. "We'll keep going east," I said finally, glancing up to align myself. Although there was a hazy layer of clouds over the spirit realm, filtering the light of Kiriah Sunbringer, it wasn't oppressive and impenetrable as it was on Eris. I started forward, determination burning in my blood. "We haven't been that way yet. There has to be an exit somewhere. It's just a matter of being comprehensive in our search."

"I think it's going to take a bit more than comprehensiveness," Mayam said softly when I pushed my way through the greyish foliage, and struck out on a path that appeared to meander eastward through sparsely forested land.

I had a horrible feeling she was all too right.

Chapter 7

"I'm sorry, Hallow—I know you want your wife back, but if this attempt doesn't work, I'm going to have to take a break. Just a short one, I promise. My mind is so muzzy with lack of sleep that I feel like my head is filled with treacle," Tygo said, his round, earnest face drawn, clearly showing he was at the end of his strength.

"We'll all take a break if this doesn't work," Hallow answered, his shoulders slumped with fatigue, sorrow, and worry. Although he managed to keep his mind focused on the spells to be cast, the runes to be drawn, and the words of the invocation to summon Thorn into the staff that stood before the three arcanists, he, too, was exhausted. "Goddesses willing, this will work."

"Arcany is a demanding mistress," Aarav said from his point on the triangle, his hands dancing in the air while he sketched the runes of power that would be imbued into the staff itself. "You must give her your all, Tygo, or she will have none of you. Complaining that you are tired and want a rest is the sign that you will never be a master arcanist, such as Hallow."

Hallow stopped worrying about Allegria for a few seconds to register irritation at Aarav's rejoinder. For one thing, they had all been working almost non-stop for three days, with only brief snatches of rest when they were ready to drop. It wasn't fair for Aarav to chastise Tygo. He reminded himself that although something about Aarav rubbed him the wrong way, he didn't need to give in to the urge to tell the other arcanist to keep his mind on his magic, and not to worry about what anyone else was doing. "Just two more spells to go. Aarav, you have the focus runes drawn on the bird?"

"Aye, and I've placed the blessing of the stars into the head of the staff, where the bird rests. Tygo ought to have done that, but since he has spent all his time on the Bellias-stone, I felt it best to do it myself so that we'd be sure it got done."

There was an unspoken accusation that it was this lack on Tygo's part that had caused the summoning spell to fail the past two times, but Hallow was simply too worried to do more than say, "The consecration of the Bellias-stone is of the greatest importance, so I'm happy to have him ensure it receives the goddess's approval before he places it."

"Almost done," Tygo answered in a distracted manner. His eyes narrowed as he wove spells of arcany around a glittering bit of blue-white crystal, one that had fallen to Genora several hundred years ago when the stars burned across an ebony night sky in blazing streaks of light. "It's just a matter—Bellias blast the thing, it won't fit where it's supposed to go—it's just a matter of placing it at the apex of the spell …there." The last word was spoken in a sigh of relief as the crystal snapped into place, held by the power imbued into the staff.

"Very nice. Very pretty," a smooth voice said from behind Hallow. He half-turned, unwilling to stop drawing the last of the wards on the spell that were needed to protect the inhabitant. A handsome, smiling man sat on an elegant white horse that picked its way carefully through the debris of rock and sparse vegetation, giving the impression that the ground sullied its glossy, polished hooves. The horse was not only pristine despite the ever-present grey dust of Kelos, but even its barding of silver stars and moons on a field of midnight blue looked as if it had just come from the hands of a groom. Both it and the horse positively sparkled. "I particularly like the focusing runes at the top. That should make for a very powerful weapon, very potent. I will enjoy wielding it against my foes. Ah, but the famed Thorn of Kelos is not inhabiting it yet?"

"This staff belongs to the *Master* of Kelos," Tygo said quickly, before Hallow could decide on the best way to respond to such provocative statements as the stranger had seen fit to offer. "Only he can wield it."

The man halted next to Hallow, making a show of looking around, the expression of distaste that crossed his face almost exactly mirroring the one borne by his horse. "Blessings of the goddesses," he said politely, continuing to layer on the last ward. "It's not often we have visitors to Kelos. Not ones who are alive, that is. Who might you be?"

"I *might* be anyone, but I am, in fact, Lyl of Starfall. Well…" The man made a face, then slowly got off the horse. That's when Hallow noticed that a company of at least two score followed the man; the sounds of the horses' hooves were muffled by the dusty air. From the corner of his eye, Hallow saw the captain of the guard materialize, his hand immediately going to the hilt of his sword. "I *was* Lyl of Starfall. Now I am Lyl, Master of Kelos. You are Hello?"

"I'm afraid you are confused about more than just my name, which is Hallow of Penhallow. I lead the arcanists, and head the guild. But I believe I've heard of you," Hallow said, finishing the ward and turning to face the man fully. The staff glowed with a soft white light, accompanied by a drawing sense in the air that made the hairs on Hallow's arms prickle. All that needed to be done was for the three arcanists to speak the words of summoning, which would hopefully pull Thorn from the spirit realm to this one. "You serve Darius, do you not?"

"I serve no man but myself," Lyl answered, eyeing the tower behind Hallow. "That appears to be the only standing structure. I assume that is my quarters? Trulane! Have the arcanist's things removed, and the chambers made ready for me."

A tall, willowy man ran forward on Lyl's command and bowed obsequiously, although he shot Hallow a wary glance. "It shall be as you command, my lord. But...er...there appears to be a spirit guarding the door."

The captain of the guard did indeed stand with his back to the door that led into the tower, his shield and sword in his hands. Lyl considered this for a moment with pursed lips.

"I don't know why you are under the delusion that you have been named Master here, but I can assure you it is not so. Not only was Exodius quite clear when he named me as his successor, but I've worked hard to bring the Arcanist's Guild to order. Or as much order as one can impose on arcanists," Hallow said in a mild tone of voice, one that belied the anger he felt. It was already beginning to waken the chaos magic inside him. The quirky side of his mind, the one that found humor in odd situations, had him adding, "And I just don't know how my chaos magic is going to manifest itself if Allegria isn't here to be the recipient of its attentions. I dread having to explain to her that I was forced into seducing you simply because you annoyed me."

Lyl looked startled for a moment before composing his face into an impassive—if somewhat haughty—expression. "Your lustful urges are as dirt to me, arcanist, although your interest in seducing me is duly noted. Trulane!"

"Aye, my lord," the ingratiating man said, quickly scribbling with a stub of a pencil in a small journal. "It is so noted."

Hallow sighed to himself and wondered how his life had gone so wrong in the course of just a few days.

"As for my delusion, as you refer to it, I fear it is you who are mistaken. I was Exodius's apprentice, and when he departed the mortal realm, it is I who should have taken up the mantle of Master of Kelos. I was busy elsewhere, so naturally, he sought a temporary replacement." Lyl put his hands on his hips as he glanced around again. "But I have returned to Genora, and now that the Starborn throne is secured, I can turn my attention to my rightful place here. Trulane, why are you not attending to your duties inside the tower?"

"The spirit—" Trulane bleated, gesturing toward the captain of the guard.

"Is dead. Dissipate his form, and do as you are ordered. The rest of you—spread out and round up any spirits who are hiding. A new reign has come to Kelos, one of order and structure, and I would have everyone present learn their place in it."

"I don't have time for this foolishness," Hallow said, hastily casting a spell on the tower before turning back to the staff, intent on conducting the summoning despite Lyl's appearance and his deranged attempt to take over. "Tygo, Aarav, are you ready?"

"Aye," the men replied in unison.

"Then let us proceed." Hallow didn't like having Lyl present while they had to focus on the delicate spell of summoning, but he'd be damned if he forced Allegria to wait even a minute longer in the spirit world than was needed. Besides, there were only forty or so soldiers—driving them from Kelos wouldn't be easy, but not impossible, especially with Aarav and Tygo to help him, along with the spirits who resided around them. He cleared his mind of worry about Allegria, the fear that the chaos power was growing in strength, and annoyance at Lyl.

"You, sergeant." Lyl beckoned at one of the soldiers, who hurried forward. "Tell the rest of the company to take shelter around the ruins as best they can. I realize the accommodations are not at all what the Starborn army is used to, but it is important that we squelch any problems that may arise with my ascension to power."

Hallow, his hands already drawing in arcane power from the stars, as well as the energy that had been absorbed by the plants and living things around them, glanced at Lyl, his eyebrows rising as he realized the company of men with Lyl was not his entire force.

"What army?" Aarav asked with a sniff. "When last I was in Starfall, there were only a handful of Starborn who'd survived the purging by the

Harborym. If you think to disturb us with two score men, you will soon see the folly of such a plan."

Lyl smiled, a gesture that made Hallow's gut tighten uncomfortably. "Which is why we were happy to welcome to Starfall the ranks of Harii who had been driven by famine from their land. We have named them Starborn, and they show their gratitude by filling out the Starborn army. Five legions will join us soon."

Aarav and Tygo slid almost identical glances toward him. Hallow continued to struggle with the red rage that wanted to break free of his control. Dread filled him, firing the chaos power until a pool of red formed at his feet. He struggled to control it, beating down panic at the thought of the army no doubt even now heading their way. There were just too many of them, and too little of him.

Lyl would be in the position to take from him the one hope he had of freeing Allegria.

"Kiriah will never rise on the day when I let my heart go without a fight," he swore under his breath. All the same, there was no way the three of them—even with the assistance of the captain of the guard and the spirits of Kelos—would be able to fight off the entire Starborn army once its full force arrived. If only Deo hadn't left...but he stopped that train of thought before it had done more than form in his mind. Deo would have helped, but there were limits to his power as well.

"Master Hallow?" Tygo asked, his gaze moving from Lyl to Hallow, clearly asking whether or not they were going to stop the summoning in order to attend to the threat of Lyl's army.

"Stay focused," Hallow told Tygo and Aarav. He noticed the latter sketching protection runes covertly over his chest and tried to ignore the sounds and sights of the Starborn company moving into Kelos. Behind him, he heard the shout of the captain of the guard, and the sound of the captain's all-too-corporeal blade striking another. He closed his eyes for a moment, whispering the spells, picturing Thorn inhabiting the staff.

"Send half of your men to the north side," Lyl ordered, now striding about, flinging orders in all directions. "Seal the crypts so that no more spirits may rise. Those of you with talismans of the dead may use them at will. This place has long been overrun with ghosts, and I intend to prune away those who do not have anything to offer. Trulane, stop wasting time with that guard. I want to get into the tower. Exodius would have taken any valuables away with him, but I wish to have his archives at hand. Sergeant! Take the staff the arcanists are working over. I will finish it to my own specifications."

Katie MacAlister

Hallow pushed down his fear and worry, and pulled hard on the arcany that surrounded him even when Kiriah was at her brightest in the noon sky. The chaos magic fought his intentions, filling him not with lust this time, but with the desire to destroy the living beings around him. Hallow worried for a moment that since chaos was the magic of death, it would taint the summoning, but the runes on his cuffs held true, allowing him to concentrate, filling the triangle holding the staff with pure arcany.

He pretended he didn't see the runes on his wrists glowing a deep, rich red rather than their usual blue.

"Don't make me repeat myself!" Lyl yelled, cuffing one of the men on the back of the head when he pointed toward Hallow and the others. "Get the staff! Has that spirit been removed yet? I want that door to the tower opened in the next ten seconds, or I will call down the wrath of the twin goddesses upon you!"

Hallow's eyes were the merest slits as binding words tumbled from his mouth. Three men had started toward the staff. Aarav and Tygo's mouths moved as well, no doubt also intoning their parts of the summoning spell. A separate part of his mind sent a prayer to Bellias to give them just a few more seconds to finish the summoning, just the time it would take to bring Thorn forth.

And what, that part of his brain asked, *will happen if the summoning fails again?*

He had no time for such thoughts. He threw all of his love and fear into the words that slipped over his lips to fly immediately upward, spinning and twirling in the air like leaves in the autumn. The staff itself broke free of its stand, lifting a foot off the ground, its runes glowing with a white-blue energy that cracked and snapped.

"Take it!" Lyl shrieked when the nearest men hesitated at the outer edge of the triangle, obviously hesitant to reach inside to grab the staff. "Don't be such a fool! It can't hurt you! I demand that you bring it to me now!"

Just as the last word of the summoning was spoken, the soldier reached into the circle, and it seemed to Hallow as if the whole of Alba held its breath, waiting for the space between heartbeats to see what would happen.

The light from the runes glowed brighter, blinding Hallow. For a moment, the light formed the shape of a woman, and then the blaze of bluish white faded, and a familiar voice sounded in his head.

It's about time! But I told you this form was too big. Although the wing size is nice. And that's an interesting tail you carved for me. Hmm. I could get used to this. Sparrow hawk, is it? Yes, yes, I see now that it has possibilities. Mind you, it's no swallow, but—

"Thorn, as Master of Kelos, I order you back into the spirit realm," Hallow shouted, just as the guard snatched the staff from his hands. "Find Allegria. Help her! Bring her back to me!"

What? The priestling is in the spirit realm? Why? Is that Lyl standing back there screaming about something? Thorn gave a disgusted snort. *What is he doing here? Why is he taking the staff?*

"Thorn, obey my command!" Hallow shouted over Lyl yelling at the soldiers. The chaos magic surged inside him. He doubled over, pain lacing his body, stabbing into him with the sharpness of a honed blade while he struggled to keep the magic from simply exploding out of him.

Someone has grown a fat head in the time I was away, Thorn said in a huffy voice. *Fine! I'll go fetch the girl, but I will have a word or two to say to you when I get back!*

Hallow dropped to his knees, his arms wrapped around his chest, agony riding him, but before the red haze consumed his awareness, he managed to whisper, "I don't think you will, no."

It took some time before he was able to stand and face a furious Lyl. He felt shaken, as weak as a kitten, and ready to sleep for at least a fortnight, but at last all the magics that lived inside him were once again subdued.

"That was a close thing, Master Hallow," said Tygo, who stood bound next to Hallow. The younger man eyed him as if he were a rare flower. "I thought for sure you would destroy Lord Lyl, and perhaps the entire army."

"Master Hallow has more sense than to do something so foolish," Aarav said from Hallow's other side, where he, too, was bound. He gave one of his annoyed (and annoying) sniffs, but even that failed to stir anything in Hallow but an abstracted thought that he'd be forever grateful both men had answered his call.

"*Master* Hallow is no more," Lyl said, storming over to them, his face red with fury. "Hallow of Penhallow, late of Kelos, I claim the title of Master from you, and name you outcast. Your standing with the Arcanists' Guild is stripped. You are no longer recognized by me or Bellias."

Hallow felt as if his horse had kicked him in the gut, and stumbled backward at the words. Tiny invisible ties that connected him to all other arcanists seemed to snap off and wither away, leaving him—for the first time in many years—with the sensation of being utterly alone in the world, with no connection to anyone else.

But he had Allegria now, even if he couldn't feel her presence.

Lyl turned to Tygo, his expression indicating just how unimpressed he was. "What is your name, arcanist?"

"Tygo Starcaller," he answered, giving Lyl a bow made awkward by the rope that bound his hands to a bit of standing stone behind him.

Hallow slid him a quick glance, a bit startled by the surname. Starcaller was the name of a highborn family, one with ties to the queen. He'd had no idea Tygo had such illustrious roots, but it explained why Lyl, with a curl of his lip, said nothing more before moving on to Aarav. "And you? Who are you?"

"I am Aarav, son of Aaram," that individual replied with a haughty tone that Hallow was coming to think was ingrained in him. "I come from the region of Dimwatch, but I was trained by Exodius, the Master before Hallow."

Once again, Hallow found himself taken aback by the men who had aided him. Exodius, Thorn had told him, had taken on only three apprentices in the centuries he had been Master of Kelos, and evidently Lyl had been one of the three. That Aarav should be another was surprising. Could it be just a coincidence, or was there a connection between the two?

"The time of your punishment is at hand," Lyl said, gesturing to one of the guards who stood in a line behind him.

"Punishment?" Tygo asked, glancing to Hallow and Aarav. He licked his lips. "Why are we being punished? We have committed no crime."

"You both have acted against me in the assistance you gave Hallow," Lyl pronounced, listening when one of the guards spoke softly in his ear.

"Hallow was Master when we answered his call," Aarav pointed out. Hallow had to give him full points for appearing almost bored by the situation, but a suspicious part of his mind pointed out that if the man was connected to Lyl, then he had little to fear in the way of punishment. "As Tygo says, we have done no wrong, and have, in fact, been treated without respect or honor by you and your men. As an arcanist of good standing in the Guild, I demand that you release us."

Lyl watched him for a moment before turning his attention back to Hallow. "Since you feel so abused, I will remove you, too, from the Guild rolls. Henceforth, I name you outcast. You are no longer blessed in Bellias's eyes."

Aarav jerked, just as if he, too, had been struck a blow.

"This is poor payment for all the help you've given me," Hallow told him softly. "You have my apologies for how things turned out, and my promise that I will do everything I can to reinstate you with the Guild."

"You are Master no longer," Lyl snapped. "You cannot help him any more than you can yourself. But I am willing to barter with you."

What was this? Lyl was willing to negotiate for the control of Kelos? Hallow gave a mental head shake. It made no sense. "What do you want of me?" he asked.

Lyl half-turned and waved a hand toward the tower. The captain of the guard had disappeared, but the door to the tower stood closed despite the four men clustered around it, attempting to use a massive stone to break it down. "You did something to the tower. Sealed it, I suspect, although I have never seen a seal like that before."

"It's one of my own design," Hallow answered, wondering what Lyl was up to. He was able to focus again now despite his exhaustion, his mind calm with the knowledge that Thorn was helping Allegria. "And you might as well tell your men to stop attempting to break down the door. Nothing can get through it until I remove the spell."

"And that is the crux of the matter." Lyl moved until he stood a few inches from Hallow, obviously attempting to intimidate him. "Open the tower, and I will release your friends."

"The captain of the guard?" Hallow asked, confused for a moment. "Or Tygo and Aarav? Never mind—it doesn't matter. The captain will return when he has regained his energy, and my compatriots are well able to take care of themselves, although I do apologize to them both for the treatment you have shown us. For a man who professes to be the head of the order of arcanists, you appear to have no respect for gifted practitioners."

"Just so," Aarav agreed, while Tygo nodded vigorously.

Lyl's face turned red. He shoved it into Hallow's, little bits of spittle flying out when he snarled, "Sooner or later, I'll get into the tower. And when I do, I will throw you and your friends into the depths of the crypt that lies beneath it, where you can molder away to dust."

Hallow considered his options when one of the soldiers ran up demanding Lyl's attention for a few minutes. Without the staff, Hallow had lost much of his power, but he was not helpless.

Despite being bound, his fingers started drawing symbols in the air behind him, symbols that he linked together in chains. Although the summoning of Thorn had left his arcane abilities depleted, he drew on the bond between living things, the changes that were wrought in them, and the complex links that formed a net of connections. There was power in those connections, magic in the links, and just as he pulled strength from them to make chain after chain, he picked through his tired thoughts.

Though he'd never sought the position of leader of the arcanists, he'd be damned if he just handed over the responsibility without so much as a by-your-leave. "I believe, on the whole," he said thoughtfully, when Lyl dismissed the soldier, "that it would be better for me to leave. The spirits can retreat should you become too obnoxious, and the tower is safe, at least for the present. Yes, I think it's reasonable for me to leave this situation to be handled at a later time. My wife is far more important to me and the future of Alba than you are. I would move the stars and moons themselves to protect her."

If he'd thought Lyl was angry before, his words seemed to trigger apoplexy in the man, leaving him sputtering with rage.

"My lord!" one of the men behind him called, pointing. "The arcanist— he's making magic behind his back."

"Spells? He's drawing spells?" Lyl shook his head. "That's not possible. You must see a spell that's being drawn. Everyone knows that."

Hallow sighed to himself, his fingers creating barely remembered symbols that he'd learned from the blood priests on Eris. He could feel the warm glow of the chains building up behind him, the magic in them contained, stored, waiting for him to release it.

"No, it's not arcany. They're...red. Long red strings of symbols," the man told Lyl. "I've never seen anything like it."

Lyl narrowed his eyes on Hallow, then moved behind him to examine the blood magic.

"Aarav, Tygo—" Hallow gave them each a quick glance. "I will not ask you to join me. The journey to find Allegria, and what will follow, is not one I would wish on anyone, and I will ask no more of you. But you will always have my gratitude and thanks."

"Where you go, Master Hallow, so I will go," Tygo swore defiantly, his gaze skittering away from Lyl when that man screamed an oath, spinning on his heel and gesturing wildly at the soldiers.

"He is attempting to bespell us all! He wears bands on his wrists and ankles giving him power!"

"I am a solitary man by nature," Aarav said calmly, his voice expressing no interest whatsoever in the sight of Lyl raging before them. "And I'm certainly not one to swear allegiance to anyone in such a dramatic fashion as my colleague Tygo. However, in this, I am in accord with him. I have no other pressing business at the moment, and can lend you aid recovering your wife, Hallow."

Hallow was warmed by the words, touched that both men would defy the leader of their order, and made a mental promise to repay them for their kindness once the situations with Allegria, the Eidolon, and ultimately Nezu, were dealt with.

"Remove the cuffs!" Lyl demanded, pacing before them. "Break them off him if you must, just get them off."

For a moment, Hallow's fingers grew still. "Oh, you *really* do not want to do that," he told Lyl. "You are not going to like me if you take off the cuffs."

"He admits it!" Lyl crowed, shoving forward a couple of the guards who had moved hesitantly to comply with his demand. "He admits that the cuffs give him this strange magic! Take them off him and bring them to me. I will examine them, and ascertain just what it is he has bound into them."

Hallow's shoulders slumped for a moment, feeling as if the weight of the world was bearing down on him. But then the quirky part of his mind pointed out that Lyl's reaction to his unleashed chaos would be entertaining, at least.

"Run," he said softly, just loud enough that Tygo and Aarav could hear him. Two guards knelt before him, pulling off his boots and fumbling with the iron pins that held the cuffs closed around his ankles.

"What?" Tygo asked in a whisper, his gaze skittering around.

"Run," Hallow repeated, his gaze not on the men at his feet, but on Lyl, who continued to pace. He gathered up the chains of blood magic, imbuing them with his intentions, as he'd been taught, charging the magic to transform destruction to protection.

"But—we're bound—" Tygo started to say.

"Where?" Aarav asked. Lyl marched around behind all three of them when two guards started to work the cuffs off Hallow's wrists. Inside him, chaos surged as the first of the ankle cuffs fell with a metallic clink.

"Frosthaven," he answered, naming a town a day's ride to the north. He had no idea where Thorn would bring Allegria back into the mortal realm, but Frosthaven was almost directly in the center of Genora, and would make a good setting off point to wherever she was. He raised his voice to add, "I give you all fair warning that you should move back. If you are too close to me when the confinement runes are removed, I may not be able to protect you."

"Confinement runes? Those aren't confinement runes," Lyl said, a sneer evident in his voice when he stomped around to face Hallow, the first ankle cuff in his hand. "It's magic, some strange magic that I have not yet learned. But I will, Hallow of Penhallow. Fear you not, I will learn all the secrets you hold."

The second ankle cuff came off, and Hallow clung tight to the blood magic in his hands, not wanting to waste it controlling the chaos, instead calling on Bellias, using the power arcany gave him to leash the red haze that started to dull his vision. "I wouldn't wish that on my worst enemy,

Lyl. This is my last warning. Get back, well back, because I only had a short time to learn from the blood priests, and my skills with their magic aren't as great as they are with arcany."

"Blood priests?" Lyl's eyes narrowed, looking at the second cuff when it was handed to him. To Hallow's amusement, the guards, after a moment's thought, slipped his boots back onto his feet. He would try to protect them with part of the net of chains he'd woven, and which even now glowed and pulsed in his hands. "You've had dealings with blood priests? But you're an arcanist! How did you learn of such things?"

"Now?" Aarav asked just as the cuff on Hallow's left wrist fell to the ground with a thump.

"Pick it up!" Lyl demanded. "Let me see it. It clearly holds much power—"

Hallow felt his knees buckle, and struggled to keep them stiff even as he fought the chaos within him. The red in front of his eyes grew in great splatters that leeched across his vision, his breath coming hard and rough while he fought. "Now." The word was ground through his teeth at the same moment he felt the last cuff loosen and fall from his wrist.

He had no time to worry about the arcanists beside him, for the chaos, freed from the control of the runes inscribed by both Allegria and Deo, filled him with rage, a fury that demanded the death of all things surrounding him. It caused him to jerk forward, snapping the rope binding him. He had just enough presence of mind to fling wide the chains of blood magic a scant half second before chaos erupted out of him, exploding outward in a wave of death and destruction.

His aim was a bit off, he noticed a half minute later, when his vision returned. He stood panting, the magic within him sated and quiet now—at least for a short while. Around him, bodies lay in a circle, with him at the center, red chaos covering everything and everyone, seeping into the gray of Kelos until it was absorbed. The bodies moaned and made short, uncoordinated movements. Hallow noted that one or two of the guards behind him lay still, too still. They were dead, and he was truly sorry that his chains of magic had failed to protect them. But the bulk of the people... Lyl, the guards, and the soldiers who had been moving in and around the ruins, were alive.

Tygo and Aarav were gone. Hallow smiled to himself, collected his four cuffs, and slipped them on again before picking his way across the moaning, twitching bodies to the stable.

"I hate to leave Kelos in the hands of a man so clearly mad, but it can't be helped," he told Penn as he fetched his saddle. Penn snorted, shook his head, then looked pointedly over to where Allegria's mule stood in the pasture, her head over the fence, her watchful eyes on Hallow.

"No," he told the mule, aware that people were starting to sit up, shaking their heads and groggily asking what had happened. "There is no time, and you are safer here. I will tell Allegria that you are concerned about her welfare."

The mule continued to stare at him. Penn nudged his back in a manner that had him stumbling forward a few feet. Hallow thought of pointing out to them both that he was master, but that word had a taint to it.

"For the time being, at least, but I'll cleanse it once we return. Fine, come then, but don't blame me if you have to walk across all of Genora!"

Five minutes later he rode out of Kelos with the mule's reins tied to Penn's saddle, the sounds of voices calling to each other drifting on the air after him.

Chapter 8

"Why did you really come here?" Idril lay across Deo's chest, which was damp beneath the harness, and heaving from the exertion he'd just made. She spent a moment in admiration of that exertion, her body humming with delightful little quivers of remembered joy at their joining. Truly, there were many things that annoyed her about Deo, but his skill in bedsport was not one of them.

Without opening his eyes, he pinched her behind, immediately rubbing away the sting with a hand that was made rough with callouses, and yet still managed to touch her with the gentlest of caresses. "Do you suddenly believe that your charms are not enough to draw me to your side?"

She smiled a smile filled with satisfied feminine knowledge. "No. I know you crave this, as do I. We have been too long parted for sexual congress to lose any of its attractions."

"We wouldn't have been apart for so long if you hadn't insisted on wedding my father," he answered.

She froze for a few seconds, her fingers stilling where they had slid under the leather and silver bands that crossed his chest in order to stroke his thick pectoral muscles. "You know that was not my choice."

"I know your father pressured you into it, but the marriage could not have taken place without your consent."

She sighed, not wanting to ruin the pleasant interlude, but knowing that she'd have to address the issue with him sooner or later. And she'd much rather deal with the fit he was bound to throw in privacy. "About that…"

"And in the end, what good came of your marrying him? The Tribe was only in the Council of Four Armies for a handful of years before your father imprisoned mine, and claimed his lands. It makes me wonder if you didn't wed him simply to goad me."

Idril made a face that, thankfully, Deo did not see.

"I am not a jealous man, Idril. You of all people should know that," he continued, shifting her to a more comfortable position across his body. She stopped stroking his lovely big chest, and started drumming her fingers on it. "There was no need to wed my father just to enrage me. I am here because I wish to be here. With you."

The very idea that Deo thought himself above jealousy when he was the most jealous man alive was beyond comical, but she couldn't point that out to him. Not now, when she had to dance around a delicate subject.

"But let us not waste our time talking about your marriage to my father. Let us instead talk about our wedding. My mother will wish to be present, so we had best do it today, before I have to return to Starfall to oust this Lyl," Deo said in a matter-of-fact tone that always annoyed Idril. He said the most outrageous things in that tone, ones that were sure to prickle on her skin like a biting insect.

"Today? Are you insane? We can't be wed today," she protested, thinking quickly.

"Why not?" he asked, opening his eyes to give her a quizzical look.

"Because—" She snatched at the first excuse that came to mind. "A wedding takes much preparation. There is the feast to be organized, and the pilgrimage to the temple, and the bounties given to the people."

"We can do without a feast," he answered, closing his eyes again, his fingers drawing wards on her behind. "As for the pilgrimage, there is a temple right here, not a hundred yards from us."

"Yes, but that's a water talkers' temple. We can't go to it to ask the goddesses for a blessing on our marriage," she argued.

"Of course we can. The water talkers worship the Life-Mother, so it's entirely suitable that we should seek her blessing instead of her daughters'."

"And then there's the bounties. You know full well it is the duty of the bride to make those, and I have nothing with me that I could use as gifts to the people of Deeptide."

"Bah," he said, gently pushing her off him so that he could rise and stride over to the small room that held the privy. He scratched his belly as he stood before the stool, giving Idril the opportunity to admire his truly magnificent ass. She spent a moment in rapt appreciation of the lovely thick muscles that curved and swooped, of the indentations on the sides that made her fingers itch to follow the smooth skin, and perhaps even give him a little love bite again. She'd shocked him earlier when she'd bitten him on one pale cheek, and had the worst urge to do it again. "I have coin with me. You can use that instead of whatever favors you would distribute. The inhabitants of Deeptide will be happier with coin than they would be with some remembrance of our marriage vows. I'll tell my parents that we will have the ceremony at noon, when Kiriah is at her strongest. My mother won't like it, but she will be in a hurry to march the army south, so I do not expect much opposition."

"Deo…I can't…I don't want…" Idril hesitated. Deo was the only person who truly saw her as she was, not a delicate, frail creature who had to be protected, but a woman whose depth of passion matched his own. But where Deo showed every thought, every emotion, Idril kept hers buried behind a mask of control, and she was sorely tempted to don that mask now.

Deo paused at a ewer, washing his face, chest, and privates before turning and cocking an eyebrow at her. "You fear our separation? That can't be avoided, I'm afraid. I would have you safe while I attend to Lyl, so it would be best if you remain with my father's company. You can join me…no, I must go help Hallow and Allegria deal with Nezu after that. But once he is taken care of, and I return to Aryia to address the problem of my Banes, we will be together then. You may join me while I dispose of your father if you like, although I won't insist you be there since it might be disturbing to watch his removal."

"I can't marry you today," she blurted out with uncharacteristic haste. She mentally damned herself for her lack of control, adding in a more measured tone, "It's not that I don't want to. You know I very much do wish to wed you. But…I can't."

"You can't want your father present," he said, scowling before he marched over to the door to open it and say loudly, "We wish to break our fast! Bring food that we might do so."

Idril fought back the urge to stab Deo somewhere non-vital with his own sword, clicking her tongue and sliding out of the bed to catch up her dressing gown, just barely managing to don it before the door opened, and two of her handmaidens entered bearing platters. "Of course I don't want him present. He's deranged, and would no doubt try to kill you, and most probably me, as well, for wedding you. Noellia, please cease that giggling. Surely you've set eyes on a naked man before, not that I approve of Deo just standing there letting you and Guen see everything he was born with."

Deo looked confused for a moment, then glanced down his body. "Do you find me unseemly? Is that why you don't want to marry me? Woman, just half an hour ago you were riding me hard, cooing in a manner that indicated you were receiving much pleasure, not to mention the fact that you climaxed so hard you almost ripped my rod right off, so I'll thank you to remember that when you are making objections to my body."

Idril took a deep, deep breath. Both handmaidens stifled giggles behind their hands. She shot Noellia a particularly quelling look when the maid evidently decided to confirm Deo's virility, but luckily for Idril's vaunted control over her temper, Noellia stopped ogling Deo long enough to deposit food on the table. Idril continued to glare at the maids until, still giggling—and with far too many admiring glances back at Deo—they left the bedchamber.

"I will admit that my mother's kin make excellent ale," Deo said conversationally, pouring out two tankards before plucking from the platters some cold meat, bread, grapes, and cheese, which he set before her. "Sit and eat, my lustful little dove. I must meet with my parents to alert them to the wedding, then I will gather supplies for my ride south to Starfall. That should give your handmaids time to do all that is necessary to make you ready."

"We are not getting married today." Idril stood before the table when Deo sat down to eat. She took yet another deep breath, deciding to get it over with quickly. "Much as I would like to, I can't wed you because I am already married."

Deo frowned and set down his tankard. "You said you divorced my father six weeks after you wed him. Is that untrue? Are you married to him still?"

"I did, it is not, and I am not." Really, it was a wonder there was any air left in the chamber, considering how many deep breaths she was taking. "My father forced me to wed Parker, one of the Northmen who helped him take Abet. I'm sure you will assign the direst of motives to this marriage, but I assure you that other than the issue of not being legally able to wed you now, it has no bearing on us, no bearing at all. We are betrothed. I wish for us to be married. I enjoy the things we do in bed together, and wish to continue to enjoy them for many centuries, without the thought of my deceased mother's spirit hovering around me being disappointed in my lack of lawfully wedded sexual congress."

Slowly, Deo set down the knife bearing the cold beef he was about to consume, giving her the exact same look she expected to receive. The words, when he spoke, had an edge to them that probably could have cut the loaf of bread in front of her. "You wed someone else?"

"Against my will. And this time, I didn't even give my consent." Idril fought the urge to wring her hands. She'd never been a hand-wringing sort of person, and she wasn't about to start. "My father had me gagged because I told the monk he forced to wed us that I didn't wish to marry

Parker. Papa held a sword to the monk, and told him to marry us or he would lose his head."

It was Deo's turn to take a long, deep breath, which he did before rising and pointing the eating knife at her. It still held the beef, which waggled as Deo shook it. Idril would have giggled, but like hand-wringing, she'd instituted a firm no giggling policy. "Do you think you could go six months without wedding a stranger? Is it too much to ask that you stop marrying everyone but me?"

The giggle slipped out before she could stop it. Deo looked even more outraged, if that was possible.

"Do not, my love," she said, sliding onto his lap, her hands stroking back the lock of hair that always seemed to fall over his brow, and which she loved to tuck behind his ear. "Do not look at me as if the goddesses called me forth just so I could torment you. This marriage to Parker means nothing to us, nothing at all. Less than nothing, really. Other than a slight legality. I will divorce him just as soon as I go to the Northlands, which my handmaids tell me is the only place one can effect a divorce to one of the Northmen. Evidently there is some ceremony where one lights a fire made up of the husband's bed. Then one walks backwards around it three times while holding a chicken, a bumblepig, and a cat, saying, 'Man of the north, husband of my bosom, and bearer of the twig and two nuts which the great god Snor hath given thee to people the lands, I shun thee henceforth and forever. No more will I receive thy body unto mine, and to my hands I restore all that I brought to the marriage,' and just like that, the marriage is broken, and the divorce complete."

Deo stared at her as if she had a chicken, a bumblepig, and a cat dancing on her head before giving his own head a brief shake and saying merely, "If it wouldn't be too much to ask, could you refrain from marrying anyone else?"

"I'm already wed," she said with lofty disregard of the low growl he made deep in his chest. "I can't be married to anyone else; otherwise I'd be wedding you today."

"Somehow," he said, tapping her on the hip until she slid off his lap, allowing him to rise, "I don't think the fact that you are already wed would stop you from marrying whoever else struck your fancy. Very well, I will tell my parents that once I've taken care of Lyl, Nezu, and my Banes, and you've walked backwards around your husband's burning bed, we will be wed. Until then, I expect you will wish to remain with my father or the queen."

"Actually," she said, watching him as he pulled on his clothes. She very much enjoyed how tight his breeches were, and the way they caressed the long lines of muscles in his thighs. It was almost as good as the way the black tunic stretched over his chest. "I believe I will accompany you."

He frowned again, just as she knew he would. "Why?"

"Because you need me. Also..." She hesitated a moment, trying to find words to capture the fleeting impressions she'd had of the queen. "Deo, what do you know of the water talkers?"

"They are my mother's mother's family," he answered, sliding on a scabbard that rested on his back and held his sword. "Water talkers are Waterborn, although they do not use that name."

"Your mother is troubled," she said slowly, still struggling to make sense of her thoughts. "She went to the temple yesterday, in the morning, before you arrived, and when she emerged, she was much disturbed. She met with Lord Israel, but neither would tell me what the priestess told the queen."

Deo gave a little shrug. "If it was something of importance, she would have mentioned it to you, or at very least to me. They said nothing last night, other than to continue to blame me for leaving Lyl in Starfall." A little flash of pain was visible in his eyes, not the physical pain she knew he always bore, but one that struck soul deep. His guilt over Sandor's death.

She moved into his arms, holding him tight, pressing her lips against the pulse point in his neck. "My love, you forget that I was there when your Banes attacked. Your father tried to reason with them, but they would have none of it. They have fallen under my father's spell, and thus, you are not responsible for their acts. You did not kill Sandor through them."

He held her for a minute, not saying anything, but she knew he felt the guilt his father had cast onto him. "It will be a long ride to Starfall. I will travel hard, with few breaks," was all he said, giving her a swift appraising glance. She lifted her chin, and was pleased when he gave a little nod, saying only, "Be ready to leave at noon."

She watched him go, her heart warmed by the fact that of all the people on Alba, he was the only one who was not deceived by her appearance. He knew just how strong she could be.

"Noellia!" she called, scanning the items in the bedchamber, making a mental list of everything that must be done before they could depart. She would travel light, with just a few garments and necessary items, and would be sure to stop by the kitchens to arrange for food for the journey. Deo frequently forgot that not everyone had the strength to go for days without eating.

"Aye, my lady?" the handmaid answered, appearing in the doorway.

"Fetch the Kingfishers," she said, naming the twin daggers that Deo had given her upon their return from Eris, his betrothal gift, one that had shocked Allegria and Hallow but delighted her.

She smiled to herself. Deo might be a little put out by her marriage to the Northman, but a long journey together would go a long way to providing balm.

One that hopefully would include more time to ride him as she had that morning. Her womanly bits highly approved of that possibility.

Chapter 9

If there was one thing Deo hated, it was having his plans crossed.

"I dislike having my plans crossed," he informed the man who staggered off a lathered horse before almost collapsing at his feet.

"Urgh." Quinn the captain said. He took a step and weaved, clutching the red-headed Shadowborn woman with one hand, while the other held onto Dexia, the small vanth in girl-form, both of whom had likewise slid from equally worn horses.

"Oh, it's you." The little vanth eyed Deo. "We could have used you earlier."

On the whole, Deo approved of the sometimes-vicious little vanth, even though he was less pleased with Quinn, an emotion that dated back to the trip out from Eris, when he'd caught wind of a foul rumor regarding the captain's blatant pursuit of Idril.

"A thousand pardons that we have ridden literally day and night without rest, spending a vast fortune on rented horses, not to mention spending so much time in the saddle that I may never have children," Quinn added, with an attempt at a bow that went a bit wonky, and almost felled him and Ella. "To upset your plans is clearly unthinkable, although the lack of waiting horses, men, or supplies indicates we have not interrupted a major campaign."

Ella giggled, then groaned when she moved to the side to allow a stable hand to take her horse.

"We rode so hard that I have a blister on my arse," Dexia said, spinning around, clearly about to hike up her dress to show him.

"I don't need to see your arse blisters," Deo said quickly, averting his eyes from the vanth in case she decided to show him anyway. He narrowed his eyes on Quinn, asking, "What is of such importance that you had to ride so hard and interrupt the decidedly major plans I had to leave at noon?"

"Lots of things, but do you think we could have a bit of wine before I unpack all our adventures for your enjoyment? Oh, and be sure to cool down the horses before they are fed. They deserve extra oats for their acts of courage to spirit us away from…well, we'll go into that once our throats are a bit less parched." The last was spoken to the stable hands, all three of whom nodded before hurrying off with their charges.

Deo sighed the sigh of a martyred man, one who had not only had his wedding canceled, but who'd learned that his betrothed had yet again married someone who was not him. He really would have to keep a closer eye on Idril. Clearly, she couldn't be trusted to go about on her own without wedding the nearest available man. "Ale. You can have ale, not wine. One tankard, and that's only because Idril is not here, where she's supposed to be." Deo frowned at both his horse and Idril's when a stableboy brought them out.

"You are all graciousness," Quinn said in what Deo found to be a suspiciously smooth tone, but he led the threesome into the hall of the house where he'd been given accommodations and asked for ale.

By the time food, bread, fruit, and bowls of sweet butter were brought, and Quinn had slaked his thirst on two quickly downed tankards of ale while Ella had fallen on the food with little cries of joy and Dexia had gone off to find something "with a bit of blood in it," Deo's patience was running out. "Well?" he asked.

Quinn belched, excused himself, and wiped his mouth with the sleeve of his tunic. "Yes, we are well, but only by the grace of both goddesses. I'll start at the beginning—"

Idril glided into the room, giving Deo a pointed look when she asked, "Deo? What are you doing here? I thought we were leaving at noon, and it's a quarter past now. Oh, hello captain. Ella. Where is the sharp-toothed vanth?"

"Out scavenging for something to eat," Ella said around a mouthful of bread and butter, a few crumbs scattering on the table before her as she spoke.

"Scavenging? But—" Idril glanced at the food on the table, narrowed her eyes in thought, and said simply, "Oh. Yes. Just so."

Quinn rose and gallantly offered Idril his chair, an act that Deo immediately resented.

"Allow me, Lady Idril," Quinn said, holding the chair for her. "And may I say just what a pleasure it is to see you again? Especially since you look so hale. Did you do something to your hair? No? Perhaps you have a new gown? Or is it just the blinding light of your soul shining that so dazzles the eye?"

"Or perhaps it's the bullshite you're spewing that is blinding you," the woman Ella said under her breath before stuffing yet another piece of bread into mouth.

"Thank you, captain," Idril said, moving over to him. She offered a smile that Deo felt was far too nice for the likes of Quinn. "I'm happy to see you again, although just what you're doing here is beyond my understanding—"

She hesitated when Deo, giving Quinn a non-too-gentle shove, took command of the chair, and with a look at Idril that dared her to comment, waited for her to sit. "That's what I've been trying to find out," he said abruptly, "but Quinn's been too busy pouring ale down his gullet to answer."

Quinn snagged a three-legged stool that sat against the wall, and plunked it down next to Idril, smiling at her before picking up his tankard. "We rode hard for three days, and barely escaped death. Well, Ella did, since Dex can't be killed and I'm lifebound, so if I'm killed, I'll just pop right back to life. Where was I?"

"Ogling Idril?" Deo asked in what he thought of as his most reasonable tone, his arms crossed. Inside him, the burn of chaos threatened to come to life, but he kept it clamped down. The captain wasn't worth the trouble of explaining to his father why he'd unleashed a power that could have devastating effects.

Quinn shot him a quick assessing glance, but relaxed when Deo did no more than raise an eyebrow.

"There is no one worth admiring more than Lady Idril, to be sure," Quinn answered.

Ella murmured something that sounded like "arse."

Quinn ignored her to pour out a bit more ale, and say, "As I was about to tell Lord Deo before your gracious presence joined us, we came from Starfall. Originally. Hallow sent us there after we defeated the thane, to see what Darius was up to."

Idril refused the offer of ale, a little frown forming between her pale blond brows. "You went to watch Darius? Why you? You're not Starborn, are you?"

"I am, actually, although my mother was from Talles," he answered, surprising Deo. Denizens of the continent to the east of Genora generally kept to themselves. "More importantly, I spent time at the court when I was young and apprenticed to a bookmaker whom the queen favored, and thus I knew the back ways in and out of Starfall. Hallow was concerned about the thane returning while he and the other arcanists summoned

Thorn to the new staff, and decided Ella and Dex would be safer if we were all away elsewhere."

"I wouldn't have thought that Starfall was such a place of safety," Idril commented.

"Normally, it would be very safe, but of course, with Darius in charge, we most definitely treaded with care," Quinn answered.

"It was especially enjoyable when they noticed me," Ella added, brushing crumbs from her hands.

Quinn nodded. "Since it's obvious Ella isn't Starborn, she drew more attention than I would have liked."

"But surely Darius would not do anything to harm you," Idril said, still frowning slightly.

"He wasn't there," Deo said before Quinn could answer.

The captain bent a questioning glance on him; then his confusion passed and he nodded. "Ah, so that's what happened to him. You took him?"

"Yes." Deo moved away from the wall against which he'd been leaning, and went to stand behind Idril, his hands on her shoulders. "I met him leaving Kelos, and brought him here."

Both of Quinn's eyebrows rose. "To see the queen?"

Deo nodded.

Quinn gave a low whistle, then continued. "Starfall was oddly empty of Starborn, but a steady influx of Harii were streaming in each day, making me believe something was up. The city itself was in the hands of an arcanist named Lyl. He's the one who took exception to Ella being there."

"He tried to make me his concubine," Ella said with apparent indifference, selecting an apple from the bowl before biting noisily into it and saying around a mouthful, "He didn't succeed."

"That he didn't." Quinn grinned at her, causing her lips to twitch in response. "In fact, he couldn't walk for a good three hours after Ella...er... convinced him that he should look elsewhere for bedsport. Since things were getting a bit uncomfortable in Starfall, and I had no idea why Darius was bringing in all the Harii, we decided to return to Kelos."

"Did Hallow get his spirit summoned?" Deo asked. "Has he found Allegria? If so, I must send them a message to meet me in Starfall."

Quinn and Ella exchanged anguished glances, Deo noted with interest.

"Er..." Quinn cleared his throat. "I don't know the answer to either question."

Ella's face took on a pale cast. She suddenly shoved the plate away, murmuring an excuse before hurrying from the room.

Deo watched her before turning back to Quinn, an obvious question in his eyes.

"There was no one at Kelos," the captain answered, his expression unusually somber.

"Hallow and Allegria weren't there?" Idril asked.

"No one was there. No one *living.*" Quinn's gaze met Deo's. "Evidently, while I went to Bellwether to check on my ship and crew before returning to Kelos, Lyl marched the Starborn army there. Why, I have no idea, or what happened to most of them. Moved on, I suspect, but when we arrived, all we found were bodies."

"Whose bodies?" Deo asked, a pang of worry gripping him. He had every faith in his abilities, but he was no fool—he couldn't take down Nezu on his own. Together with Allegria and Hallow, yes, he had every confidence that they would destroy the monster, but he needed them by his side.

"A few score of soldiers, members of the Starborn army Lyl had led out from Starfall. Deo—" Quinn glanced briefly at Idril. "The spirits there, those who hadn't been driven away to the spirit realm by fear, told me that the Eidolon thane had returned and raised the remainder of his warriors. It was they who slew everything in sight—the spirits that lived peacefully in Kelos, the soldiers that Lyl had left, and the people of several nearby villages."

Deo had a moment of nightmarish guilt when he remembered Hallow pleading with him to remain in Kelos in case the thane returned. He closed his eyes against the pain following the knowledge that once again his actions were responsible for the deaths of innocents. "And Hallow?"

"Was not there. The spirits said he and two other arcanists escaped shortly before Lyl left."

He felt the softness of a woman pressing herself against him, her breath warm on his neck. He opened his eyes, looking down to where Idril had wrapped her arms around his waist, her lush body providing wordless comfort. "Thank the goddesses that they got away. And Allegria?"

Quinn shook his head, his expression still grave as he toyed with a tankard. "The spirits said there has been no sign of her since we drove out the thane."

"It's not your fault," Idril whispered, her amber eyes filled with such warmth that for a moment Deo wanted to get on his knees and thank the goddesses for her. But he was never one to give in to soft emotions, not when there was work to be done.

"Perhaps not, but Hallow answered my father's call when he sought aid in finding my mother, and I will not abandon him when he needs us. Much though I wish to locate this traitor Lyl and bring him before the queen, we will instead go to Hallow's aid in finding Allegria."

"I think there may be a bigger problem facing you," Quinn said slowly, turning the tankard in his hands, his gaze on the depths contained within.

"To do with Lyl?" Deo asked, feeling momentarily bereft when Idril released her hold on him to move to his side. "He is no threat to me. He is an upstart, a lackey, nothing more."

"No." Quinn looked up when Dexia appeared in the doorway, wiping her mouth as she slipped inside. "My ship needed repairs after the trip from Eris, so we had to ride here rather than sail, as I would have preferred. All of which meant we came by the North Coast Road. And three days' ride from here we came across two men riding like the stone giants themselves were pursuing them."

"What two men?" Idril asked.

Quinn's gaze met that of Deo. "Two Banes of Eris. They were disinclined to pay attention to us at first, until they caught sight of Ella and recognized her as a Shadowborn. Then we barely made it away from them, and the only reason we did is because our horses were fresher than theirs. As it was, they destroyed Dex's form, which meant she had to take another."

The vanth smoothed down her dress. "Luckily, there was a form handy."

"A form handy?" Idril repeated, looking confused. "How do you mean?"

Deo had a very good idea of just how the vanth assumed the forms she wore, and considered whether or not it was something Idril should hear, then remembered the time Idril threatened to geld one of Quinn's sailors because he insisted on calling the hours in a manner that was highly disruptive to their bedsporting. He decided she would be fine hearing the truth.

"Dex...er...assumes the physical form of someone who's passed into the spirit realm," Quinn said, looking mildly uncomfortable.

"How very interesting," Idril murmured. "How is it you only find the forms of small girl children handy?"

Deo was destined never to hear the answer, for a shouted warning had him running out to the cleared area that served as a central square. A water talker sentinel pulled his horse to an abrupt stop, waving one hand behind him. "Attackers!" he panted. "Attackers slaying the army! Where is the priestess? We must lock the gates!"

"Who—" Idril started to ask the sentinel, but he raced past them, disappearing into the temple, where the priestess, the Queen's cousin, resided.

Deo didn't wait. He ran toward the west gate, the chaos inside him lighting his blood, filling his mind with visions of destruction. He knew exactly who was attacking the army of water talkers that his mother had raised.

Two solitary figures approached, both halting when Deo moved to the middle of the road, arms crossed, watching and waiting for them.

One of the figures dismounted, hesitated a minute, then came forward slowly. "Lord Deo?" he asked, a look of disbelief clearly evident on his face. Deo recognized him instantly, a bit shocked because Eset—and his brother Kell, who was even now dismounting—were two of his staunchest supporters, amongst the first who had volunteered to become Banes.

"You are the two who killed Lady Sandorillan?" Deo shook his head, not willing to believe it, but seeing the proof in the black lights that glowed along the runes on their wrist cuffs. "My father said it was three Banes who had betrayed us to Jalas. I assumed it was the men he had spirited away after the Battle of the Fourth Age. Not you. Not the first of my Banes."

"You live?" Kell moved alongside Eset, his gaze searching Deo's face. "But—how can this be? We saw Lord Israel encase you in crystal. We heard him tell the guards to bury you deep where no one would find you. Lord Jalas said that you were lost to us forever."

"Jalas was the one calling loudest for my father to destroy me," Deo said dismissively. "Regardless, he did not."

"But we saw—" Kell stopped, his brow furrowed. "We saw you in crystal."

"You saw what my father wanted others to see, nothing more," Deo said, very aware of the chaos burning deep inside him. Thus far it wasn't struggling to slip his control, but he suspected that control would shortly be tested. He hadn't decided until the moment he saw the Banes how he would deal with their actions, but at the light that glowed from their runes, he knew their fate was written as surely as the runes had been etched into the cuffs. "Jalas was wrong."

"Lord Jalas is wise in many ways," Kell reassured him. "You do not know him as we do. We have spent time with him, and learned much from him. Did you know he has taken Abet? Your father tried to retake it, but we knew you would not wish for him to regain his power, and thus we helped Lord Jalas defend the keep."

"You did me no service then." Deo shook his head at the dark path of his thoughts. Was it too late to save the men? He felt obligated to try to do so. "It pains me greatly to say this given my history with him, but my father is not the enemy."

"No? And yet, Lord Israel is the source of much sorrow in Alba," Eset pronounced. "Jalas told us how he has abused the Fireborn, and how he—Jalas—rescued them from your father's tyranny, and in thanks, all of Aryia swore an oath to become members of his tribe."

Deo ignored that statement, knowing it to be untrue. The Fireborn were many things, but stupid was not one of them.

"You do not know, because you were buried in crystal until your father saw fit to bring you back, but Lord Jalas has sought to free the Fireborn from the curse cast upon them so long ago," Kell said, taking a step forward in his eagerness. "You must join him. He would welcome your help, of that I am certain. We have promised to do what we can, of course, knowing that you would want us to lend our aid to him, but—"

"What curse?" Deo interrupted, assessing the men. Eset looked angry, and Deo didn't like the red lights in his eyes, but he couldn't damn the man by that fact alone. Still, either the Banes would have to accept the truth of the situation and atone for their actions, or be destroyed lest they wreak further destruction.

"The Grace of Alba. Lord Jalas has engaged abjurors, men from a distant land, to unmake the curse Kiriah Sunbringer laid upon us." Kell's eyes lit up with a glint that Deo had no trouble recognizing as that of a fanatic. "With the abjurors' aid, he will free us, all of the Fireborn, and allow us to become what we were truly meant to be."

"And what would that be?" Deo was unable to keep from asking, giving the men one last chance to prove that redemption was not beyond their grasp.

"Masters," Eset answered, almost biting the word in half.

Deo stared in horror for a few seconds, wondering what it was Jalas was up to, and how he had so quickly brought the Banes over to his mad way of thinking. For that matter, why would he want to strip from the Fireborn the power to wield magic? He shook his head, dismissing the question. Now was not the time to ponder the actions of a madman—he had his own problems to deal with. The fact that both men had moved so far from the core beliefs he had instilled in the Banes made his path clear. "You have failed me, but I do not hold you to blame for that. Your fall is a sin on my soul, just as are the acts you have committed since the chaos corrupted you."

"Corrupted us?" Eset's face twisted into a mocking smile, and his hand slid toward his sword.

Deo settled into a relaxed pose, ready for the fight that was sure to come.

"Just because we agree with Jalas that we were meant to be masters of the Fireborn does not mean we are corrupted, Lord Deo," Eset continued, red flaring to life in the man's eyes. "They do not hold the power we do. In all things, we are their masters—after all, we control the chaos magic, harnessing it, using it as you created us to do. Corrupted?" He gave a harsh little laugh. "Enhanced. Strengthened. Perfected—all that and so much more, yes. But *not* corrupted."

"You, of all of us, know what the chaos can do," Kell added, his face earnest, and in it, Deo saw with certainty the madness that had called to him before Allegria had filled him with the light of Kiriah. "Without it, we are but useless bags of meat parading around believing we are masters of our own destiny, but in truth, only the chaos gives us the ability to take charge. Using it, we are gods amongst beings of clay and dirt, and for this gift, we will be forever in your debt."

"You will be forever dead," Deo said, regretting that the Banes could not be allowed to continue, but knowing their madness must come to an end. Too many innocents would suffer if he did not do what must be done.

Voices behind him called from the temple, voices he recognized.

"Dead?" Kell looked confused.

"You think to stop us?" Eset sneered, shaking his head and gesturing with a wave behind him. "We have learned much since your apparent death, my lord. You simply have to look at the remains of the so-called army that was camped outside the gate to see proof that we have grown in strength even as we've learned how powerful chaos can be. We will let nothing stop us, not even you."

Kell frowned at his brother, a flash of uncertainty flickering across his face. "Eset! We owe all to Lord Deo. You must not speak to him in such a manner. He is clearly overset, something to do with his rescue from crystal death—"

"He has changed. Can you not see it?" Eset interrupted, pointing with his sword to Deo.

Deo calculated quickly. It would take his father a little time to organize the town's defense, but his mother—the more experienced warrior—would be faster. He judged he had a minute or less before others would hamper his ability to take care of the two Banes.

"Look at his runes, Kell—they are yellow, just as the lightweaver's were. He's been infected by her, his magic tainted. He's no longer worthy of leading the Banes of Eris to their rightful destiny."

"But we swore fealty to him," Kell said quickly, his gaze darting from Eset to Deo and back. "We owe him our—"

"We owe him *nothing*," Eset snapped. "We will destroy him just as we will all who are unworthy. We—"

Deo didn't let him continue. He'd been carefully nursing the anger inside him, using it to fire the chaos magic while at the same time giving it a focus. Just as he heard the sound of horses coming up the hill from the town itself, he allowed his control to slip. The runes along his harness lit up reddish gold, filling him with a familiar sense of power, one that demanded sacrifices.

Usually he fought the urge to destroy and to bring about the deaths from which the chaos fed, but this time, he spread wide his arms, and allowed the chaos to flow out of him.He didn't expect much resistance.

He was wrong.

"Kill him!" Eset snarled, leaping forward, his sword in one hand, while with the other he released a red wave of chaos that immediately consumed Deo's magic. "Kill everyone in the town. We will wipe clean the entire continent of the infection that stains it if we have to!"

Deo stared for a moment in absolute surprise. Never had his magic failed him. Not even when he'd called upon it to face Nezu.

But now—long years of training had his sword in hand before he realized it, parrying Eset's blow that would have taken off his head.

"Deo! What is he doing out there by himself? Captain, you must help him—oh, Queen Dasa, thank the goddesses. Deo thinks to face his men by himself." The words were carried up to him by the wind coming from the shore, the voice unmistakable.

The Banes both jumped him, red magic flying in the air, and for a moment, for one infinitely short moment, he wondered if this was the time when he would finally be defeated.

"Not this day," he growled, and slammed the hilt of his sword upward into the jaw of Eset, sending the man staggering backward even as Deo's other hand wove an intricate symbol that glowed red-gold in the air for a second before it wrapped itself around Kell. "And not by your hands!"

"You see?" Eset panted, his eyes glowing red in a manner that Deo remembered Allegria describing when he had gone berserk. "Look to his runes, brother! He is tainted! He does not even possess chaos magic any longer. He has diluted it, weakening it until he is a useless blot of nothing."

"I've been called many things, and by many people, but 'a useless blot of nothing' is, I think, by far the most insulting," Deo said in between short grunts of pain when Eset attacked again, this time with chaos wrapped around his sword. At the same time, Kell danced around him, slashing and stabbing in a manner that just infuriated him further.

"Deo!" He heard the voice before the two Banes realized Idril was there. Deo swore under his breath, knowing with the foresight of a seer what the next few seconds would bring.

Once again, he was wrong.

Just as Eset turned to face Idril, who was armed only with the daggers he'd given her, the chaos magic roared to life within him. If he'd thought it had been weakened before, he was mistaken, for suddenly, with the mere act of Eset lifting his sword to strike the woman who had held Deo's heart for more years than he could recall, he ceased being himself, Deosin Langton, useless blot of nothing and so-called savior of the Fourth Age, and became instead a tool of vengeance.

Idril reached him, one hand clutching the back of his tunic just as chaos exploded out of him with a sound that he was certain had deafened him. The blast of magic eradicated not only the two men in front of him, but also the stone gate beyond them, a massive structure that stood a full three stories tall.

Bits of stone, rock, and twisted metal rained down on them, echoes of the concussion bouncing off the cliffs surrounding the town in repeated waves of noise. Deo spun around, curling his body protectively around Idril, his eyes widening when he looked beyond her to where the town lay.

Or where it should have lain.

The entire east side of Deeptide was rubble, with a dense cloud of dirt and dust hovering over the remains. Bits of brick and stone walls slid and crashed to the ground, leaving partially-standing shells of buildings. The other half of the town, the part that was caught in the cone of magic that had erupted from Deo…it was gone, swallowed by the sea that surged and withdrew in massive blue-grey waves gilded with the golden red residue of his magic.

"Grace of the goddesses, Deo," he heard Idril murmur against his chest. "My ears are ringing. What did you do—"

She had extracted herself, her eyes widening when she saw the destruction he had wrought. "That…the town…was that—"

"Yes," he said, glancing back to where the Banes had stood.

Nothing of them remained. He felt a moment of sadness at losing men who had sworn to devote their talents to ridding Alba of evil, only to be consumed by the result of once-good intentions. Or rather, the power he had imbued in them.

"Are you harmed?" he asked Idril as he braced himself for what he must do. Within him, chaos simmered, subservient and quiet once again, but at the same time making him aware that he didn't have nearly the control over it he thought he had.

"No." She continued to gaze at the destruction he had wrought, then wrapped her arms around him, holding him for a moment, filling him with everything that was good in the world before releasing him.

More than just buildings had been knocked down with the blast. Horses struggled to rise, some with riders being dragged by feet caught in stirrups, while others who had been on foot now lay stunned.

Deo fervently prayed they were all alive, and rushed past Idril to assess the damage, searching amongst the bodies that lay scattered across the road for those who were familiar, quickly righting the unharmed, while assessing the extent of the injured.

Thankfully, there appeared to be very few of the latter.

"Deo!" He heard his father's furious roar even as he spotted him helping the queen to her feet. She looked livid, her eyes sparking silver lights that he could see from where he stood. "By Kiriah's ten toes, what did you do?"

Deo ignored the question, yanking aside bits of rubble, helping the couple of water talkers who had started digging survivors out of the remains of their houses.

Beyond, where part of the town was missing and waves lapped at a newly made shoreline, figures straggled out of the water before standing and staring in abject horror at the remains of the town.

"Thank the goddess they are Waterborn," he murmured, and hefted half a wall from where a woman and her child were huddled under a bookcase. "Are you harmed?" he asked the woman.

"No...no," she stammered, her face expressing the same mingled horror and confusion that he had seen all around him as the townspeople recovered. "We're just—what happened?"

"My son happened," he heard his father growl behind him. "As usual, he has rained death and destruction where a simpler solution presented itself."

"Destruction, yes," Deo said, shooting his father a sharp look. "But not much death. At least not that I've seen."

"The people in the part of the town that you sent crashing down into the sea—"

"Are even now rising from the waves," Deo said, nodding toward the fresh stretch of shore where other townspeople, covered in the dust and dirt of the debris, met their friends and family who stood shivering and wet. "They are water breathers. They can't drown."

"They can if they had been knocked senseless, or injured beyond healing," his father snapped, turning and lifting a hand when Dasa called to him. "What in the name of Kiriah Sunbringer did you think you were doing?"

"Taking care of the Banes." Deo leashed his anger and annoyance. Would the day ever dawn when he did not arouse his father's wrath? He pulled aside bits of broken furniture, jerking one of the water talkers forward when the red clay tiles of a roof came slamming down in front of them.

"Could you not have done so without destroying everything in the area?" his mother asked, picking her way through the debris.

Deo cast his gaze momentarily skyward, wondering if the twin goddesses took enjoyment in blighting his life. "No," he answered, deciding that explanation would have to wait until such time as all the citizens of the town had been accounted for.

"Bellias help me, Deo, if you can't control your magic, then I will give your father my approval to banish you somewhere you can do no harm!" Dasa helped an old man and his dog out from where they were sheltered by a table while Deo put his shoulder to a wall that leaned drunkenly inward, blocking a door, and shoved until the wall slid backward, collapsing with a loud noise, and dense cloud of brick dust.

"I will not be banished again," he said in a voice made gritty with both annoyance and the polluted air. "Not by anyone. Are you harmed? Good. No, do not go back in there. The walls are not safe. I will fetch what you need."

Deo waited with what patience remained him while an old woman croaked her request. By the time he fetched her basket of knitting and returned it to her, his parents had moved off, helping to rescue other residents, pets, and valuables.

Idril had summoned her handmaidens to help the people of Deeptide, and the women now moved amongst them with pitchers of wine, food, and baskets of ointments and herbs to heal their hurts.

Deo cast a curious glance at the temple, noting that although a few windows had been broken, it had suffered no other damage, whether by chance or because of the Life-Mother's protection, he knew not.

Darkness had fallen by the time everyone was accounted for, and places to stay had been arranged in those structures still deemed habitable. Deo had expected censure by those affected, and wouldn't have been in the least bit surprised to be further castigated, cursed, and spat upon as the one who had brought such trouble down upon their heads. But oddly, although he met with many a wary expression, the water talkers did not treat him as a villain.

"Not that you deserve anything but scorn heaped upon your head," his father said when Deo, exhausted, sat at a long table in his mother's chambers inside the temple, with Idril at his side, while the captain, Ella, and Dexia were seated on the other side of the table. "Of all the—but no." Israel took a deep breath, and cut off his rant in mid sentence, a fact that would have taken Deo by surprise if he had any energy left to express such an emotion. "I've said enough about that subject. I can see by the stricken look in your eyes that this time, at least, you are fully cognizant of the damage you have done."

"*You* might not have more to say to him," Dasa said while pacing past Deo only to turn at the far end of the room to pin him with a potent glare. She'd been pacing ever since Deo's presence had been requested, and Idril and the others had followed him in to the queen's rooms. "It is not *your* kin who have been almost destroyed."

"*Almost* being the key word," Quinn murmured, giving Idril a sleepy-eyed smile.

Idril missed it, being at that moment occupied with staring down at her hands where they rested in her lap. Deo wasn't misled by her apparently subservient demeanor. Idril was at her most inventive when she looked humble. No doubt she was even then planning some particularly arousing way to end what could only be described as one of the worst days of his life.

The queen whirled around to glare at Quinn. He lifted his hands in apparent surrender, adding, "I meant only that no one died. None but the two Banes, that is."

"And the soldiers they killed in the camp outside the city," Ella added softly. Deo heard an odd note in the Shadowborn's voice that made him glance at her. Her expression showed nothing.

"Don't forget about the swath of destruction they left coming here," Dexia added, her gaze resting on Idril for a few moments before she picked up a small cloth doll bearing a few braided strands of hair that bore a startling resemblance to the blond tresses that fell in a silken shimmer down Idril's back.

"How you could believe that destroying the home of my kin was a solution to the issue of your out-of-control Banes—" the queen started to say, but stopped when Deo rose to his feet.

"Come," he told Idril, holding out his hand for her.

Her eyebrows rose slightly, but she obediently put her hand in his, and got to her feet. "Where, my lord?"

Deo took a deep breath, acknowledging the debts he owed. They seemed to grow with each passing day. If he didn't start paying them off, soon they might threaten to drown him. "Kelos. Or near there, assuming Hallow took sanctuary somewhere safe nearby."

"You're leaving now?" Israel asked frowning, casting a look at the now glassless window. "It will be deep night soon. You wish to depart at such an inauspicious time?"

Dasa snorted, and stomped over to Deo, her eyes still blazing. "Never did I think the day would come when my son would run away from his responsibilities. If any man had told me that you would do so, I would have slain him where he stood. And yet, that is exactly what you are doing!"

"I am leaving because I must," he told her as Idril's fingers tightened around his in warning. "I owe it to Hallow to help him now, when he needs my aid."

"*He* needs your aid?" Dasa's voice rose. She gestured toward the window. "And what of Deeptide? Does my kin—your kin—not matter? You destroyed their town, their homes, their lives! Do you not feel any obligation to help them?"

"Their buildings are damaged, yes," he said, wondering at the fact that the magic inside him was not raging against the tirade directed at him. "But they can be rebuilt, just as the town can. For those who were injured by the destruction of the two Banes, I am very sorry, and have left with the bursar as much coin as I can spare to help rebuild their lives. But beyond hewing stone and cutting down trees, I am of little use to them here. There are bigger threats to their future—"

"Deo, hear me well," Dasa interrupted, stepping close to him, so close he could see the black streaks in her silver eyes. "If you leave here now, when my people—*your* people—need you most, then you will no longer be my son."

"Dasa," Israel said, standing up as his frown grew blacker. "You allow your emotions to rule your reason. Deo, for the first time in my knowledge, has admitted his blame in the happenings today. He has made what reparations he could, reparations that I will contribute to in his name because he did what was needful, even though the Waterborn were ill-used in the process. But beyond that, he speaks with reason. He can be of no use here while Lyl is on the move, and Allegria is lost to us."

"These are *my* people," she snarled, spinning around to glare at him. "It is *my* kin who have suffered by Deo's hand, and I will not have it said he simply walked away in their time of need."

"The Starborn are your people, too," Israel said, narrowing his eyes on her. "Do you forget them in your rush to placate your cousin, the priestess?"

She spat a word that Deo knew would enrage his father. With a shake of his head at the futility of it all, he simply started for the door, calling over his shoulder, "Disown me if it makes you feel better, but I must have Hallow and Allegria if we are to have any hope of stopping Nezu from destroying Alba."

"Do not expect me to rush to your assistance when you need it," Dasa said loudly over the sound of scraping chairs. Quinn, Ella, and Dexia all rose and followed silently after Deo. "Your Banes have seen to it that my army has been destroyed, so even if I wanted to—and I assure you that at this moment, you are the very last person I would consider aiding—I will have nothing with which to help you. Go now, and you will find yourself alone, with no army at your back, hopeless in the eyes of the goddesses!"

He paused at the door and looked back at his parents. Dasa's face was red, her hands fisted, waves of animosity all but rolling off her. He wondered for a moment why she was suddenly so willing to disregard her beloved Starfall, and the Starborn whom she ruled, but that, too, was a puzzle for another day.

With a nod to his father that, to his surprise, was returned, he said simply, "I might be without many friends, and have no great company, or the blessing of the goddesses, but I am not hopeless."

"Nor are you alone," Idril said, pressing herself against his side.

"You have me," Quinn told Deo with a wry smile. "The goddesses have blessed me...or cursed me, depending on your point of view...and that should count for something."

"Nor do you need a great company," Ella said, her gaze flicking between the queen and Deo. "You simply need people who aren't afraid to do what needs to be done."

"And a vanth," Dexia said, smiling in a way that showed every single one of her pointed teeth.

He met his mother's furious gaze. "I will return to lend what aid I can once I have rid Alba of the threat of Nezu."

"Deo!" she yelled after him, but he turned and walked through the door, the others falling into place behind him. "I mean what I say! If you leave Deeptide now, I will make it known throughout Genora that you are no longer my son."

"Whereas I will make it known to the very same people that you go with my blessing," Israel called after him. "I will gather what help I can, and follow you as quickly as may be."

The door closed on the sound of Dasa unleashing a verbal tirade on Israel.

"Is your mother always that...volatile?" Quinn asked a few minutes later, as he and Deo saddled the horses while Idril and the others gathered supplies.

"No."

Silence followed that word, one that lasted until Deo led the horses out to the yard.

"Odd, that, don't you think?" was all Quinn said.

It was a question that remained with Deo for some time.

Chapter 10

"This is a disturbingly bleak place." I stood with my hands on my hips and surveyed our surroundings. "What did you say it was called?"

"Me?" Mayam stood up from where she'd bent to examine a small flowering plant. Like the ground beneath our feet, it was black—everything from the stem to the leaves and flowers all bore slightly different hues of the same color. "Did I say what it was called? I don't remember."

I disregarded that statement. "I don't remember" had become a frequent refrain the last few days. I frowned at that thought, something niggling in the back of my mind, something disturbing, but whatever it was refused to come forward and let me see it. "I suppose it doesn't matter. I just thought you called it by a specific name."

Mayam glanced around. "The stones here are pretty. What would you call it, if you could name it?"

"The stones, or this place?" I scrambled to the top of a black rocky outcropping, noticing that the texture of the stone was oddly smooth, as Mayam had pointed out. It was almost glass-like, glistening onyx in the dulled daylight.

Black lay before me: black ground, black rock, a few scrubby black plants, and black skeletons of scorched trees long dead, their jagged, naked branches resembling the fingers of a withered crone.

Or those of a...of a...my mind came to a stuttering halt at the word I wanted to draw forth. "Kiriah blight it," I muttered to myself, having the same sense of something trying to get my attention and feeling irritated with my inability to think properly.

"It's not very descriptive of the land itself, but I agree that as a sentiment, it suits," Mayam said, climbing up onto the ebony remains of a fallen tree that looked like it had been blasted by lightning. "Blighted is a good word for it."

"No, that was meant for myself. There's a word I want—the people who were affected by those big red ones—they were all shrunken in on themselves, and had claw-like fingers."

Mayam wrinkled her forehead in thought. "Night talkers, you mean?"

"I have no idea what that is." I glanced behind me, in the direction we'd come. The edge of the forest was dull grey, as was right and proper in the spirit realm. This blackness that consumed everything was not. "It's just wrong, and yet at the same time, it feels oddly...right," I said aloud.

"No, they really are called night talkers. I'm certain that's the right name for them. They were well known on Eris, and highly sought after. It's said they could summon the shadows, and slip into them to hide from view. My mother said she had a night talker in her family, but I never saw him." Mayam picked up a smooth bit of polished onyx stone, examined it, and, after a moment, tossed it aside. "The rocks here are pretty, though."

"Well, whatever this place is called—and to answer your question, I think I would call it *deep night*, since it reminds me of that time when Bellias is hiding, and the night seems to consume everything—we're finally here. What was it that you wished to do here?"

Mayam looked startled. "I don't...did I want to do something here?"

"You must have, else we wouldn't have come." I jumped down off the rock and strode forward, climbing a narrow, barely visible track to a small hilltop. Below us, a dip in the landscape led to a small scooped-out area where a massive black block stood, ringed by twelve smaller stones. "This is a disturbingly bleak place. What did you say it was called?"

Mayam moved to stand next to me, frowned, then gave me an odd look. "Didn't you just ask me that?"

"Ask you what?"

"What I called this place?"

I considered the landscape that surrounded us. It was uninspiring, and yet, it definitely felt as if we should be here. "I don't think so. Did I?"

She rubbed her temple, murmuring to herself, "I could have sworn you asked...oh, never mind."

"Shall we go down to that big block?" I pointed down to the depression ahead of us. "That must be what you wanted us to come here to see, yes?"

"I suppose so," Mayam said, her voice hesitant and unsure.

We headed down the rocky path to the depression, the muted sound of waves reaching our ears. "Do you hear that? We must be very near the coast," I said, pausing to sniff the air. There was no salty tang, just the smell of death, blackened, scorched death.

"We've come a long way," Mayam agreed, picking up a stone to examine it. "The stones here are pretty. Like glass."

"We have that. It seems like forever since we left...erm..." I gave up trying to remember the last place we'd been, and looked around. "This place is odd, don't you think?"

"Bleak," Mayam said, nodding. A considering look crossed her face and she amended the statement. "No. Blighted. Wasn't that what you called it?"

"Blighted is a good description for it. What's this region called?"

Mayam gave me a look out of the corner of her eye, a smooth stone clutched in her hand. She opened her mouth to answer, but at that moment, there was a massive rush of wind, and a man shimmered into view.

He had short, spiky black hair, and bristling eyebrows with piercing blue eyes. "Allegria! What are you doing here? Have you no sense, priestling? No common sense? Well, I suppose it doesn't matter, I found you, and that's what's important. Ah, you have a Shadowborn with you. Blessings of Bellias, my good lady. I am Thorn of Kelos."

"I am Mayam, sir," she said, making a deep curtsey.

"Thorn?" I frowned as that familiar wriggle in my head made me annoyed again. "That's an odd—" I stopped, a shadow flitting through my mind like a bird sweeping and wheeling in the air.

The man stared, his eyebrows bristling in a way that made me want to giggle. But there was no humor in the eyes that watched me. I had an odd feeling that he was assessing me, and that I had been found lacking. "It's an odd what?" he asked.

"I..." I closed my eyes for a moment, trying to pin down the image that flickered just on the edge of my memory. I shook my head, giving up. "No, it's gone. I thought for a moment I had it, but it flew off like a bird."

"Yes!" Thorn shouted, smiling and patting me awkwardly on the shoulder. "You remember? Thank the goddesses. I thought I was going to have to explain to Hallow why I was returning to him a wife who wouldn't recognize him. You've been in the spirit realm for a long time, according to the spirits who've seen you, but clearly you haven't suffered as other mortals have. Well, that's all for the good."

"Hallow?" I asked, the name making a little curl of warmth burn in my belly. I liked the name. It sounded...pleasant.

"Who's Hallow?" Mayam asked.

Katie MacAlister

Thorn stared at me for a minute, then with an oath under his breath, started drawing symbols on the air. "I wish I had my staff now, the one I gave over to the Master, but I'm not so feeble that I can't do this the hard way."

"He's an odd man," Mayam said softly in my ear, giving the stranger a worried look. "Think you he's mad?"

"No doubt," I whispered back, and without a word, we both sidled past him, moving along a path that sloped downward, toward an indentation where a big black slab lay. "He's probably harmless, but we'd best let him be. Besides, we came here for you to do something, and we should get that done. Er...what did you say this place was called?"

"Me?" Mayam followed while I marched resolutely onward to the black slab.

The man Thorn caught up to us a short while later, as Mayam and I were having a discussion about what we would call this area if it were up to us to name it. In each of his hands sat a glowing ball of blue-white light about the size of a large apple.

"—think blight is a good name for it..." Mayam stopped speaking when Thorn stopped in front of us. "Oooh. Pretty."

"Very pretty," I agreed, feeling that a few kind words toward the obviously confused man might urge him to move on. "Is that something for us?"

"You could say that," he said, and to my surprise, hurled the ball at my head. It hit me with the impact of...well, I couldn't think of the word that I wanted, but I staggered backward, my arms cartwheeling wildly. "Kiriah's ten tiny toenails, what was that?"

I rubbed my temples, my head tingling, my vision blurred for a few moments. I heard Mayam call out in surprise, and spun around to help her, in case the madman attacked her, too.

"No, not madman," I said slowly as the tingling faded, and with it, the cloud inside my head lifted. "Thorn!" Joy filled me as I beheld the man before me, now standing with his arms crossed.

"Ah," he said, a smug look on his face when I dashed forward to give him a hug and kiss on his cheek. He patted me on the back, saying, "Just so, my dear, just so. Remind me to tell that annoying apprentice of mine that I can still perform the old magic, which is more than he can do."

"Old magic?" I rubbed my head again, feeling oddly lightened, as if I'd been wearing chains of solid lead that had suddenly been cast off. My spirit sang with unfettered joy until I glanced around. "Where's Hallow?"

"Allegria?" Mayam suddenly appeared at my side, also rubbing her head. She looked at Thorn, her gaze sharpening on him. "A spirit? What did he do to us? Who is he? Is he a friend of yours? Have you sought him to bespell me? I won't have it! My lord Racin shall hear of this mistreatment!"

"Alas, Hallow did not come with me," Thorn said, his expression of self-satisfaction fading. It took me a few minutes to reconcile the image of him as a man with that of the wooden bird he inhabited when he was in the mortal world, but there was something about him, an air of mischievousness that was all too familiar. "There was…er…trouble at Kelos when he sent me to find you."

"Trouble?" I had my swords drawn, and whirled around just as if I expected to see whatever it was that threatened the man who was everything to me. "The thane? He attacked again?"

"Where are we?" Mayam asked, spinning in a circle, scowling when she saw me resheathing my swords. "What are you doing with those? I thought I took them away from you! Give them to me at once. It is not fitting for a prisoner to be armed when the captor is not!"

"Again?" Thorn asked, one hand ruffling his hair. "The thane attacked Kelos? The one who sleeps in the crypt beneath my tower? That thane?"

"Yes, he…erm…" I gave a little cough and gazed into the distance. "He woke up some time ago."

"He's never woken in all the centuries that I ruled Kelos," Thorn said, puzzlement sliding into suspicion. "The only time I heard of him stirring was a tale my master told of a thief who was foolish enough to break into the crypt with the thought of stealing the thane's sword. And the Eidolon went back to sleep as soon as the man died. After twelve days. It really is remarkable how someone skilled at torture can keep a person alive despite all the various—" He waved his hand in a gesture I didn't want to explore.

"Yes, well, all of that aside," I said, still not able to meet his eye. "The point is that if the thane has attacked again, then I must go at once to Hallow. He and Deo can't handle the thane by themselves. How do we get out of here?"

"I am not going anywhere," Mayam said, crossing her arms. "And neither are you. You are my prisoner, given into my care by Lord Racin. I demand that you give me your weapons, and place yourself in my charge."

"Who is this Shadowborn woman?" Thorn asked, giving Mayam the same look of disbelief I was fairly certain covered my own face. "And why does she feel that making outrageous statements of that sort has any value, conversationallyspeaking?"

"She's Deo's former…well, friend, I guess. We met her on Eris. Then she betrayed us."

"I simply realized that Lord Deo was being unreasonable with regards to Racin," she said with an irritated sniff.

"How do we get out of the spirit realm?" I asked Thorn. "And how fast can you get to Hallow once we're out? He's probably going mad worrying about me, and if he's coping with the thane, that's the last thing he should be doing."

"Coping with the thane?" Thorn asked, obviously confused.

"Worrying."

"About that—" Thorn looked thoughtful. "Yes, I think we're going to have to call in my apprentice to help with that. The irritating one, not the traitorous one."

I stiffened. "I realize that Hallow may not have been your choice for the position of Master of Kelos, but to refer to him as irritating is just unfair. He has tried very hard to accede to your demands, many and varied as they are, and he does a wonderful job keeping not only the spirits of Kelos happy—excluding the Eidolon, and that wasn't his fault at all—but also organizing the arcanists."

"What are you talking about?" Thorn asked, a distracted expression on his face. "Of course I chose the lad to be Master. I knew the minute I saw him with Exodius that Hallow would be perfect for the position. Far more perfect than Exodius ever was, but don't tell him that. Not until he does what we want."

"I don't know who Exodius is, and to be honest, I don't much care. I wish to be returned to my lord Racin," Mayam said stiffly, sitting down on a large black rock that was oddly smooth and glossy.

We both ignored her. "What do you want Exodius to do? Something for Hallow?" I asked Thorn.

"No, something for me." He frowned at nothing for a moment, then nodded, as if coming to a decision. "Yes, it has happened. The connection to Kelos feels different, which means Hallow...but that is neither here nor there. Come, priestling. We have tarried too long. I do not wish for the Askia to notice you here. They will want to know who you are, and why you are here, and both of those are questions you will not wish to answer. I will see you to the mortal plane, but then I must find Exodius."

"He's that way," I said, pointing over Thorn's shoulder. "We met him... hmm. I don't remember how long it's been. We met him a few days ago, I think, in a town next to a river. It had a great hall perched at one end."

"Trust Exodius to claim the grandest residence he could find," Thorn murmured, shooing me forward. "Yes, yes, I know the town of which you speak, and I will go there henceforth, but first we must get you out of here before the spell wears off, and you return to a state of insensibility. There is an exit down there, by the altar where the barrier between the two realms is the weakest."

"There's an altar here?" I asked, moving forward down the path. "Who are the Askia that we need to be wary of them? I haven't heard of such a people."

"I will not have you escaping!" Mayam called after us, and with a hrmph, leaped up and pushed her way past Thorn to march beside me. "Lord Racin would never forgive me should I let you slide through his fingers."

"You really are delusional if you believe I will let you hand me over to that monster again," I told her in my most polite voice before turning my head to ask over my shoulder, "Thorn?"

"Hmm?"

"The Askia?"

He blinked at me, his eyebrow tendrils waving gently in the breeze.

"Who are they?" I prompted when it was clear he hadn't been paying attention. "And just where are we? Does this place have a name, or is it just some desolate stretch of the coast?"

He was silent for a moment, his expression unusually grave. "This is the Altar of Day and Night," he finally answered.

"And the Askia are the twelve maiden warriors who guard the All-Father." Mayam gave a disgusted snort. "Really, your ignorance is almost breathtaking in its scope."

I opened my mouth to dispute the label of ignorance, but had to admit that in this instance, she was correct. "What are they doing here if they guard the All-Father? I thought the goddesses—"

"And Nezu!" she interrupted.

"Banished him," I finished, rubbing the goosebumps on my arms."The Altar of Day and Night. I assume the name refers to the twin goddesses? It's a fitting name, regardless. This whole area is so...so..."

"Desolate?" Thorn suggested, stopping next to the altar, and sketching a few symbols on the ground.

"Bleak?" Mayam asked, and bent to pick up a small stone, which she examined with apparent interest.

"Familiar," I said, finally putting my fragmented thoughts together.

Thorn shot me a questioning glance, but said nothing, just continued to draw symbols on the ground in the shape of a circle.

It took another six minutes before Thorn managed to get an exit opened that led out to the mortal world—this was despite Mayam's constant complaints and demands that we take her immediately to Nezu.

"I will look first," he warned, moving in front of me as I was about to pass through the opening he'd made in the fabric of being that separated the physical from the spirit realms. "In case the Askia have noticed you were here, and wish to make trouble."

"I have no fight with them," I said softly, glancing over my shoulder. For some reason, my skin felt prickly, like someone had used a piece of silk to rub a glass rod, then passed it over my arm. "There is no reason they should wish to interfere with us."

"You are Fireborn," Mayam said with a one-shoulder shrug. "They need no other reason to hate you."

"Why on earth would the fact that I'm Fireborn matter to them? I've never even heard of them, so why would they take umbrage with me?"

Mayam's lip curled with scorn, but she answered readily enough. I had a suspicion she liked the opportunity to flaunt her knowledge in front of me. "The Fireborn are children of the goddess Kiriah, who was in her turn a child of the Life-Mother. The All-Father believed the Life-Mother was behind her children's first attempt to banish him, which failed because it was just the twin goddesses together. It wasn't until Nezu joined them that they were able to succeed. The Askia haven't forgotten that. It's said they roam the coast, searching for men and women whom they can train up as soldiers to fight on behalf of the All-Father."

"They have an army, these Askia?" I'd never heard of any other people inhabiting Genora but the Starborn and the water talkers who lived on the northern coast. I wondered whether or not they would be helpful in the fight against Nezu.

"Not here. Their warriors are sent to the Vinlands," she said, naming the continent to the south of Genora. She grimaced and added, "My old master said once that he had been there to learn from the warriors—the Harii—but the people he found had broken with the Askia, and aligned themselves with the Life-Mother."

I shook my head, more than a little baffled that I had not heard of these people, wondering if Sandor knew of them and kept the knowledge from the priestesses, or if she, too, was ignorant of what went on in foreign lands. "It's a shame they are so far away. If they are aligned with the twin goddesses, we might have used their help with Nezu. Or at the very least, Darius."

"Help with Nezu?" she repeated, suspicion sharpening her gaze. "What do you mean? Do you plot against Lord Racin? Do you—"

Thorn reappeared, gesturing for us. "Come quickly. I saw an Ask, but she was alone, and appeared to be preoccupied watching a ship on the horizon. You should be able to avoid her if you are careful."

"I'm not afraid of a battle." Mayam lifted her chin and pushed past me to slip through the barrier between realms.

"Nor am I, but I do not seek them when they are not necessary." I pulled up both swords and pushed my way through what felt like a dense, warm wad of wool before emerging back into the mortal world.

Cold, salty air slapped me, causing my hair to whip around and immediately stick to the edges of my eyes and mouth, the cold sting of it making my eyes water and my nose run, but even so, I took a deep breath. My sense of relief at returning to normalcy was so great I wanted to sing.

"Ugh. The weather was much nicer in the spirit world," Mayam groused, rubbing her arms.

I glanced around, curious to see what this area looked like in the real world, but to my surprise, it was the same. Mostly.The colors were sharper and deeper in hue, the air was both lighter and had more substance, and Kiriah overhead sent little ripples of warmth down my back. But other than those differences, we stood in a black landscape of twisted, dead ebony trees and glasslike rocks. "It may have been nicer, but I much prefer this world to any other. May the goddesses bless you for all your help, Thorn. I can't—oh."

A wooden bird flitted around me; the handsome sparrow hawk design that Hallow had chosen for Thorn's new physical body fitted him well.

Such a nice priestess. I'm glad I found her for the lad. I hope she finds him soon, since it's clear he needs her. Now to go find that old fool Exodius and convince him to relay her whereabouts to Hallow...

I gasped at the voice that spoke directly in my head just as the bird was about to slip back through the entrance to the spirit world. "Thorn! I can hear you!"

What? You can? Thorn flew around my head a few times, causing Mayam, who was glaring around us, to shriek and duck, covering her head with one arm, while using the other to flap wildly above her. *How extraordinary. Especially since I'll have no other way of communicating with the lad until he regains the staff. Do you need me to guide you to the nearest town? It's to the north, along the coast.*

"No, we can find it."

"Find what? Lord Racin? He's back in the spirit realm, as I have told you a number of times," Mayam said, still batting at Thorn when he swooped over our heads.

"Thank you for everything," I told the bird, and held out my arm. He alighted on my wrist, his wooden talons gentle on my flesh. I gave him a little kiss on the head before drawing a blessing on him.

The symbol flared with a brilliant golden light, one that had me seeing black spots for a few seconds. The intensity of the blessing took me a little aback.

Now, now, don't you go falling in love with me, Thorn said with a ribbon of amusement in his voice as he took to the wing, making a big circle around us. *Hallow wouldn't understand that at all, not to mention the fact that it wouldn't be appropriate, not with you being a priestess of Kiriah, and me being me.*

I laughed aloud, watching fondly when he disappeared, slipping back into the spirit world.

"You are a very strange woman," Mayam snapped.

"So it's been said, but I have yet to let that bother me. We had best be off before these warriors of the All-Father find us. Thorn says there's a town to the north. I'm going to head that way and see if there are any horses to hire. Are you coming with me, or going off on your own?" I didn't particularly care what she did, not now that I had one of the moonstones and my weapons back. Uppermost in my mind was finding Hallow, and making sure he was unharmed.

Mayam's lip curled with scorn, but she evidently bit back the comment she wanted to make, and instead, with an abrupt gesture, marched past me northwards. "I have no other choice but to go with you. You're my prisoner. I can't just let you wander around free. But don't expect me to be so accommodating once Lord Racin finds me."

"You just told me he was in the spirit realm," I pointed out. I made my way through the circle of large black rocks that seemed to stretch upward toward Kiriah with inky, jagged fingers. I glanced back when I found a game trail going north, wondering at the oddness of the Altar of Day and Night. Why was it so horribly bleak, and yet at the same time so familiar to me? "And it's not likely that he's going to come out of there until the thane calls the All-Father forth. Speaking of which, why does he want the All-Father—"

As we rounded a particularly large rock, I came face to face with a massive man whose skin was tinted red, his long black hair lifting gently in the breeze from the shore.

"Well, shite," I swore.

Surprise flitted across Nezu's black eyes for a moment, followed immediately by a calculating look that assessed and dismissed me.

"Lord Racin!" Mayam pushed past me to bow low before him. "I knew you would find me. I told the priestess that you would, but she scoffed at me. At *you*. And yet, here you are, and here she is, and despite her having me removed from the spirit realm, she is still my captive."

Nezu glanced at Mayam, annoyance dripping from his voice as he said, "What are you doing here? Who brought you to the altar? I was told you ran off with the Fireborn priest."

I may have felt like my brain was wrapped in swaddling clothes for the last week, but at that moment, my mind was as sharp as the straight razor that Hallow used to scrape the whiskers from his face. I was a lightweaver, once again blessed in Kiriah's sight, and I had in my possession one of the powerful moonstones that were the focus of so many people's attention. I would be damned if I did not use those weapons to their fullest potential.

"My lord, I did not run off; I was taken by this one—" Mayam started to say, but I pulled the moonstone from where it was tucked away in an inner pocket, and started a prayer to Kiriah. The second the words formed in my head, heat licked my flesh, the power of Kiriah flowing through me so strongly that for a moment I panicked, fearful it would simply consume me. Hastily, I directed the light, sending it to focus through the moonstone.

Nezu's eyes widened when a golden-white light formed a corona around me, his gaze settling on the moonstone I held in my hand. "That's mine!" he bellowed and lunged toward me. In the distance, I could hear the deep, grating calls of the Harborym answering him, and beyond that, the sound of a battle horn, and knew I had very little time to do what was needful.

"By the grace of Kiriah Sunbringer, I send you back to where you belong!" I shouted, holding the moonstone aloft as if it was a beacon. "Bound once to Eris you were; so you shall be bound again!"

"You cannot—" Nezu stopped and tried to lunge at me, but hissed in anger, drawing back with a furious expression.

Light filled my mind, the power of not just the sun, but of Kiriah herself. It burst forth from the moonstone with a whip crack of sound that echoed off the scorched stand of trees just beyond the altar. Next to me, Mayam screamed and fell to the ground, immediately curling into a protective ball.

"I can do anything," I told Nezu in a voice that was foreign to me, the syllables rolling off my lips with a slow, weighted cadence that was not my own, and yet as familiar as the breath in my lungs. Power flowed from and through and around me. I was light, I was creation, I could give life or take it away depending on my whim. I wasn't just a priestess of Kiriah—I *was* Kiriah. I was a goddess, creator of the race of Fireborn, and there was nothing and no one who could stop me.

My gaze moved from the moonstone, focusing on the man before me, and for a moment, his form shimmered, changing from the red monster to that of a being cloaked in shadows, his eyes glittering silver. "Nezu," I said in that strange yet familiar voice, the word resonating through me.

Anger chased the sorrow that followed the word, anger and an intention that filled my being.

"No," he snarled, snatching the front of my tunic and pulling me up to him, his eyes glittering when he gazed deep into mine, burning a cold path down to the very depths of my soul. "I will not allow this. Not again."

"Not again," I repeated, agreeing, and before he could react, jerked myself out of his hold and allowed the light flowing through me to focus through the moonstone once more. This time the light didn't just snap out at him, it slammed into his chest, sending him staggering backward a few feet.

"This is not over," he swore, his head lowered as if he was about to charge. Several Harborym had reached him by that time, Harborym that melted into red puddles on the ground when I flicked a glance at them. "You will not disrupt my plans. Not this time."

"I can do anything," I repeated and started to gather up the power of sun; the sensation of it, like the heat of a thousand infernos,was as natural as the beat of my heart. I lifted the moonstone again, calling forth all the intention, sorrow, and pain that fed the magic inside me before sending it into the moonstone.

It shattered in my hand, cracking into four pieces just as Nezu, with a snarl of profanity, stomped forward and ripped open the fabric of being that hid the entrance to the spirit world, disappearing into it without so much as a look back.

I stared down at the broken bits of crystal lying across my palm, the power of Kiriah slowly fading from me, leaving me bereft and shivering without it.

"What have you done?" Mayam asked, her voice penetrating my dark thoughts. I continued to stare at the moonstone, aware of her slow movements as she got to her feet. I did not care about the expression of horror and fear on her face.

"It broke," I said in disbelief, prodding the crystal with one finger, trying to push the pieces back into place. It lay heavy on my hand, nothing more than a broken bit of crystal, lifeless and without any resonance. "It was whole. It was completely fine. Then I used it as a focus, and...it broke."

Mayam took a step back, shaking her head. "What *are* you?"

"Lightweaver. Former Bane of Eris. Priestess of Kiriah Sunbringer," I said wearily, feeling drained by the withdrawal of Kiriah's power.

"But you—you glowed! And Lord Racin seemed..." She clearly struggled to find the word she wanted.

"Insane?" I suggested.

She slid me an unreadable glance. "Wary," she finally answered. "Of you."

"It's because I channeled Kiriah herself. I did once before, when Deo and Hallow and I closed the master portal Nezu opened in Abet." I glanced down at my arms, where the faintest scars still remained. "Although I'm very happy that this time, I didn't hurt myself doing it."

"What you did—" She stopped when the horn I'd heard before sounded again, this time much closer.

"Askia," I said, stuffing the bits of moonstone into my inner pocket, and turning to see how close they were.

My eyes widened as I took in the surroundings. What had been black, burned, and twisted trees, rocks, and plants now glistened with life. Little green tendrils peeked out between the black glass rocks and birds flitted from dead tree to dead tree, bringing the air alive with birdsong. Even the scrubby black grass that had dotted the area was now interspersed with minute thin green shoots. As I watched, a colorful snail crawled up the top of the huge altar stone. I plucked it off, examining it for a minute before dropping it onto the nearest rock, pulling up my swords as human-shaped shadows flickered amongst the twisted trees to the south. Battle cries lifted high into the air to join the gulls that wheeled overhead, adding their own haunted calls to the nightmare scene.

"Goddesses!" Mayam said on a gasp, her eyes huge as she backed away. "We should...we should..."

"Run," I said, nodding, then spun around and ran after Mayam, who had bolted to the north. Strident voices followed us, indicating the Askia had caught sight of us running from the altar.

I slid on a smear of red that dotted the path, leaping over rocks and fallen trees while I drew as many protective runes as I could, my mind filled with not only the All-Father's guard, but the question of how I was going to tell Hallow I had broken one of the precious moonstones needed to help defeat Nezu.

And just what had he meant by telling me he wouldn't allow me to do something again? Do what? Had he felt the nearness of Kiriah, as I had when I channeled her power? I shook my head at my thoughts even as we raced through the slowly changing landscape, my ragged breath drowning out all but the highest cries of the Askia. "They're getting closer," I yelled to Mayam, a few yards ahead of me.

"How far is it to the town?" Her words drifted back to me while I dodged a leafy tree branch that snapped back after her passing.

"I don't know. Thorn didn't say." I risked a glance back when the game path we'd followed curved inward, away from the shoreline. Behind us at a distance of a few hundred yards, I caught sight of two women clad in black leather armor, their long black hair streaming behind them as they raced after us. But it was what I saw in the distance that had my blood turning cold in my veins. "Blessed goddesses above, I hope not far, because they have horses, Mayam!"

She screamed something unintelligible, disappearing into dense foliage when the path swung to the left.

I dug deep, running after her while sending prayer after prayer to Kiriah Sunbringer.

I had a horrible feeling that we were going to need every blessing she could spare us.

Chapter 11

"Master—"

"I'm not absolutely certain you can call me that. No, to the right."
Hallow finished weaving a shadow spell over the trench that the good
citizens of Nether Wallop had helped dig across one section of the Great
East Road and stood back to squint critically at the results. There was a
distinct suspicious darkness lying across the ground, but he hoped that
the spell he'd just woven over the trench, along with the natural protection
cast by the cedars lining the road, would help conceal it. "Thorn, is there
anything you can do to conceal this trench?"

The bird, which had taken to perching on Hallow's shoulder since
it seemed to be reluctant to return to the staff now held by Lyl, gave
a harsh squawk.

"Fine. This will just have to do. Would you mind checking the road again?"

Thorn took off without so much as bobbing his head, and Hallow
wondered for what seemed like the fiftieth time how, when Thorn had so
often driven him nigh unto madness with his endless chattering, he could
actually miss hearing the arcanist now that he was no longer Master of
Kelos. "Bellias blast that Lyl."

"If only it was that easy," Aarav murmured, passing with an armful of
balls made up of arcany.

Hallow turned to go see how the other defenses were holding up, and
almost ran down Tygo.

"My master always told me that Bellias blesses those who don't call
on her for every little want," Tygo said in a self-righteous tone that he
immediately countered by adding in his normal voice, "I always thought

that was a lame excuse. If I have the chance to ask the goddess for help, why wouldn't I? She's a goddess! She has unlimited power, and I'm her devoted worshiper, so why shouldn't she want to aid me?"

"A sentiment I heartily endorse," cooed a female voice. Hallow turned and made a little bow to the buxom woman who stopped before him. She ran a quick assessing eye over first Tygo, then him. "Blessings of Bellias, Lord Hallow. I am Red Eva. I was told you were seeing to our defenses, and wanted to offer you not only my thanks, but the hospitality of my house. That's it there, the one with the shifts hanging out the window."

"Er…" Hallow glanced at the woman's black hair. "*Red* Eva?"

"Aye." She ran her gaze over him again, then smiled, invitation visible in her eyes. She leaned forward until her mouth was a scant inch from his ear and whispered, "It's said that my love grotto can tighten so hard around a man that it makes him see red."

"Love grotto?" Hallow almost choked with a sudden urge to laugh, but he kept firm control of his lips, simply shifting a few steps away from the woman.

"You know." She gave him a look that wasn't so much an invitation to come hither as a demand that he fling himself on her. "My birth cannon."

He stared at her, unable to speak lest he lose the scant control he had. Next to him, Tygo gave an abbreviated snort that was more than half laughter.

"You can't possibly be a man who does not enjoy women to the fullest, but perhaps they use another term where you are from?" She edged closer, stroking a hand down the front of his jerkin. "Mount Pleasant? Penis sharpener?"

Hallow wondered idly what bad choices he'd made to land him there at that exact moment.

"Fur-backed turtle," Tygo said, his eyes narrowed in thought.

"Crotch cobbler," Red Eva all but purred. Her voice dropped an octave. "Mother of all souls."

"Much as I appreciate the offer to visit your…er…establishments—both personal and structural—I am not only busy at the moment making sure that a deranged arcanist doesn't destroy this town as he did the last one that gave us shelter, but I am also married. Happily.*Very* happily. So thank you, but if you will pardon me…" Hallow stepped around both Tygo and Red Eva, and ran over a mental checklist of items.

"Later, then, after you have seen to the attackers," Red Eva called after him. "Your wife is welcome to join you. I have three man minxes she can enjoy while you are sampling the wares my ladies offer, and I'm willing to give her a discount, too."

Hallow ignored the offer, focusing on the defensive line he and the townspeople had been working on since before Kiriah had risen that morning. The trench on the road was sure to catch at least a score of men, hopefully Lyl included. The townspeople had been busy making what they colloquially called fire mops, small twists of rag and rope soaked in fat, which could be lit and tossed onto invading parties. "Aarav, are the arcane traps set?"

"Aye, although I don't know what good they will do," the older man said, his expression morose. "I made them weak, as you ordered. They won't kill anyone, just knock them around a bit."

"I have no intention of killing Lyl's army," Hallow said evenly, turning to find Tygo once again standing right in front of him. "Not unless we have no other choice. They are not responsible for his decisions. What is it you want, Tygo, that you must constantly try to trip me?"

Tygo straightened up, his earnest face slightly flushed with exertion. "Master Hallow—"

"He's no longer Master of Kelos," Aarav interrupted. "You can't call him that anymore."

"He should be Master," Tygo argued, looking mildly annoyed. "He did nothing to warrant removal of the title!"

"That is neither here nor there. My point is—" Aarav placed the balls of magic inside several of the paper lanterns that had been strung above the road in a zig-zagging pattern, so that they glowed with the gentle light of the starshine captured by arcany. "You cannot call him that anymore."

"What is it you wanted?" Hallow asked, taking pity on the young man, whose face turned an even darker red at Aarav's chastisement. "Did you complete the protection wards on all the houses?"

"Aye, master," Tygo said, casting a defiant glance toward Aarav, whose shoulder twitched in response. "All the houses, and the hall, and the well, and the stable, and the—"

"Excellent," Hallow interrupted, not wishing to take time to inventory all the structures standing in the small but picturesquely named Nether Wallop. "And the south road is clear?"

"It is. I just ran back from checking it myself. Jordan, the headman, says that no one uses it because it goes to an uninhabitable land, but I made sure there was nothing blocking it, no magic or pitfalls or even stray cattle making it impossible to pass. If your wife comes via that road, she should have no trouble getting here."

Hallow fought the need to leave everything to chase after Allegria... or at least where he thought she would be, given what Exodius had told him. He reminded himself that she wouldn't thank him for leaving Lyl's army to ravage yet another town when she was perfectly safe. "Although I wish she'd get here. She's had enough time, judging by the map—what?"

One of the local men he'd sent as a scout galloped toward them, riding up onto the narrow verge of grass to avoid the pit that lay across the road. Thorn flew behind him, his wooden wings flapping furiously.

"They're coming!" Hallow turned and bellowed back toward the town. "To arms!"

A deep bell rang in response, and the people of Nether Wallop raced toward their appointed places. The old and young would be herded into the caves a quarter mile away, while everyone who could wield a weapon would be stationed around the village.

"Let us hope Tygo is as effective at setting slowing spells as he is at currying favor with those in command," Aarav said acidly, his white robe fluttering as he dashed past Hallow before leaping into one of the trees alongside the track.

"Tygo?" Hallow called, taking up a stand in the middle of the road, about five yards from the trench.

"In place, Master Hallow." His voice was muffled, but filled with excitement.

Hallow shook his head to himself. "You'd think he would have had enough excitement in the three days it took us to get here—how close are they?" he asked the scout, who had pulled up beside him, his horse snorting and sidestepping.

"Less than half a league, and moving fast," the man said, glancing over his shoulder.

Thorn flew overhead, circling Hallow a few times until he held out his arm, allowing the bird to alight. "Did you see Lyl?" he asked the scout.

"Aye, he rode at the front." The scout frowned, dismounting when another man dashed out to take the horse. "There were men with him—men I'd never seen before. Piebald, they were."

"Piebald?" Hallow asked, confused.

The scout waved his hand around vaguely. "Their skin was mottled in shades of brown and tan. Just like my best cow."

Hallow blinked a couple of times, realized he was doing that, and forced himself to stop.

The scout's voice grew grim. "They were also warriors, bristling with swords and lances and morning stars."

"I've never seen people who have such coloring." Hallow dug through his prodigious memory, but came up with a blank.

"You're about to," the scout said, watching the road anxiously.

"I suppose so. Get to your place," he instructed the man, pulling out his sword and wishing for the sixth time that day that he had the staff upon which Thorn normally sat. "Thorn, you saw these strange men?"

The bird bobbed his head a few times, watching him with his strange, unblinking eyes.

"Do you know who they are?"

Thorn flapped his wings wide for a second, then bobbed again.

"Blast it to the stars and back, I wish you could talk to me. Are these strange warriors from Genora?"

Thorn sat silent, tipping his head to the side to watch Hallow.

"Wonderful. Lyl has picked up supporters from somewhere unknown, as if his chasing us for the last three days wasn't enough of a trial. Very well." Hallow pulled down the leather jerkin he'd donned over his normal tunic and leggings, and pushed hard on the chaos power that had been buzzing inside him, making him feel like an entire hive of annoyed honeybees had taken up residence in his chest. "I know you are bound to the master should he call on you—damn Lyl's hide—but does that mean you can't stay here and help us?"

Thorn squawked and leaped into the air, circling Hallow three times before alighting on his head, his wings flapping with excitement.

Hallow had a picture of just what he looked like with a big wooden bird perched on his head, and fought a profound feeling of martyrdom.

A dull rumble echoed down the road. "Be ready! They approach!" Hallow warned before bracing himself, gathering arcany around him, all the while keeping a nervous eye on the runes on his wrist and ankle cuffs. "I wish I'd had time to add to the runes—ah. There they are."

A horn sounded behind him as a warning to the people who were headed to the caves, followed almost immediately by harsh cries and shouting. The people of Nether Wallop, while determined to help the arcanists deter Lyl's army, had never seen such a battle, and were no doubt terrified by the reality of the threat they faced.

"I invoke that which created the night and day, bound by my hand, by my breath, by my blood, and unto it, I imbue my intention," Hallow intoned softly, casting symbols into the air, locking them together into chains of blood magic. He ignored the sounds of panic behind him, keeping his attention focused on the body of men who rode down the narrow road. "That which no man has seen I cast before me, bound to this place, no more to be changed."

The chains of magic fell to his feet, glowing a rusty reddish color before melting into the road, long tendrils reaching toward the hidden trench. A cry went up from the men approaching, as several voices lifted at the same time.

"By Bellias' toes, what is that?" Hallow stopped casting symbols for a moment, his gaze narrowed on the men. He saw instantly what the scout had meant about the odd coloration of the warriors' skin, but his sharp eyes had picked out what the scout hadn't. "They aren't piebald—they're simply decorated. With runes, I believe, drawn onto their flesh."

Thorn hopped up and down on Hallow's head, flapping his wings.

"I have a very bad feeling they don't need the swords they carry," Hallow told Thorn, bracing himself as the first of the men was about to reach the trench. Behind the two score or so warriors, he caught sight of a familiar banner, and knew that Lyl had hidden himself in the middle of his company. "If something happens—if our defenses fail—you'll find Allegria and warn her, yes? Get her to Deo or Lord Israel. She'll be safe with them if Lyl strikes me down."

Thorn gave a great cry, hopping again on Hallow's head before he took to the wing, making a circle overhead.

"I invoke the bornless," Hallow yelled once he judged the men in the front could hear him. He spread wide his arms, his sword in one hand, a ball of arcany in the other, while Thorn made high, piercing cries as he flew faster and faster in a circle over Hallow's head. "I invoke the sightless. I invoke the breathless. Before you, I do commit them to my protection!" The words were ancient ones that his former master had taught him, an invocation that preceded even the arrival of the Fireborn to Alba, words that resonated with the elements of nature, and those beings who had been born of them.

The road was wide enough only to allow three men to ride abreast, but although the men clearly heard him, they didn't slow down. In fact, Hallow saw them spur on their horses as they started to chant. "No, not chant," he said a second before the first of the men reached the trench. "Sing. How fascinating."

Chaos—both magical and physical—broke out just when the lead men reached the trenches. Reluctant to harm innocent animals when it could be avoided, Hallow had caused the road a few yards from the trench to be graven with a spell that caused fear in animals. He'd used it before to keep Penn from wandering when there were no hobbles at hand, and he was pleased to see the horses of Lyl's army react in the same way. They whinnied in high, unnatural tones, bucking and kicking, instantly unseating the men before they turned and bolted into the woods. The first three men went down into the trench, no doubt looking as if they'd disappeared to those who rode behind.

The chaos within Hallow surged, but he held it leashed, watching twenty or so of the nearest horses go crazy, either because their compatriots were doing the same, or because the magic woven on the road reached them. Regardless, the warriors with the runes etched into their flesh in great brown shapes were thrown, and rose to their feet, no longer singing. A couple cursed and went after the horses, while the others rushed toward Hallow, shouting battle cries.

"For Bellias!" Aarav cried from where he was perched in a tree and cut the twine that held aloft the paper lanterns filled with arcany.

"For the Master of Kelos!" Tygo answered from his tree and cut a second string.

The effect of pure arcany splashing down on the front part of the army led to madness within its ranks. Horses screamed and attempted to twist aside to avoid the onslaught. Hallow, prepared for that, threw high the chains of blood magic intended to soothe the pain of the horses. Thorn caught the chains in his talons, flying swiftly over the pandemonium that lay before them in order to drop the blood magic on horses driven to near madness.

"What is this? Why are all the horses running—for the love of the goddess, someone stop them! To the trees! You, Deter, fetch back those horses. The rest of you, come with me!" Lyl bellowed over the noise of horses panicking and men yelling, calling out questions or imploring the goddesses to protect them.

A half dozen more men who had rushed toward Hallow disappeared into the trench. One teetered on the edge, but with a tremendous leap managed to land heavily on the other side.

"Impressively done. I don't suppose you'd like to tell me what you are before we proceed?" Hallow asked politely, lifting his sword in case the attacker decided to forego conversation.

The man, as tall as Hallow but much thicker in the torso and shoulders, paused for a second. "You what?"

"Who are you? I've never seen anyone with runes…er…etched? on their flesh. You're not a runeseeker, for I've met one of those."

The man straightened the arm bearing a small shield, and pointed to his forearm where a patch on it was made brown with coiled sentences. "That's a dirge, mate, not runes."

"Dirge?" Hallow searched his mind while noting with satisfaction that the arcane balls Aarav and Tygo rained down on the army were causing a break in the ranks, just as he'd hoped. Only a few men rushed forward now, and those that did were instantly swallowed up by the trench. "That's a type of song, isn't it?"

"It is. I'm a dirgesinger. Have you never heard of us? We are the greatest warriors on Alba," the man told him without a shred of modesty.

"Sorry," Hallow said, shaking his head. "Never heard of you."

"Blessed by the Paean? Children of the All-Father?"

"Well, we're all technically that," Hallow pointed out.

"Aye, but we're his special children," the dirgesinger answered. "Paean— his son, who was god of the sun before the Life-Mother cast him from the celestial realm—asked the All-Father for brothers, and he created the song which gave life to us."

"Song," Hallow said, wishing he had time to fully discuss this new form of magic. He'd never heard of either dirgesingers or another sun god.

"This here is my life song," the dirgesinger said, tracing a collar of brown words that wrapped around his neck. "Granted by Paean himself, you understand."

Clearly, the man took much pride in that. Hallow, in the interest of possibly swaying the dirgesinger over to his side, away from Lyl, donned an expression of admiration.

"Most impressive. Er..."

"Aye," the man said, nodding quickly. "We have gotten a mite distracted, haven't we? Well, onward, eh?"

Hallow tossed the ball of arcany he held into the air, catching it in a way that the dirgesinger couldn't help but notice. "I don't suppose you'd care to join my forces?"

"Oh, we couldn't do that," the man said with a little frown and shake of his head. "'Twouldn't be fitting, you know? His lordship back there, he called us forth from the Vinlands, and we swore fealty to him."

"You're a Harii?" Hallow asked, having heard once of the Southerners, a race of people his old master Wix had said were more than half feral.

"Aye, although we prefer the name dirgesinger." He paused, and added with a little shrug, "Except the painsingers. But we don't hold with their kind. They keep themselves to themselves, which is for the best, if you ken me."

Hallow didn't even want to know what people called painsingers did, especially since the warrior before him clearly wished to avoid them.

"You know—this is just a thought—you could always foreswear your fealty to Lyl." Hallow gave a little grimace at the scowl the man sent his way, then sighed and lifted his sword again. "As you like, but be warned—"

He attacked before completing the sentence, catching the dirgesinger by surprise, slamming the hilt of his sword alongside the man's head. He dropped to the ground, issuing a low moan that had a hint of a tune to it. Hallow turned to move to the verge so that he could throw himself into the heat of the battle.

His feet refused to move.

He frowned down, but the dirgesinger was clearly unconscious. However, that moaned song he'd managed to vocalize had done its job. "Bellias blast it all. Fine. But if my magic gets out of control and singes you, you have no one to blame but yourself," he snapped, and let the chaos inside him slip its leash just a little, directed downward at his feet.

The resulting explosion threw him back a good fifteen yards, so that he collided with the side of one of the houses across the village square, causing his head to ring. He slid down the wall, slumping on the ground for a few minutes while he struggled to draw air back into his lungs and to clear the black blotches from his vision. Slowly, both his vision and hearing cleared, and he scrambled somewhat painfully to his feet, only to notice two important things.

The cries and yells he'd heard from the townspeople weren't prompted by the threat of Lyl's oncoming army, but by the arrival of the woman who stood on the stone well, calling down streaks of sunlight. His heart sang a song of sheer and utter joy.

"Allegria," he called, stumbling forward, wanting nothing so much as to take her in his arms and kiss every inch of that dear, adorable face.

She turned, staring at him first in surprise, then with matching joy. "Hallow! Thorn said you were close, but I didn't know you were right here!"

"Thorn said—" The words dried up when a woman wearing a banded leather skirt and form-fitting bodice rushed forward, a bow in one hand, a long dagger in the other.

The chaos within him rose even as he gathered arcany, blasting the woman with both before she got within a few yards of Allegria. "What do you mean Thorn said? He spoke to you? In the spirit realm, you mean?"

"Yes, but here, too. I heard him in my head just like you do." She slammed down another column of light, this one causing the woman who'd attacked her to scream and curl into a little ball.

"That's fortunate, because I—well, we'll deal with that later. Who is this?" he asked, gesturing toward the woman who now lay on her back.

"Ask," she said, turning back to face the south road that trailed along the coast into Nether Wallop.

"I just did," he said, moving to her side even as he checked to make sure Lyl's army wasn't getting any closer. He noted the villagers left behind lurking in the shadows, waiting to defend their town should the army make it past Hallow and the arcanists.

"No, that was an Ask. She's one of the Askia, the All-Father's elite guard, or something like that. Mayam stopped providing information after I threatened to leave her behind because she wanted to rest and I wanted to survive. The Askia are tireless," she added with an annoyed glare down the south path. Two women emerged from the shrubs on either side of it, one shooting a hail of arrows in rapid succession.

Allegria slammed down a wall of golden light, causing the Askia to shriek and leap backwards. The woman who had been knocked back by Hallow's magic started crawling toward a wagon that had been turned on its side to provide a barrier.

"They appear to be impervious to arcany, as well," he noted, frowning at the woman. By rights, she should be dead, with at least a fist-sized hole punched through her middle.

"They are. It's something to do with the Life-Mother and All-Father. They don't like Kiriah's blessings, though," she added with a swift grin.

At the sight of her standing on the edge of the well, all long legs, ample breasts, and hips that could convince him to do anything, he leaped up behind her, pulling her backward against his chest so he could bury his face into the nape of her neck.

"Hallow!" Allegria sounded both shocked and amused. "You can't do that now! Can't you see I'm in the middle of a battle?"

"As am I, my heart." He lifted his head from where he was drawing in the scent of her and cast another glance to the west road. Lyl's men were using long branches wrenched from the trees combined with their own belts to try to reach their friends in the trench. Tygo and Aarav, using balls of arcany from their perches high up in the trees, kept the bulk of the company from proceeding forward.

"I'm very glad to see you, though," she answered, turning in his arms to kiss him, the gold flecks in her eyes glittering brightly. "I've missed you."

"And I you," he answered, groaning when she wiggled against him in a way that had the chaos—amongst other things—surging to life. "My heart, if you make that particular move again, I will damn all my responsibilities and take you to the nearest bed—"

"I have quite reasonable rates for empty rooms," a voice called out from a doorway to his left. "Slightly higher for one with either one of my ladies, or if your wife wished to have her own fun, one of the man minxes."

"—and pleasure you like you've never been pleasured," he finished, trying hard not to glare at Red Eva.

Allegria laughed, sliding her hand down to where his passion was indeed giving in to the urge to claim her. "I'll hold you to that, my love, but let us first take care of these pesky attackers so that I can try a new technique Mayam told me about."

He blinked, unsure whether he'd heard her correctly. "You learned a new sexual position from Mayam? The Shadowborn woman who betrayed us to Nezu?"

"Discussed, not learned, and yes. I'll tell you about it later."

"I'm willing to give you a discount on the rate if you don't mind taking the room with the peephole," Eva called when he, with much regret, released Allegria, and leaped off the well. "I'd also be interested in hearing about this new technique."

"Who—" Allegria started to ask, casting a quick glance back at the bawdy house.

"Later," he promised, and with an assessing glance at the south road, decided Allegria had the Askia under control. His attention was better focused on driving back Lyl and his army.

And just in time. To his horror, he realized what he'd assumed was an army scattered by disarray and the attacks of Tygo and Aarav was in reality one that had spread its forces to breach numerous spots on the wooden wall that circled the village.

"Fire! Fire on the north wall!" the headman yelled, emerging from behind the largest of the structures where he had been on guard. He yelled to others to join him, snatching up a bucket and plunging it into the well before dashing off; two other men and a woman did likewise.

Hallow spun around to help them, but took only one step before a voice called from the east. "They're taking down the trees!"

"Why would—" Hallow started to ask, but just then a loud crack echoed off the cliff that rose to the north, followed by a tremendous crash when a tree was allowed to fall directly onto a section of the wall. "Bellias blast him, he's smarter than I thought. Tygo! How many are out there?"

"What's going on?" Allegria asked, her hands full of light. She paused in the act of throwing balls of it at a growing group of women who had gathered at the slight curve of the south road. "Who is tearing down the wall?"

"Lyl," he said, more or less grinding the word through his teeth.

"The magister?"

"Arcanist," he corrected and ran toward the front gate. To his horror, the men who had been trapped in the trench were now crawling out, assisted by rope and branches held out by their compatriots. "Tygo!"

"He's not here," came a weak voice from a dense clump of foliage that grew through the wooden barricade of the village wall.

"Aarav?" Hallow shoved aside a small stack of ale barrels, and found the arcanist covered in blood, his body slumped crookedly against the wall. "Kiriah's nipples, man! What happened to you?"

"Lyl," he said, the word coming out slow and hesitant. Aarav closed his eyes, and for a moment Hallow thought he'd died, but he opened his eyes again, pinning Hallow back with a look that he knew would haunt him for years. "He's not as stupid as we believed him to be."

"Stay here," Hallow ordered when, with a groan that hurt to hear, Aarav tried to rise. "Rest. I'll send a healer to you as soon as I've dealt with Lyl. Which direction did Tygo go? I'll need him by my side to get rid of Lyl."

"Banishing spell?" Aarav asked, a spark of curiosity replacing, for a few seconds, the pain visible in his pale blue eyes.

"Yes. Hopefully." Hallow grimaced. "I've never done one on my own, but together with Tygo, I should be able—" He stopped when Aarav shook his head. "He's dead?" he asked, dreading to hear the answer.

"Worse." Aarav coughed, blood speckling his lips. "He's joined Lyl."

"What?" Rage coursed through Hallow, immediately firing his magic, *all* his magic. Chaos warred with the pull of arcany, while the symbols of blood magic danced in his mind, his fingers sketching the symbols even before he knew it.

"Traitor, no doubt sent to spy on you. Us. Knew something was off about him," Aarav said with another groan. "He didn't feel right."

Hallow spun around, racing toward the gate, intending to find Tygo and show him how betrayers were dealt with, but at that moment, three things happened simultaneously. The first was a handful of dirgesingers breaching the village gate, charging in with strange, grating sounds emerging from their mouths. Their song seemed to scrape across the sky itself, and Hallow had a horrible feeling it was their form of magic. The second was an answering stream of bodies from the south road, where ten women rushed forward, headed straight for the well and Allegria. The third thing was a familiar bellow that rose along the road occupied by Lyl's army.

"Thorn?" Hallow called, pointing to the swell of men that suddenly ran forward, most of whom immediately fell down into the trench.

The bird, who had been darting at the lead dirgesingers, his claws scratching their faces, wheeled around and raced over Hallow's head, skimming over the swell of men who still charged forward, as if driven by madness.

"Where? Hallow!" Allegria took one look at the Askia rushing her, and threw down a wall of light before leaping off the well and running directly toward him. "Thorn said—"

A repeat of the bellow interrupted her, causing Hallow's lips to curl even as he started weaving together binding spells that he flung out in a crescent before him. "Deo has excellent timing. Can you handle those Askia?"

"Long enough, yes," she said, turning her back to his. Little flashes of sunlight slamming down into the ground caught his peripheral vision.

His lips moved silently while he spoke the words of binding to aid the blood magic, ignoring the screams of horses running mad, some mowing down Lyl's own men while others, thoroughly spooked, burst into the dense foliage and disappeared into the woods.

"Who—you!" Lyl's voice, filled with rage, rose half an octave when he caught sight of Deo. Thorn returned as the rush of the Starborn army lessened. The trench was now almost filled with the bodies of those who had fallen in, tangled up amongst those who struggled to get out.

Thorn perched on Hallow's shoulder, clearly there to help focus his magic. With his eyes on the dirgesingers, Hallow lifted his hand to cast an arcane compression blast, but a strange silence filled the square for a few seconds.

The lead dirgesinger stopped, staring at the Askia while they streamed around Allegria's shafts of sunlight. The first couple of Askia stumbled to a halt as well, staring back at the dirgesingers.

To Hallow's amazement—and delight, and gratitude—the Askia, with a cry that raised the hairs on Hallow's arms, threw themselves on the dirgesingers, who likewise lifted their voices in a horrible song, one made up of words that seemed to be made of granite grinding upon granite. The very act of hearing them seemed an abomination against nature.

He stared at the battle that unfolded before him while the arcany gathered in his hands tingled his fingers. He shook it away, half-turning to face Allegria. "Er..."

"Yes," she said, lowering her hand as well. "It is odd. Just about the last thing I expected to see."

"Am I—I'm not hallucinating, am I?" Hallow asked, rubbing a hand over his head in case he'd been struck on it without his knowing. "I'm seeing this correctly?"

"You are if you are seeing the Askia attacking your friends," Allegria answered.

"They most definitely are not my friends—they belong to Lyl. Speaking of which, I suppose I should help Deo, since that sounds very much like the sounds of a transmogrification spell being spoken." Hallow turned back to the gate, where a small cluster of people stood on the lip of the trench, their backs to him. Beyond, the dappled light of the road revealed a large man accompanied by a few smaller shapes, surrounded by golden-red chaos magic that glinted in the sun for a few seconds before it evaporated.

"Do you think it's safe to just leave them?" Allegria said, sidestepping quickly when one of the dirgesingers, who had been flung to the side by an Askia, skidded to an abrupt stop a few feet away. "They seem to be engrossed with each other, but I'm not sure who your lot is. Or, for that matter, why they are so angry with the Askia. Not that I object, since they've been chasing me for the better part of the day."

"The enemy of my father's enemy is the truest friend I have." Hallow quoted an old proverb as he considered the fighting. The Askia and dirgesingers appeared to be fairly matched, he was interested to note. Both wielded swords, and every time one of the men tried to sing a few words of their terrible song, the Askia responded by screaming and attacking the singer, effectively shutting him up and rendering his magic impotent. "So long as the villagers remain out of the way, I believe we could spare a few minutes to help Deo."

"Does he need it?" Allegria asked, a smile curving her delightful lips as she looked past him to where Lyl, surrounded by four guards, stomped out to confront Deo.

His amusement faded when he thought of just what Lyl had cost him. "He may not, but I have a few things to impart to Lyl." With a glance at the villagers who stood clustered on their rooftops and hidden in doorways, all of whom were engaged in watching the battle between the Askia and the dirgesingers, he wrapped an arm around Allegria, holding her tight against his body.

Instantly, the chaos magic surged at her nearness, but after just a few a few highly erotic thoughts, he spoke the words of a protection bubble, sending them both flying forward ten yards until they stopped on the far side of the trench.

"That will never get old," Allegria told him with breathless delight, her eyes alight with pleasure.

"It's one of the perks of being an arcanist," he told her, giving her a swift kiss before releasing her, lest the chaos magic—and his own emotions— demand he do more.

"Do you come on the Queen's order?" Lyl demanded of Deo, taking up a stance in the middle of the road, obviously intent on stopping Deo from proceeding further. "If so, you may take to her the message that I will no longer be a pawn in her games. The Starborn deserve a better monarch than one who would side with the very beings that almost destroyed us."

Deo marched up to Lyl, stopping to look him up and down. "Who are you?" he finally asked.

Lyl looked outraged for a minute. "Who am I? *Who am I?* Who are you that you do not know who I am?"

Deo's eyebrows rose in mock surprise. "You don't know who you are? Have you sought help for your befuddled mental condition? Is that why you're out here in the middle of nowhere, apparently laying siege to a small village whose inhabitants dally in a trench?"

Lyl's face turned red as he sputtered out an incoherent response.

Allegria's breath touched Hallow's ear as she gave a little giggle. "Deo does that so well."

"Annoy people, you mean?" he asked without moving his lips, feeling someone present had to maintain a dignified mien. "He is a master at it."

"I am Lyl!" the man responded, having worked the worst of his unintelligible oaths out of his system.

"Who?" Deo asked, looking unimpressed.

A burble of laughter rose in Hallow, but he quelled it with a firm hand.

"Lyl of Kelos, late of Starfall." Lyl drew himself up to his full height, which was a good head and a half shorter than Deo. "I was the queen's chancellor for many years, until she sold the Starborn to the invaders."

"Oh, he did not just say that," Allegria exclaimed with a little shake of her head, sliding her hand into the crook of Hallow's arm and leaning on him in a way that made him feel like the happiest man on Alba despite the grave threat hanging over their respective heads. "Wait, did he say Kelos?"

Hallow sighed. "He did."

She squinted at Lyl, who was telling Deo just how important a personage he had been in Dasa's court. "He has Thorn. Or rather, the staff part of Thorn. Why does he have it instead of you?"

"He seems to feel that he is Master of Kelos because he was Exodius's apprentice back when he—Exodius—was alive," Hallow answered.

"And I would like to be named the smartest person on Alba, but declaring myself such does not make it so," she snapped in return. She would have marched forward to confront Lyl if Hallow had not pulled her back against him.

"We are of the same mind concerning that, my heart, but I'm interested to see what Deo does with him."

Allegria slid him a long look. "What *Deo* does with him? What's this, Hallow? You've never been afraid of a fight before."

"Nor am I now, but there is such a thing as knowing when to fight and when to stand back and allow an enemy to wear himself out first. You see? He's pricked Deo's anger by telling him he has no right to be on Genora. And now Deo has angered Lyl by dismissing him as unimportant. Ah. That was a very foolish move on Lyl's part."

"Shoving Deo just makes him mad," she agreed. She watched with interest when Lyl was sent flying backward into the nearest tree. His guards rushed to his side at the same time Lyl slid down the tree trunk to disappear into the waist-high foliage. "Should we help this Lyl person up? I don't want to if the man clings to the deluded belief that he is Master of Kelos when you hold that position, but I suppose Kiriah wouldn't like it if I stood by and watched a man be smashed to a pulp against a tree, even if he deserved a little pulping. Oh, no."

Disgust sounded in her voice. Hallow smiled, wondering when she'd notice that one of the figures who had stood half-hidden behind Deo was that of Idril.

"Deo," Idril said, moving forward with a little frown between her brows when she gestured toward the spot where Hallow and Allegria stood. "I insist that you stop toying with Queen Dasa's flunky, and attend to what is important. There is Hallow. There is his priestess. Please do whatever is needful with them so that you may banish the monster Racin, thus allowing us to sail to Aryia to deal with my father."

"Hello, Idril," Allegria said, almost drawling the last word. "What are you doing here, out in the unsanitary world where you might soil one of the many gauzy layers of your gown?"

"Envisioning death and destruction, for the most part," she answered Allegria, giving Hallow a little nod of acknowledgement when he made his courtliest bow. "Also considering the best way to geld a man, and finally, wishing I could engage in sexual congress with Deo, but he refuses since the captain and his child are with us, and Deo claims he can't perform to both our satisfaction knowing the child would be right on the other side of the tent."

Dexia smiled a sharp-toothed smile at Idril.

"That didn't seem to stop the captain and Ella from congressing in their tent whenever they weren't bickering, but Deo, evidently, has finer feelings," Idril added with a little sniff.

Deo, who had been in the process of picking up Lyl with one hand clamped around his neck, turned back to glare at Idril. "Mayhap your latest husband would be able to stiffen his rod knowing that a vanth was lurking just a few feet away, listening to every grunt and moan, but I am not so made."

"*Latest* husband?" Allegria asked, her eyes wide.

Idril waved away the question. "It's nothing. The merest of nothings. A minor legal point that will be taken care of just as soon as I locate the appropriate campfire and my husband's bed."

Hallow, while enjoying, as always, the interaction among Idril, Deo, and Allegria, had been keeping one eye on Lyl. Deo might have been under the impression that the man was a bumbling fool, but Hallow knew better. He'd felt the power that crackled around Lyl when he claimed the position of Master, and he had no doubt that Exodius had trained his former apprentice well.

Which was why just as Quinn, Ella, and Dexia were about to approach, Hallow's fingers started drawing blood symbols.

Allegria, feeling the movement of his hands, glanced down in surprise. "What—" she started to say at the same moment that Idril started forward toward Deo, but before more than a second passed, the air suddenly took on a charged, prickly feel.

"Down!" Hallow ordered, yanking Allegria to the ground and covering her body with his after he flung the half-finished chain of symbols toward Deo and Idril. He hoped the others were far enough away that they wouldn't be too badly injured.

Allegria squawked, a noise that disappeared into a concussive blast that seemed to echo again and again from the rock walls that faced the north edge of the woods. Pain seared through Hallow's head and shoulders as small bits of rock and wood rained down on them.

He groaned and uncurled himself. The sharp sting of pain, accompanied by a suspicious wetness along his back, alerted him to the fact that some of the sharper bits of debris had pierced his leather jerkin. "My heart! Were you injured?"

"No, not at all, although by Kiriah's ten toes, I will roast that annoying Lyl alive for that. My ears are still ringing."

Allegria rose and started forward toward a now clear circle that held three figures. Around them, for a radius of twenty feet, everything that had been standing was now flattened.

"No," Hallow said, struggling to get to his feet. Pain struck so deep that it caused him to gasp, and black splotches ebbed and flowed in front of his eyes. "Do not...Allegria, he is too..."

"Just a little smiting," she said, stopping in front of Lyl and lifting her hands. "Just enough to teach him not to claim he's master when you are, or to use an arcane concussive blast right on top of us, not to mention the fact that he's just generally annoying."

"Hallow?" Another woman's voice came as if from a great distance. Hallow staggered forward a few steps, intending to warn Allegria to keep away from Lyl, but the inky blotches that obscured his vision were just too pervasive, and he gave into their promise of respite.

"Blast it! Kiriah, now is not the time to withhold your favor from me—Thorn, quiet your chatter. Can't you see that I'm fighting to get Kiriah to hear my prayer, as she did with the Askia? What do you mean Hallow has collapsed? He is right behind—blessed goddess!" was the last thing Hallow heard before he allowed the blackness to swallow him up.

Chapter 12

"Draught or no?"

I looked up at the woman who'd informed me her name was Red Eva; she stood holding a dark blue bottle. I hesitated, wanting to tell her that Hallow needed sleep in order to recover from all the injuries he'd sustained in the arcane blast, but knowing a discussion was necessary. "Hallow?" I asked softly, leaning down to his ear. He lay on his belly with his head turned away from me, his bare back covered with clean strips of linen stained with a green balm that smelled surprisingly good. It was sort of a lemony mint, oddly refreshing, and according to Red Eva would work miracles healing his torn flesh. "My love, I need to talk to Deo and Quinn. I'd prefer that you rest while I do so. If I promise to repeat everything they say, would you stay here? Red Eva has a draught that will help you relax."

Hallow moaned softly into the pillow, but lifted his head and turned it toward me, his beautiful blue eyes now clouded with pain. "No, I don't need a sleeping draught, although this bed is surprisingly comfortable. Blissfully so. I feel like I could lie here for a good thousand years."

I bent down to kiss him. The pain medicine that Eva had given him before she started cleaning his back was slowing Hallow's reactions. His lips made kissing noises five seconds after my mouth had parted from his. "I had a feeling you were going to be stubborn about this," I said with a sigh, but rose from where I was sitting on the edge of the bed.

Eva left the draught on a small round table and departed with a murmured offer of further help if it was needed.

"Not stubborn," Hallow said, his face twisted with pain when he rolled onto his side and swung his legs to the floor. He weaved for a few seconds, and I braced myself to catch him in case he swooned again. "Foolish for letting Deo tackle Lyl, perhaps, but that was not due to being stubborn. I need to be up because I have news to impart to Deo, and I suspect he has some for us. Odd."

"What is?" I asked, fetching his boots, and helping him on with them. I decided that he'd have to forego his tunic, despite the fact that Idril would no doubt ogle Hallow's fabulous chest.

"You. When did you become twins?"

I glanced up in surprise. "Are you seeing double? Oh, Hallow, your head is damaged. I knew it! That son of a whore's left buttock! If he hadn't run away like the coward he is after blowing you up, I'd hang him by his balls. Then I'd geld him, sew his balls back on, and hang him by them again! Lie back down, love. You need rest more than anything else."

He gave a little laugh, rubbing his thumb across my bottom lip. "Many people have told me I'm not right in the head, but I never expected my beloved wife to do so. No, my heart, I am not injured. At least, not in the way you mean. My vision is just a bit wobbly right now, no doubt due to the pain syrup you gave me rather than a blow to the head." He frowned for a few seconds, glancing around the small room. "You did say Red Eva, didn't you?"

"Yes. She's the local harlot, but she's also evidently a healer. A very good one, I think, since she didn't do anything that Sandor wouldn't approve of, and Sandor is the best healer I know. Can you stand if I'm at your side?"

"Always," he said, giving me a slightly lecherous look, despite drooping eyelids that told me just how sleepy the moonflower syrup was making him. He paused when I took one of his arms, helping him out to the common area of the bawdy house, now thankfully empty of the regular occupants. "Why do I hear no sounds of battle?"

It took me a moment to understand what he was asking. "The Askia slew the dirgesingers."

His eyebrows rose. "All of them?"

"All of them." I pushed away the memory of the remains they'd left behind. "Once they made sure that the only survivors were a few Starborn in the trench, they took off themselves. The headman said the last he saw, they were heading south, along the road that we'd come on."

"Interesting," he said, his fingers twitching as if they itched to make notes. "And I take it Lyl ran off after he blasted us all to Bellias and back?"

"In the most craven fashion, yes." We negotiated the several wooden stools and chairs scattered around the low-ceilinged room to where a small grouping of softer furnishings were arranged by the fire. "And by that I mean that not only did he *not* remain so that Deo could beat the peewadding out of him, but he left most of his army."

"He left his men?" Hallow asked, nodding at Quinn when the latter rose and offered him the comfortable chair upon which he'd been sitting. "He just left them behind?"

"They're outside now," Quinn said, tipping his head toward one of the small windows. "Trying to make themselves comfortable amongst the people they said Lyl intended to attack. You can imagine how welcome the villagers are making them feel."

"All but Red Eva," Ella said, bringing a three-legged stool forward for me and setting it next to Hallow's chair. I made sure he had a goblet of wine before I sat beside him, my worry for him battling with my need to be chasing down Lyl and making him pay for almost killing us. "She's out there with her ladies and three men she calls man minxes, all of whom are doing a brisk trade."

"Right out there in the open?" I asked, a sudden desire to see such a thing causing me to get back onto my feet. "Where anyone can see? And she has male harlots, too? What sort of services to do they provide, exactly?"

"Wife," Hallow said in what I'm sure he intended to be a stern tone. He caught my hand and pulled me back down onto the stool before I could take more than a step toward the door. "Now is not the time to investigate harlots, male or female, nor their range of services, although if the rates posted on the wall are anything to go by, they must be quite comprehensive."

"Hmm," I said, eyeing Hallow.

"What does that hmm mean?" he asked, leaning toward me to whisper in my ear, his eye crinkles making me feel—as ever—both hot and cold at the same time.

"It means I'm wondering how long it will take you to heal, and if the harlots hold any sorts of classes that I might attend," I whispered back. Cool air swirled around us when the door opened and Deo and Idril came in arguing loudly.

"—don't care how good you feel *Tribe of Idril* sounds, we must take care of the god Nezu before we return to Aryia. Is that wine Hallow is guzzling? Has he left any for the rest of us?" Deo marched over to where we sat, a familiar martyred look upon his face.

"Yes," I said, lifting the ewer of wine Red Eva had provided us, asking in the sweetest tone I could, "Would you like to drink it, or wear it?"

"And *I* say that since Nezu has apparently retreated to the spirit world, then we have time to go back to Aryia to cast my father out of Abet and claim the tribe." Idril smacked Deo on the arm, giving him a pointed look until he gestured toward one of the chairs, and offered her the goblet of wine I'd just poured him.

"Tribe of Idril?" Hallow asked at the same time that Deo, with a glare at me, held out a second goblet. I poured him wine as well, before retaking my seat next to Hallow.

"You have to admit, it has a nice ring to it," she said with her usual placid expression, sipping delicately at the wine.

Deo looked as if he wanted to argue the point, but instead he sat and considered Hallow. "If you are able to sit and drink, and make sheep's eyes at Allegria, you must not be as near death as I assumed you were when I carried you here."

"He isn't making sheep's eyes," I responded, my temper running high for some reason. Ever since we'd left the spirit realm, I felt as if my hold on it was fraying. "He never makes sheep's eyes!"

I turned to look at Hallow, only to find him watching me with eyes that held mingled desire and sleepiness. "That's not sheep's eyes," I told Deo, pointing at Hallow. "That's the moonflower syrup to take away the pain."

"Looks like sheep to me," murmured Quinn, who'd been down to the cellar to help himself to a small cask of Red Eva's rum. He poured some for himself and Ella, and even Dexia when she held out her mug expectantly. "Lady Idril, might I offer you some of this truly excellent rum? It will lighten your heels and gladden your spirits."

"Thank you, no," she replied with a gracious nod of her head toward him. "My mother would be restless in her afterlife if she thought I was indulging in rough spirits."

"How does she feel about your wedding every man you meet?" Deo asked in a smooth voice that had me giggling to myself.

Idril narrowed her eyes at him.

"What sort of classes?" Hallow's whisper tickled against my ear.

"Hmm?" I frowned, confused for a few seconds, until I remembered the earlier part of the conversation.

His breath brushed my ear. "If you are under the impression that you need instruction in the art of lovemaking, I'm happy to tell you to save your coin, because you are perfectly versed in that particular field. So much so, you leave me as limp as a bumblepig in the heat of the sun."

I allowed a little bit of pride to show in the smile I gave him. "You get some of the credit. I admit my part is harder, because all of my bits are tucked away where they can't get into any trouble, but I don't want you thinking you're shirking your share of the work."

He tried to give me one of his normally smooth bows, but the movement had him flinching in pain. "You are graciousness personified. Also, seduction personified, and delightful, endless nights of pleasure personified."

"And you're delightfully silly when you've had moonflower syrup," I said, leaning over to kiss him. I stopped when Deo cleared his throat loudly.

"If you could refrain from having your way with Hallow right here in front of us, we have a few plans to make." Deo ignored the sour look I flashed his way, waiting until I pressed a not-so-chaste kiss to Hallow's cheek and sat back on the wooden stool. He took a moment to let his gaze wander over all of us. "Idril's desire to claim the Tribe of Jalas as her own notwithstanding, I wish to return to Aryia as soon as possible. Thus, we need to send Nezu back to Eris, so that I may do so."

"I wish you wouldn't," Ella said in her soft voice. I slid her a glance, not having had much opportunity to see how she fared. She looked well enough, her color a bit high, but there was something in her eyes, a shadow that had me curious as to why she had arrived with Quinn and Dexia. When I'd been dragged into the spirit realm, I had assumed that Hallow would keep an eye on her, but it seemed that Quinn had taken over the job.

The others all turned to look at her.

"Oh. I...er..." Her blush deepened, her hands fluttering a little as she stammered out an earnest, "I'm sorry, I didn't mean to interrupt this important conference, but if you could possibly *not* send Lord Racin—Lord Nezu, that is—back to Eris, we would all be so grateful. The Shadowborn, that is. The family I lived with suffered most grievously under his rule, as did our entire village, and I imagine all the other villages. To be freed from that tyranny only to have it thrust back upon us is unthinkable."

"She has a point," I said, glancing at Hallow. "We saw well enough the sort of devastation he wrought upon the Shadowborn. I can't blame them for not wanting him back."

"The question then becomes where *will* we send him if we don't return him to Eris?" Hallow frowned, one of his long fingers rubbing absently around the lip of the goblet. Little fires kindled within me at the memory of the touch of those fingers, making me wonder how quickly Red Eva's healing herbs would work.

"Does it matter, so long as he is rendered without power?" Deo asked, making an impatient gesture. "I would prefer that he be killed outright, but since it's impossible to kill a god, the best we can hope for is to confine him somewhere that he can live his life out of our way, where he can do us no harm."

Hallow's brows continued to pull together in a little frown as he considered Nezu's fate. That look of worry was a familiar one, at least since I had seen him at the Altar of Day and Night. "If only Kiriah hadn't forsaken me again," I muttered, still fuming over the way she was toying with me.

"Kiriah has forsaken you?" Deo, who had been in the middle of telling Idril that if she could just stop marrying random men long enough to wed him, he would be able to take up her cause, paused to shoot me a look that pierced me down to my soul. "You are no longer a lightweaver?"

"Of course she's a lightweaver," Hallow said quickly, coming to my defense. "Just because she hasn't been able to weave light exactly the same way she did before the portal appeared in Abet doesn't mean she's not still blessed in Kiriah's sight. As I keep pointing out to her."

I gave his cheek another kiss, this time accompanied by a quick fondle to his thigh. "Thank you for believing in me even when I doubted that. As it happens—" I hesitated a minute, then decided there was no reason not to tell everyone of my experiences. Quickly, I recounted my time spent in the spirit world, followed by the appearance of Nezu, and how Kiriah's power seemed to flow in and through me.

"You channeled Kiriah Sunbringer again?" Hallow asked at the same time Deo leaped to his feet. "You have one of the moonstones?"

"Yes, to both." I dug into the inner pocket of my tunic, and pulled out the bit of cloth wrapped around the stones. "Sadly, it broke when I tried to banish Nezu."

Six heads bent over the four broken bits of crystal that lay on the table before us.

"They look…" Idril prodded one of the pieces with the tip of an elegant finger. "Dead."

"You killed the moonstone?" Deo asked, outrage dripping from his words. "Do you *know* how important a tool those are to us?"

"Of course I know," I snapped, guilt pricking my temper. "I was there when your traitorous follower stole them and gave them to Nezu, after all."

"It wasn't my fault that Mayam betrayed me. She wasn't one of my Banes, and thus wasn't officially a follower—" Deo started to protest, but stopped when Hallow held up a hand.

"I believe our time would be better spent focusing our attention on how to defeat Nezu now that we know he's close, rather than flinging accusations about." Hallow looked tired now, his shoulders slumping as he tried to make himself comfortable in the chair. "In fact, I have a feeling that we would be best served to hear just how everyone ended up in this town at the same time."

"We came from Deeptide to find you," Idril said, sipping again from her cup. I couldn't help but notice that even though she'd evidently been on the road for days, she looked as pristine as if she'd spent the day in her solar. "Deo insisted we help you after he killed his Banes, so that is what we did, despite my pointing out you are a great arcanist, and no doubt had no need of our help."

"On the contrary, I have every need of it. But let's back up a step. Why did you kill your Banes?"

Deo told a long tale about how his father had tried to oust Jalas from Abet, ending with the death of Sandor.

"Blessed Kiriah, no!" I said on a gasp, pain lancing me at the words. "Sandor—she can't be—Deo, was your father sure she was dead? Entirely dead? She is the head priestess of Kiriah, and much learned in the ways of battle. She is said to have fought the stone giants who remained when the Fireborn were first brought here. Perhaps she was just gravely wounded, and Lord Israel thought she was dead…"

My words trailed off at the truth evident in Deo's face. Although many thought of Deo as a hardened warrior, incapable of any emotions save those suited to battle, I knew better. Guilt was visible in his eyes now, guilt and regret. No doubt he blamed himself for the loss of Sandor.

I choked on the thought, tears burning the backs of my eyes. I reached blindly for Hallow, and suddenly, he was there, holding me close to his magnificent chest, allowing me to sob onto his shoulder, his hands warm on my back while he comforted me.

"Really, Deo," Idril said, her voice as light as a morning breeze. "Was there no other way to break the news to her?"

What was this? Idril was chastising Deo on my behalf? I stopped crying long enough to glance over at her, mopping my eyes on my sleeve.

"I take no pleasure in delivering bad tidings," he told her, but his gaze, tinged with worry, was on me. "I felt it was better to get it over with quickly. Allegria is not weak. She will grieve as we all grieve for the loss of Lady Sandor, but she knows that nothing can be done to change what happened."

"No," I said with a few more sniffles, glancing up at Hallow. His eyes, too, were filled with sadness and regret. "Nothing can change the past. But I'm going to risk Kiriah's wrath by saying I hope the Banes you killed suffered just as Sandor did."

Wisely, Deo did not answer that statement, gazing instead into the fire with a pensive expression.

"Considering the magic Deo unleashed on them also flattened half of Deeptide, not to mention sending the rest of it sliding into the sea, I believe you can be assured that they suffered," Quinn said with only the slightest twist of his lips.

Silence fell for a few minutes, long enough that we could hear noises from the square outside: voices raised in song, the murmur of people talking quietly, and occasional raucous laughter followed by feminine squeals.

"And where are the queen and Lord Israel?" Hallow asked at last. I was about to sit back on the stool, but he pulled me down onto his lap, instead. I arranged myself carefully, making sure I didn't lean on him in a way that would harm his healing back.

Idril and Deo exchanged glances. "My father, I believe, will be sailing down the coast. I sent him a message as soon as we heard you were spotted heading eastward along the Great East Road, and he planned to raise whatever company he could and follow."

"And the queen?" I asked, pushing down the sorrow that threatened to swamp me. Later, I promised myself, I would send prayers to Kiriah for Sandor. But I knew the priestess would not welcome dramatic professions of grief. I could almost hear her telling me not to lose focus, and get on with what was important.

Another glance was exchanged, but this time Quinn and Ella were in on it, as well.

"Why do I have the feeling that you are about to impart something that, while not nearly as devastating as your news of Lady Sandor, will be almost as shocking?" Hallow asked in a voice that was both weary and yet resigned.

"The queen is…indisposed," Deo finally said, abruptly getting to his feet and moving over to peer out the window, his hands clasped behind his back.

Silence fell as we all waited for him to continue.

He didn't.

"Indisposed how?" Hallow asked, turning to Idril for the answer.

She made an indefinable gesture. "It's difficult to say. She is…much changed. I thought at first it was because she was amongst her kin, but later, I thought it was because of Deo obliterating half of Deeptide."

"It was neither of those," Deo said, turning to face us. His expression was as grim as his voice. "She has been bewitched."

The silence that followed that statement was so thick, it could have been cut with my eating dagger.

"Bewitched how?" I asked, moving when Hallow shifted uncomfortably. I was mindful that although he might want the comfort of us snuggling together, his wounds meant he needed a little extra care. Accordingly, I slid off his lap to return to the wooden stool, my gaze on Deo.

"And by whom?" Hallow asked, giving me a sad little look at our separation.

Deo was silent for a few minutes before he made a disgusted noise in his throat and reclaimed his chair. "Her own kin. How, I know not. I am not wise in the ways of the water talkers. But Idril is correct in that she's changed since she went there to recruit her kin to help her retake Starfall. She refused to leave when my father would have come with us to find you and help you free Allegria. Have you ever heard of my mother refusing a fight?" He shook his head, leaning forward with his elbows on his knees while he stared into the fire. Idril scooted her chair closer, placing one hand on his arm.

"Your mother is the greatest warrior of this age," Hallow said simply.

Deo nodded.

"For her to spurn a cause that directly affects her is…" Hallow stopped, clearly trying to find the words.

"Odd," Idril said.

"Sinister," I suggested.

"Indicative of something unprecedented," Hallow finished. "A spell, you say. Hmm."

"Know you something of these waterwalkers?" I asked.

"Water talkers, my heart," he answered, his gaze shifted inward. It was obvious that he was sorting through his prodigious memory. "Some call them water witches, but although Master Wix had met some, he knew little about them. They do not share their magic with outsiders."

I rubbed my head, the strain of the last few hours pressing down on me like a leaden weight. "I don't want to sound callous, but does the loss of the queen and her army affect our ability to remove Nezu from Alba? Obviously, Deo will want her de-spelled, and back in Starfall, where she is away from the influence of the water talkers, but I don't see that the loss of her sword arm will directly impact us here and now."

"Perhaps not," Hallow said slowly, still obviously thinking things through. His ability to weigh situations was one of the things I admired most in him. Where I leaped in without thinking, he much preferred to study situations from all angles before committing himself to a course of action. Suddenly, he looked up and leveled a gaze at Deo. "When you left Kelos, you said you were anxious to retake Starfall in your mother's name. What has happened to change that—your mother's current situation? Or something else?"

"I had Darius," Deo answered with a shrug. "I took him to my mother. I did not know at the time that another remained in Starfall, manipulating appearances to hide his true intentions."

I got lost a bit in the pronouns, but decided Deo was referring to Lyl.

"And now Lyl has slipped away," Hallow said slowly, his eyelids drooping even more. I wanted badly to tuck him into bed, where his body could rest and allow Eva's herbs to heal the worst of his hurts, but knew he would not be willing to sleep until a plan of action had been made.

"It was not my fault he ran," Deo said with another of his scowls. "The man is a coward. I can hardly be blamed for that."

"Is Lyl going to be a threat to us in the next few days?" I asked Deo.

"I doubt it," he said, glancing at Hallow, who shook his head.

"If he's been run off without most of his army, it's doubtful that he will wish to strike again. Not without more men. He knows Aarav and Tygo…" Hallow stopped, making a choking noise. "He knows Aarav is with me, and I have no doubt he saw Allegria, and of course, he is well aware you are here, Deo. No, he would be foolish beyond belief to attack without some sort of army behind him, and of all the things I can say about him, I would not number foolish among them. We will be safe enough until he gathers a new force."

"Then I suggest we let go the subject of Lyl, just as we postpone our concerns about the queen right now." I eyed Idril, who was murmuring soft things in Deo's ear. "And, for that matter, Jalas. Nezu is the one who poses the greatest threat to the well-being of Alba. Nezu and the Eidolon."

Idril straightened up and gave me a lofty look, but after a moment, she nodded. "The priestess is right."

"I'm delighted you recognize that fact," I told her, more than a little surprised. Idril and I seldom saw eye-to-eye, although I had realized over the last few months that she wasn't quite the frail, delicate ornament I had first thought her. "And I appreciate the support."

"The situation with the queen is unfortunate, but I cannot see that it will harm us in any way, and Deo handily defeated Lyl—"

"Hey!" I said, outraged on Hallow's behalf. "Hallow, his men, and the villagers did the bulk of the work. All Deo did was come along behind and scare everyone half to death."

Deo adopted a modest expression. "Scaring people is what I do best."

"That is not even close to being true," Idril said, giving him a long look that had him doing a double-take.

Ella muttered a rude word that shocked me for a few seconds until I realized she had intended it for Quinn. I made another mental note to have a long talk with her. She wasn't exactly an apprentice, but I felt a certain amount of responsibility for her, since she was young and untried.

Quinn leaned over to whisper something in her ear. She made a show of ignoring him, caught sight of me watching her, and immediately straightened up, donning an expression of rapt attention while Deo held forth on all of the many and varied things he intended to do to Lyl when he next saw him.

"I particularly applaud the inventiveness of your tortures," Hallow said, his words coming more slowly now. "The idea of stuffing him into an archery butt before wheeling it over to a training ground so that he could be killed slowly by his own men is particularly bone-chilling. I had no idea your mind ran to such heinous depths."

Deo nodded toward me. "Allegria gave me that idea last year. It was right after you joined us, and she still had doubts about your intentions."

When Hallow slid me a long look, I opened my eyes wide, smiling with as many teeth as I could show. "It's just something that occurred to me one day."

"Mmhmm. I agree that splitting our focus is going to weaken our ability to banish Nezu, so assuming Deo agrees, perhaps we can move on to making a plan to do just that."

"Do you propose we all enter the spirit realm?" Quinn asked, frowning when Ella, with quick little worried glances my way, moved off to fetch another ewer of wine. "I will admit to being curious about it, since I've yet to be dead long enough to find myself an inhabitant there, but I don't know that charging in and demanding to see Nezu is going to be the best of ideas."

"No," Hallow said, blinking a few times. I had a feeling he was about to fall asleep. "That would not be wise. From what Allegria has said, I don't believe he suffers a loss of his powers while he's there, unlike other living beings. We will need to lure him out somehow."

"How?" Quinn asked, looking at each of us in turn.

"We could simply send in a note that we are waiting for him," Idril offered, brushing a speck of dirt from Deo's sleeve. "He seemed to dislike Deo quite a bit. Perhaps he would emerge from his hiding spot to face him."

"Oh, I have no doubt that he wants his revenge on Deo," I mused, my hand on Hallow's. His fingers curled around mine briefly, but he didn't stroke my hand as he normally did. "But I'm not sure that's the path to take."

Hallow glanced at me. "You have an idea?"

I hesitated a moment, assessing him. His eyes were glazed now, and I knew he desperately needed sleep. "Yes. I got it from the Eidolon."

He blinked a few more times, as if that was helping his mind work. "What, exactly?"

"Nezu made some sort of a pact with the thane to destroy the All-Father if Nezu summoned him. Why Nezu wants the All-Father dead is not clear to me, but what *is* clear is that if such an act makes Nezu happy, then we must do everything we can to stop it."

"Then we fight the Eidolon again. I approve of this plan." Deo looked pleased. "So long as this time, they do not escape into the spirit world."

"Not fight them, no." I bit Hallow's shoulder. He'd been starting to topple over to the side and jerked himself upright, swearing under his breath. "We're not going to let the thane fulfill Nezu's deal."

"How can we stop him?" Idril asked, frowning slightly. "Do you plan to first destroy the thane and his army, and then do the same to Nezu?"

"We won't have to do either. That's the beauty of the plan." I heard an intake of breath next to me. Hallow, quick-witted as he was, no doubt saw where I was headed. Everyone else looked puzzled, so I smiled and added, "We're going to summon the All-Father ourselves."

Silence greeted that statement, a silence that I felt did not reflect well on my idea.

"And then?" Deo glanced at the table where the broken moonstone rested.

"What do you think? We're going to ask him to help us banish his son to somewhere he can't hurt anyone. If not Eris then...then...well, somewhere. Maybe that island you went to?"

"He would get off that in an instant. The only reason he didn't escape Eris was because of the protections bound around it," Quinn pointed out.

I made a face, but agreed it wasn't a great suggestion. "I'm sure we can think of somewhere safe if we all put our minds to it."

Deo still frowned at the moonstone pieces. "Why do you think the All-Father would help us? He destroyed the Eidolon, and swore to destroy everyone on Alba."

"Mayam told me something about that, but it has to be wrong." I shook my head, unable to believe it. "He created us—or rather, Alba, and the first peoples who lived here before we were brought forth."

"Those who create often feel justified in destroying that which does not meet their standards," Idril said softly, her fingers tracing a bit of embroidery on her sleeve.

"He wished to destroy all that existed, yes," Deo answered me. "That is why the twin goddesses had him banished. I do not see that the All-Father will want to help us save the very same people he wished to eliminate."

"How do you know this? I heard about it from Mayam, and she called me stupid for not being conversant with the ancient lore of Alba. Does everyone know about the All-Father but me?" Five pairs of eyes looked at me with mild astonishment. I made another noise of irritation. "Kiriah's blessed knuckles, Sandor has a lot to answer for, keeping us in the—" I stopped speaking, my heart feeling as heavy as lead at her loss.

"While it is true that summoning the All-Father might serve as a lure to bring Nezu out of the spirit world, beyond that, I can see no good coming of such an act," Hallow said carefully, his eyes on mine. "He is far more dangerous than Nezu, and to have two such gods loose on Alba with destruction on their minds..." He shook his head, listing slightly.

"More importantly, how are we to defeat Nezu with one of the moonstones broken?" Deo asked, pinning me with a pointed look. "We three together are powerful, but I had counted on having my mother's forces behind us, and now that option is not open to us. If you are no longer blessed by Kiriah, then we are even weaker. We need at least one of the moonstones."

"Surely there are other ways to defeat Lord Nezu than by means of the moonstones," Ella said, taking me by surprise. She seldom contributed to group conversations, obviously feeling as if she lacked the experience to offer a comment. She turned now to face me, her brows drawn together. "How was Nezu originally banished to Eris?"

"The twin goddesses joined their powers together to confine him to Eris," Hallow said tiredly, his shoulders drooping. I swore to myself at the pain etched on his face. This long drawn-out discussion was doing him no good.

"Oh." She looked disappointed, glancing hesitantly at me. "I don't suppose...if you made entreaties to Kiriah Sunbringer, and perhaps Lord Hallow or Lord Deo did likewise to Bellias...?"

"No," I said quickly when she let her sentence trail off. "Entreaties made by me will have little effect on Kiriah. She might have listened to Sandor, perhaps, but not me."

"Not to mention the fact that we are all to blame that Nezu has been released from his prison," Hallow said, stifling a yawn. "Even if the goddesses were of a mind to hear our pleas—and I agree with Allegria that it's doubtful they would—it's up to us to find the solution."

"There's my boon..." Deo said slowly, his gaze on Hallow, but I had a feeling he was looking inward.

"Your boon!" I said, sitting up straight. "I forgot all about that! Do you still have it? Where is it? Is it with you? Is it something that we can use? I can't believe I completely forgot it."

Deo gave me a look that held both amusement and annoyance. "Are you done?"

"Not quite," I said, returning his look. "What exactly *is* your boon?"

"Yes, Deo, tell us about this boon. I don't believe I've seen it," Idril said, looking thoughtfully at me. "And how is it that the priest knows of it?"

"Everyone at the temple knew about it. It was a gift to Queen Dasa upon Deo's birth, and given into the care of Sandor when he was a babe and sent to live with Lord Israel," I answered, my gaze on Deo.

He rose and went to the door, checked to be sure no one was lurking outside it or the open windows before taking up a position in front of the fire, facing all of us. "It is as Allegria says—the boon was a gift to be bestowed when the Fourth Age dawned. It symbolized the peace of Alba, and the joining of the Fireborn and Starborn."

"But the Fourth Age didn't happen until last year," Quinn said, rubbing his chin. "There was a battle in Starfall—we heard about it from a traveling merchant—when the Harborym were driven from Genora."

"That was Deo's doing," Idril told the captain with obvious pride.

I stifled the urge to protest that Hallow and I had had as much to do with it as he did, but I was far too worried about the two pink spots that had appeared on Hallow's cheeks. I badly wanted to get a fever draught into him before I poured him into bed.

"It was not my doing alone," Deo said, his gaze back on the moonstones. "Without Allegria and Hallow, that battle would have gone much differently."

"That is old history," I said, wishing I could hurry him along. "What is the boon, and how can we use it?"

He looked up at me, one shoulder rising and falling in a half-shrug. "It is a gift from Bellias Starsong. The boon is her promise of aid at a time when it is most needed."

I stared at him in surprise. Even Hallow shook himself awake, gazing at Deo with amazement. "A boon from Bellias herself? You are favored, indeed, Deo. And I agree that using the boon will be exactly what we need. Alone, lacking the moonstones and your mother's army, we would have difficulty banishing Nezu even if Allegria had Kiriah's blessing and her full complement of powers. But with Bellias lending her aid...yes, that should just do it."

"Then we are agreed," Deo said, nodding. "We will challenge Nezu, and I will invoke Bellias' aid via my boon. Together, we will banish him to whatever location the goddess feels suitable."

"Yeees," I drawled, my mind spinning and flailing like a bumblepig rolling downhill. "But where are we to challenge Nezu?"

Deo gave another half-shrug. "You said yourself he was at the Altar of Day and Night, and that he plans on summoning the All-Father. There is no other place he can do so. We will meet him there, and banish him before he can issue the summons."

I could think of any number of problems with that scenario, but one look at the love of my life made the decision for me. "Hallow needs to rest," I said, rising from the stool. "We will continue this discussion in the morning."

"No," he said, giving a little shake of his head when I tried to urge him to his feet. "I would that we make our plan tonight. We don't know how long it will be before Nezu summons the All-Father for the Eidolon. We must have our plans in place before Kiriah rises."

"We have a plan," Deo said, handing me the broken moonstone. "I will use the boon. Together, we will banish Nezu. It's simple."

"It's not even remotely simple, but I agree the boon is going to be part of the solution." Hallow protested, but got to his feet when I more or less pulled him out of the chair. "Very well, my heart, I will go to bed. I can rest even if we haven't worked out quite everything. But I agree with Deo that what we must do can only be accomplished at the altar. We will ride there in the morning, and goddesses willing, be there before Nezu has summoned his father."

I gave him gentle pushes toward the door to the room that I'd rented from Red Eva. He stumbled twice, but made it into the room without falling. I turned back at the door and glanced at Ella. "I'm sorry, I didn't make accommodations for a sleeping chamber for you tonight. Do you have coin? Red Eva appears to be most obliging, although don't let her give you the room with the discount. It has a most unsavory feature."

"I'm fine," she said, her cheeks growing pink. She steadfastly avoided looking at Quinn, who, I couldn't help but notice, looked interested.

"What sort of unsavory?" Idril asked before he could do so. "Unsavory as in the sort of shocking that would make your mother raise her eyebrows and murmur things about no gentlewoman performing such acts, or the sort of unsavory that includes body parts used in a manner out of the norm?"

"There are depths to you that surprise me even now," I told her. "Red Eva offers a discount because there are hidden panels that allow others to view the occupants of the room in action."

"Oh," she said, looking disappointed.

Quinn made a dismissive noise, also apparently losing interest.

"Also, there are restraining thongs attached to the bed, the wall, and, apparently, the ceiling, although how one is supposed to get up to the ceiling to perform the sorts of acts that Eva mentioned is beyond me. She said something about people who are very limber being given a bigger discount than those who simply confine their sport to the bed."

"Oooh," Idril said softly, eyeing Deo, who looked mildly startled in return.

Quinn beat her to the front door, clearly on a mission to find Red Eva before Idril could do the same.

Idril called loudly while she hurried after him, "Captain! I must insist that you stop thinking selfishly of your own base needs, and instead think of mine!" I entered our room and found Hallow asleep face down on the bed, fully clothed, and snoring softly.

Chapter 13

The voice pierced my awareness before I was half-awake.

—and I nearly wore my new wings to nothing before I realized that he was, indeed, making for the Old Coast Road. You can tell the lad that Lyl is slinking away like a cur with his tail between his legs, and won't be returning here anytime soon. Not after we dealt him such a drubbing. Where are you? You aren't out here having porridge with the vanth and your large friend.

"Hrn?" I asked, pushing my hair off my face to squint at Hallow. "What was that?"

He made an inarticulate noise of comfort, and one of his legs moved a little over mine, but other than that, he didn't wake. I scooted out from under him, pulling back the shutter that covered the window next to the bed, using the light to examine Hallow's back.

There was an oddly light tapping sound at the door that I ignored for a few minutes while I peeled back the linen bandages and examined the wounds. "I'll say this for Red Eva: she is almost as good a healer as Sandor. There's no sign of redness, no swelling, and no foul smell. In fact—" I gently pressed the flesh next to one of the deeper slashes. Hallow didn't even flinch. His back felt cool to the touch, without any of the red streaks that Sandor had always said were a sign of infection. "In fact, I'd say that you are further along in healing than you should be. I'll have to leave Eva more than I planned as a thank you. What?"

The last word was spoken when a proper rap sounded at the door. I snatched up the bedclothes to cover both myself and Hallow's bare behind, but the door only opened wide enough for a hand to wave at me. "Someone wants you," Ella's voice said, followed by Thorn swooping into the room.

There you are! By my shiny pink spleen, what happened to the lad? Are those wounds from the arcane explosion? He looks like he's been mauled by a pack of behemoths. Feral ones. Is he insensible? Can you wake him and tell him I chased that traitorous arcanist almost to the coast? He'll want to know that, and of course, all the other news I have, which is that there's a rumor the queen is being held prisoner in the land of the water talkers, and also that Lord Israel has set sail for Aryia, leaving Genora to Nezu's mercy, although why he'd do that is a mystery. For one, he'd never leave the queen a prisoner, and for another, once Nezu wiped Genora clean of Starborn, he'd simply turn his eyes to the Fireborn, and although I have many things to say about Lord Israel—he came to power just as I was preparing to diminish into the spirit realm, so I only met him a few times—he's never been what I'd call outright stupid. Stubborn, yes, and single-minded when it came to doing what he thought was right and proper, but not stupid.

"Kiriah's blessed toes, Thorn!" I made an exasperated noise while the bird flew around the room, his non-stop chattering leaving me mentally reeling. "Can't you stop for a breath?"

I'm dead. I don't have need for breath, he pointed out, alighting on Hallow's behind, tipping his head first one way, then the other to examine his back. *That looks like it's healing very well. Should leave no scars. Whoever made that green salve knew what they were about. I didn't realize the lad had been damaged quite that much, else I wouldn't have spent the whole night chasing after Lyl.*

"The head of the harlots is responsible for the healing, and I agree that she is very talented, for which we will be most grateful. What's all that noise?" I asked, aware, now that the shutters were open, of pounding noises that drifted in through the window. Men's voices rumbled in as well, their words unintelligible, but I didn't hear any notes of panic or fear.

I wonder what the harlot put in the salve, Thorn said, bending close to Hallow's back. *Hmm? Oh, the villagers are putting the men we captured last night to work, rebuilding the part of the wooden wall that was destroyed, as well as two homes that also were damaged. What did I miss while I was gone? Did Hallow tell everyone about all the work we did, and how that arcanist he trusted betrayed him?*

"What arcanist? Aarav, you mean? He's in a room upstairs. We carried him there after we found him next to the wall. He said something about helping Hallow summon you, but if he's betrayed us—"

Not him, the other one. The one who looked so innocent. Take a word of advice from one who has seen two ages pass, priestling, and never trust anyone who looks innocent. They'll always sell their loyalty for a few coppers if it pleases them.

"I'll keep that in mind...Kiriah's blessings, my love." Hallow rolled over onto his side, his lovely blue eyes blinking sleepily at me, his cheek creased with wrinkles from the pillow. "How do you feel?"

"Tired," he said, rubbing his face. "And yet stiff like I've lain in one position for too long. Why do you have that look on your face?"

Tell him I chased Lyl to the Coast Road, Thorn demanded, having been dislodged when Hallow rolled onto his side. He flew to the headboard and squawked a few times, bobbing his head as he did so.

"Ah," Hallow said, giving me a wry half-smile. "I see why now. Good morn to you, Thorn. I assume you are still bound to that bastard Lyl?"

Unfortunately, I am until we can get my staff away from him. I'd have you make a new one, and bind me to it, but it took me almost eighty years to spell that staff, and I don't have the time to do that again. Tell him, priest!

"Are you always this pushy?" I asked Thorn, twirling my finger in the air. "Because if you are, I feel for Hallow, having to put up with it."

Put up with it? No one puts up with me, Thorn said indignantly, but obligingly turned around, giving us his back. I used the opportunity to hurry into my clothes, watching with one eye while Hallow swung his legs over the edge of the bed, flexing his shoulders and back experimentally.

"I can only imagine how he's chattering away at you, and yes, assuming he is, he's always that way. What does he want you to do?"

"Tell you that he chased Lyl to the Old Coast Road." I duly repeated the tidbits of information that Thorn had told me, ignoring his interruptions while I did so.

"I had no idea the staff took so long to spell, but I agree that it would be a waste of time to remake what has been done already. We'll simply have to get it—and Kelos—away from Lyl once we've dealt with Nezu. What's that?" Hallow frowned at the cup of wine I held before him.

Nezu? What's this about Nezu? Why would you have to deal with him? I thought he was in the spirit world. He went into the spirit world. We saw him go into the spirit world.

"Fever draught." I stood before Hallow until he—with a grimace—swigged it down as quickly as possible, coughing hoarsely once he'd done so. "I know you don't have a fever, but I'll feel easier knowing you've taken the medicine Eva left for you. I take it you're not in pain?"

You are here, in the mortal realm, where it is right and proper you stay. There is no dealing with Nezu to be done. Tell Hallow that he is in no sort of shape to take on someone as tricky as Nezu.

"I am, but not nearly as much as last night." He rose and accepted the clothes I handed him. "I hope I haven't held us up by sleeping too long. We have much to do today."

I can't help you with Nezu, Thorn stated abruptly, flapping his wings in agitation before patrolling the mantel over a small fireplace. *Rather, I could, but I won't. Tell Hallow that, priestling. Tell him that I will lend him no aid should he be so foolish as to think Nezu will not destroy him with the tiniest flick of his fingers.*

"It's barely past the seventh hour," I answered, glancing out the open window, where I spied two familiar figures. Evidently feeling they were hidden from sight, Quinn had Ella pinned against the wall of a small cottage that sat next to Eva's house of harlotry. I was about to yell at Quinn, warning him to leave Ella alone, but to my surprise, she grasped him by the shoulders, pulling him closer. A scant second before I could turn away, Quinn's breeches hit the ground, and Ella's legs wrapped around his waist. I spun around, swearing under my breath, "Kiriah's blessings above and below!"

"What's wrong?" Hallow asked, pulling on a boot with a little grunt of pain before he stood up and turned toward the window.

Hello? Can you hear me? Why are you not responding? Don't you understand how important this is? Allegria Hopebringer! Hear me!

"Nothing other than the fact that I badly underestimated Quinn's persuasive powers." I thought for a few seconds, then allowed, "And Ella is not as young as I first thought. She has seen nineteen summers, and that is older than I was when I lost my maidenhead. Still, I'd thought she had more sense, and they always seem to be arguing...Thorn, I do hear you. I can't possibly help but hear you—you fill my head with your words!"

"Ah," Hallow said, looking out of the window, his eyebrows going up. "That's almost as good as the position we used the day we arrived at Kelos, although Quinn appears to be using his hands on her breasts. And did he just rock her hips forward? How is that even possible at that angle?"

Well that, at least, eases my mind. Thorn sounded distinctly disgruntled, still flapping his wings in an annoying manner.

He followed me as I collected my weapons, slipping on my scabbard and swords, and grabbing my bow and quiver. "I'm sure we can try hip rocking if it looks like something we'd both enjoy. Have you any silver?"

"Now he's bending her over backward…while he's still inside her. She must be exceptionally limber. Hmm. You're quite limber. I wonder if we could—what?"

I peeked around his shoulder to see what it was that had Hallow hmming, my eyes widening when Quinn swung Ella down into some sort of a scissors position. "The blood must run down to her head. I'm not sure I'd like that, but perhaps we could do a modified version of it if we had some large pillows, a pile of furs, and a handful of silk scarves," I commented before closing the shutters. "I asked you if you had any silver. I spent all of mine to get this room and board."

Hallow stared at me, his eyes smoky with passion, sexual interest, and calculation. No doubt he was working out a way to achieve that scissor position without discomfort to either of us. "Er…yes, I have silver."

Ask him what he meant about Nezu, Thorn insisted.

"I don't have to ask him. I know what he's referring to," I told the bird, then helped Hallow gather up his belongings before we departed from the room. "And I'm sorry to disappoint you, but we can't leave Nezu where he is in the spirit realm. He can come out of it at any time to launch an attack."

"Is that what Thorn's bothering you about?" Hallow frowned at the bird as he held the door open for him to fly out. "Thorn, this is of vital importance. Nezu is free because of us. Naturally, we will not rest until we have ensured Alba will be safe from his retribution."

Tell him! Thorn all but yelled at me.

I sighed, moving over to a small round table where Deo, Idril, and Dexia were all finishing up breakfast. "Fine, but if you could go steal your staff from Lyl so Hallow can go back to being Master, I'd be very grateful. Good morning, everyone. Please excuse us for the next few minutes." I accepted some bread, cheese, fruit, and a mug of weak ale from one of Eva's workers, seeing the woman herself in the far corner of the room, a box of coins in front of her that she counted and tallied on a stick. In between bites, I hurriedly told Hallow of the protests that Thorn had made.

"You said you wouldn't help us?" Hallow asked the bird, his golden brows pulling together as he studied Thorn, now perched on top of the ale barrel.

"Do we need him?" Idril asked us when Deo went off to use the privy. "I know he helps the Master of Kelos, but if Hallow no longer holds that position, then is he even effective?"

Of course I'm effective! Thorn sputtered with outrage. *I'm incredibly effective! I'm the most effective being in existence! Tell her that I have more power than she can conceive of!*

I repeated his comments, adding to him, "I don't doubt that you have much power, but really, Thorn, you aren't the most powerful being in existence. You couldn't even get yourself out of the spirit realm, and had to have Hallow summon you."

That was different! he said with an injured sniff, turning his head to groom his shoulder just as if he was a real bird. *I am a translocated spirit, one bound to a suitably spelled physical object in this realm, and thus, I have no presence unless that object exists. Which it didn't until the lad and his traitorous friend created the new form.*

"He's a translocated spirit. He's bound to the staff," Hallow said at the same time, slicing an apple and offering me a piece, popping it into his mouth when I shook my head. "But that does bring back the question of what we will do to draw Nezu out of the spirit realm and into ours. Thorn, if you—"

No! Thorn shouted into my head, then flew in a tight circle over Hallow's head four times before going out the window. *I will not stain my soul with your death and destruction! What you plan is foolish and unworthy of the Master of Kelos. If you insist on pursuing this path, then you will do it without me!*

I stared out the window, then cast a worried glance at Hallow. "Erm… Thorn's angry."

"So I gathered. That was his "shite upon your head four times" maneuver, wasn't it? I take it his disapproval of our plan has sent him off in a snit?"

"You could say so." I repeated what Thorn had said, giving voice to the worry that had gnawed in my belly. "Hallow, perhaps we should rethink this plan. Maybe Thorn is right to urge caution. After all, Nezu is a god, and even with Deo's boon, it took *both* goddesses to banish Nezu the first time. Will Bellias have the strength to do so on her own if she only has us to help her?"

"You are favored in Kiriah's eyes. You have channeled her, and joined with us—it will be just like having Kiriah Sunbringer there, herself," Deo answered when he returned, holding up a pair of maroon pink scarves. "Idril, did you wish to bring these with you as well as the cerise ones? And what of the rope swing you insisted I purchase from the courtesan? I have no room in my bags for it."

Idril, with a slight lift of her chin that accompanied a cool look my way, rose and took the scarves from Deo, disappearing into a short hall that led to the back of the house.

"A rope swing?" Hallow looked interested. "Was it worth the coin?"

Deo smiled a wolfish grin. "Definitely. You'll want one, possibly two if Allegria is particularly enthusiastic, which she is from what I can recall of the many times she's kissed me."

"Twice," I said with dignity and a warning look to Hallow. "I kissed you twice, that's all, and Hallow, don't you dare make a comment about Deo having been my boyfriend, because if you do, then I won't want to use this rope swing that you seem to covet. Also, please see if Red Eva has two available."

Hallow gave me a lascivious look. "We shall definitely set it up once we get home. We could put one in the tower, and perhaps hang one from a tree for a little outdoor enjoyment."

"Home." I repeated the word, consumed by sadness. "Assuming Kelos is still our home."

"My home is anywhere you are, my heart," he said with gallantry that was heightened by the love shining so brightly in his face. He kissed my knuckles before popping the last piece of apple into his mouth. "Will you be ready to leave shortly?"

I nodded, slicing several pieces of bread and cheese and wrapping them along with the fruit in a bit of cloth. "Yes. I don't have anything but what I'm wearing, and that I got from Red Eva. I'll fetch Buttercup and Penn if you wish to wash."

He nodded, then stopped by the table where Red Eva was sitting, pulling out the small leather bag tied to his belt and giving her a few coins. I studied Deo for a moment where he stood with his hands on his hips, staring out of the open doorway. He was watching the men Hallow had captured as they toiled under the watchful eyes of the villagers, cutting wood, hauling in water to make mud, and removing burnt sections of the fence that protected the village from marauders.

"What?" Deo asked, obviously having felt my scrutiny but not bothering to turn to look at me. "If you want instructions about the swing, you must look to your arcanist."

I made a face at him. For two people who hadn't spent much time together in the last few months, we had a surprising affinity; our connection went back to the days when we had both been young and filled with dreams. "Curious as I am to know just how a swing can give so much pleasure, I have every confidence Hallow will know what to do with it. Deo, I have doubts about this plan. I may have been favored by Kiriah in the past, but I'm not so certain I hold her blessing now," I said, moving over to stand beside him so I could speak softly. I didn't wish for everyone to know just how gravely I doubted my abilities.

"You said you had your powers back." After a few moments of moody glaring at the former army, he turned to look at me, his black eyes searching mine. With one finger, he traced the line of dots that circled my head. "It's too bad Kiriah saw fit to remove the chaos magic from you, but we must assume she knew best."

"I did get my light weaving powers back," I said slowly, reaching for Kiriah even as I spoke. I held out my hand, intending to summon a light fawn, one of the animals I'd delighted in creating when I was a child. I could feel Kiriah's presence, not just the warmth of the sun, but her being around me, and yet the fawn refused to form on my palm. "But they don't seem to be very reliable. I'm worried that when we face Nezu, I will not be able to assist. Thorn seems to think—"

"Thorn is a long-dead arcanist who is just as mad as all the others of his ilk. Well," he said with a little shrug before turning back to the square outside the house, "Hallow is less mad than the others, but even he isn't quite sane."

"The same can be said about someone not a million miles from me," I murmured.

"If you are referring to Goat, he was an excellent companion, and offered much sage advice while I was imprisoned on the Isle of Enoch," Deo said with obvious ire. "I would have brought him with me to Genora, but my father insisted he would not be able to keep up with the horses. If Jalas has harmed him in any way—"

"I'm sure Goat is just fine in Abet," I said soothingly, biting back a giggle at Deo's defense of a scrawny animal who had evidently been his only friend for the eleven months he'd been banished. Deo seemed more stable these days than when we'd first rescued him, but regarding Goat, he was definitely a bit eccentric. "Do you think we could stop Nezu from summoning the All-Father without banishing him? Nezu, that is?"

Deo thought about this, taking the bag that Idril carried out and shoved at him before returning to her room. I couldn't help but notice a bit of plaited rope poking out of the top of the satchel, and wondered if that was the swing. "Possibly. But I don't see the point of doing half the job."

"Half the job?" I frowned a little. "What do you mean? If Nezu is banished—"

"The Eidolon will still remain. I take it you have angered them, and they no doubt seek vengeance against you, personally. And possibly Hallow. Much though I wish to return to Aryia to stop Jalas, and hopefully to place Idril on his throne—although why she wants to lead that group of near-feral savages is beyond my understanding—I can't leave this job half-done.

Nezu must be banished or destroyed. The Eidolon must be vanquished. Lyl must be removed from my mother's throne."

"And Queen Dasa?" I asked, watching him closely.

"She will have to be dealt with, too," he said grimly.

Something about Deo had changed since he'd been imprisoned and tortured on Eris. Before that time, he'd been a warrior, bent on fighting whatever battle came his way, laying his plans with deliberate detail. But now—now I got the same sense from him as I did from Hallow. Deo had gone from being a warrior who lived for battle to a man determined to protect those who needed it. That thought warmed my heart, causing me to stand on tip-toe and press a kiss to his cheek.

"No," he said with as much surprise as I felt at my action. "I will not show you how to use the swing, so do not try to seduce me."

I poked him in the arm. "As if I want any man swinging me but Hallow. That was simply a kiss of approval. You've become almost as heroic as Hallow."

"Almost!" he said with an indignant gasp.

"Yes, almost. Hallow doesn't have to care about helping other people, but he does. He gives everything he has to make Alba a better place. You were born to do that—he wasn't."

Deo grimaced. "My parents would be the first to tell you just how inaccurate were the prophecies concerning my birth."

"And yet, you've gone a long way toward fulfilling them," I pointed out.

"Not far enough," he answered.

"Will you please confine your lips to your husband, and leave mine alone?" Idril asked with a sharp edge to her voice that gave me much guilty pleasure. She returned with yet another satchel that she gave to Deo while raking me with a look that by rights should have stripped all the hair from my head.

"Husband?" I asked, deciding the opportunity was too good to miss. I'd heard all about how Idril had married another man at her father's behest, and although I knew it was beneath me to tease her, I couldn't help myself. "I thought that was one of the Northmen?"

Idril's pointed look could have skewered a wild pig. "That is an unfortunate circumstance that can't be rectified until we return to Aryia, which we will do as soon as *you* do your job and dispense with Nezu." She spun on her heel, and marched back into the room she'd used.

"She's a mite testy on the subject, isn't she?" I asked Deo. He had a martyred expression that I knew well. "Are you really going to wed her?"

"I will if I can catch her between husbands," he said, then took me by the wrist and pulled me out of the house. "Let us get the horses. Where's the captain and his harem?"

"Dexia is in the form of a child, so let me stop you from ever using that word in connection with her." I followed when he wove his way around the Starborn who had been put to work. "Quinn and Ella were...er...occupied a short while ago. Hopefully they will be quick about it so that we can leave, although Deo, I truly am worried—"

"And that's where you are at fault." He went to the area where the horses were tethered, thumping his stallion on the shoulder when the horse lifted a rear hoof at him. "If Kiriah has removed her blessing from you, worry won't restore it. If she has not, then it's a waste of time. Therefore, you must stop fussing about that which is beyond your control, and focus instead on achieving our goal."

"I withdraw my label of heroic, and replace it with annoying," I told him, and quickly gave both Penn and Buttercup their breakfast before hurrying off to make my own ablutions.

Chapter 14

"Where did Mayam go?"

Allegria, who rode next to Hallow, glanced up at him with an odd expression: part chagrin, part annoyance. "I'm not sure. We parted ways before we got to Nether Wallop. She said I was running around in circles, and that the Askia would get us sooner or later, and she wouldn't remain to be slaughtered by them when Nezu needed her." Her lips thinned for a moment. "I know it's wrong of me to be glad she went off on her own— Sandor would never let me hear the end of such callousness when I should show only compassion to others—but by Kiriah's ten tiny toenails, Mayam was beyond irksome. Why do you ask?"

"I was just curious as to what happened to her." He was silent for a few minutes while they rode. The sun was now past prime. For the last six hours, conversation had been desultory, as each member of the company became lost in his or her own thoughts. Hallow certainly had been consumed with his. He'd considered and discarded many plans to draw Nezu out into the mortal world; he had no patience to sit around and wait for the god to emerge. He said more to himself than to Allegria, "I wish I had Aarav at my side for what is to come, but he was much too badly wounded to accompany us."

"You were far more grievously wounded, and yet you don't seem to have a problem riding," Allegria pointed out, running yet another assessing eye over him.

He smiled to himself, feeling both cherished and loved. "That is no doubt due to your ministrations, my heart. I couldn't fail to heal simply from your nearness."

"Mmhmm." She didn't give him the scathing look that such blatant flattery deserved, indicating she was deep in thought. The others appeared to be likewise occupied; only Quinn and Ella chatted quietly ahead of them. Deo rode at the head of the line, with Idril close behind him and Dexia behind her.

"Is something worrying you?" he couldn't help but ask his wife. He hated to see her looking as if she'd lost her best friend. He liked it much more when she was teasing him, her eyes sparkling with humor and desire. "If you are still worried that Kiriah has forsaken you—"

"No, I think that concern, at least, has been struck from my list of things to fuss about, as Deo so insensitively put it." Allegria held up an arm. Not just her hands, but both her arms now glowed with a golden light that dazzled the eyes. As they moved south, drawing closer to the Altar of Day and Night, she'd started to glow, the intensity growing with each passing mile. She hesitated a few seconds, casting him an unreadable glance. "Hallow, doesn't it bother you that Thorn has left us?"

"Bother me?" He shook his head. "He's always been volatile, emotionally speaking. You must surely realize that by now if he's been chattering in your head for the last few days."

"It's not the scene he threw...it's what he said." She fell silent again.

Hallow considered what Allegria had told him regarding Thorn's tantrum. "His form had been destroyed when we faced Nezu on Eris, therefore, he had no idea of what happened. It could simply be that he knows Nezu as a god, and can't conceive of us defeating him, while we know that it is possible, so long as Deo's boon can be invoked."

"I think it's more than that," she answered reluctantly.

"Do you believe he has knowledge that he's keeping from us?" he asked gently, not wishing to distress her further.

"Yes. No. Oh, I don't know." She rubbed her forehead, and he noted signs of weariness on her face. He sorely wished he could erase that tension and return her expression to one of happiness and enjoyment of life, but he didn't know how to do that.

Short of banishing Nezu.

"You said Mayam told you a tale about Nezu and the goddesses. I have not heard that account—Master Wix mentioned Nezu only in passing as the god who was responsible for the shadows—and I would be interested to hear what she had to say."

Allegria recounted a tale that was fascinating in its implications and made Hallow wish he could call a halt so that he could write down the details, but as the road swung to the east toward the coast the air took on the tang of the sea. Given Allegria's description of her journey north, he guessed they were only a handful of hours away from the altar.

What would they find once they arrived?

"This is not what I imagined," he said several hours later when Deo held up his hand for them to halt. "But I'm pleased nonetheless."

"Two ships?" Allegria, who, like Hallow, had been leading her mount, gave Buttercup a gimlet glance when the latter attempted to nip her arm, and moved ahead a few feet to gaze down the white chalky cliffs to where a ramshackle stone pier staggered drunkenly into the sea. "He must have convinced the queen and her army to come with him after all."

"Perhaps, although I doubt if much of her army remains after the Banes got through with them." Hallow's gaze moved from the ships to the few bits of broken stone that served as the pier. That the town was abandoned was quite evident from the crumbling remains of a few wooden structures. Idly, he wondered who had lived there, and what had happened to the occupants even as he lifted his hand in greeting when a man in a white and gold tunic called out. Israel led his company up a twisting, narrow path to the clifftop, but there were not nearly as many men following him as Hallow expected. "I count only two score."

"Then why two ships?" Allegria asked, disappointment in her voice. Like him, she'd noted that the queen did not ride with Israel.

"I suspect we shall find out soon enough. How close are we to the altar?"

"Less than an hour. I remember seeing that broken pier when we were running from the Askia. I thought briefly of going down to the shore, but Mayam dashed into the trees and I had to go after her," Allegria answered, sidestepping when Buttercup swung her head around, clearly intent on showing her annoyance at being kept standing. "I will admit I had hoped Lord Israel would come with a larger company. Not that they can do much with Nezu, but if the Eidolon are at the altar..."

They mounted and rode after Deo and the others to a fork that met the path climbing the cliffside. "Worry not, wife. We have something that even the Eidolon dare not face," he said, smiling to himself. Despite his own concerns, despite the grave situation that faced them, despite even the discomfort of his wounds, which he had to admit were healing at a tremendous rate, he was inexplicably filled with joy. Allegria was once again safely at his side, hale, hearty, and extremely delicious.

The chaos magic inside him stirred. He'd been grateful for its slumber, no doubt brought about by the gravity of his wounds, but now it seemed to realize that he was healing, and in the presence of the woman who made his libido sing songs of lust, fulfillment, and love. Still... "None of that, now," he murmured softly to himself, pulling arcany from the sky so that it filled him with its glittering white light. After a moment's struggle, the chaos subsided again, but he had a nagging feeling that should it rally to its full strength, he would lose the battle to control it.

Lord Israel's expression was dark when they met at the fork.

"You come without the queen's blessing?" Deo asked, forthright as ever.

Hallow gave Lord Israel a sympathetic look. The latter appeared to have aged since Hallow had last seen him, no doubt due to the strife with the Banes, as well as the trouble with the queen. "We've heard that the queen has lost her interest in combatting Nezu," Hallow said, hoping to smooth over the rough greeting Deo had offered his father. "We are pleased to have you and your company nonetheless. The battle ahead of us will be a hard one, and every eager heart will be welcome."

Israel acknowledged Hallow's diplomatic words before he eyed his son, the look of dislike quickly fading to one of annoyance. "Your mother, as ever, will not be led. She has chosen to remain with her kin. I managed to rally a few of the water talkers who were not under the sway of the priest, as well as the refugees who sought me out."

"Refugees?" Deo asked, glancing past his father to the two ships. "What refugees?"

"Ours," Israel answered before pressing his heels to his horse, causing Deo to step back lest he be trampled. "They will remain on the ship, however. They are tired, and many were wounded as they escaped Jalas's Tribe. They must have rest and time to recover."

"That is unfortunate," was all Deo said.

"I take it that, as usual, you have no company with you?" Israel asked, his gaze moving quickly over each of them. He paused for a moment on Allegria, who was now almost completely bathed in the glowing light of Kiriah. "Not that any company can do what you three together are capable of doing, but still. It seems to me that you never seem to have an army around you."

Deo rolled his eyes and mounted his horse, his runes glittering in a way that had Hallow glancing down at his own. They were quiet...at least for the moment.

"Why would I waste time with a company? Such things are for you and my mother. Allegria and Hallow and I travel much more speedily without a complement of men."

"Ahem," Idril said in an uncharacteristically forceful tone of voice.

"You do not bear powers to protect yourself as the others do, my dove," Deo told her, his voice softening as he spoke. "I would not have you battle Nezu, lest you take harm where we would not."

"Hallow was most decidedly harmed just yesterday, and yet today he is fine," Idril pointed out, but Deo ignored her protestations, urging his horse forward until he rode at the head next to his father.

Hallow exchanged a glance with Allegria.

"It's going to be a very long ride with Deo posturing, and his father antagonizing him," she told him. "Not to mention Idril trying to convince everyone that she's perfectly able to take care of herself in battle."

"I *am* perfectly able to take care of myself!" Idril yelled back, twisting in the saddle to send Allegria a glare.

Hallow sighed heavily at the same time that Allegria did the same, causing him to chuckle. "At least you can't say our lives are boring."

"Not even slightly, and remind me, in case I forget again, just how good Idril's hearing is."

Luckily for Hallow's control over his various magics, they were too far back to hear the obvious argument that Deo and Israel conducted while riding to the altar.

"We're almost there," Allegria warned a short while later and urged her mule into a trot to move up to tell Deo. Hallow followed, one hand automatically drawing arcany to him. "Deo! Hold up a minute. If the Askia are present, we need to wait for Lord Israel's company."

"—have asked you three times what else you think my boon should be used for if not sending Nezu from this world—what?" Deo paused when Allegria and Hallow joined him as the road widened into a black, lifeless track. Hallow couldn't help but rub the back of his neck, trying to dispel the odd feeling that they were being watched.

"The altar is just over that crest," Allegria said, pointing to the path ahead. She, too, glanced around with quick little movements of her head.

"This is a place of nightmares," Israel said, his expression showing that he felt the same sense of foreboding Hallow felt in his bones. "It's as if all life has been leached from the land, and it cries out in sorrow and contrition."

"Yes," Allegria said, rubbing her arms. She edged Buttercup a bit closer to Penn. "It's not a good place, although it feels so..." Her words trailed away as she continued to scan the track before them.

"Feels what?" Hallow asked, dismounting and leading Penn and Buttercup over to a relatively clear spot. A few blades of black grass grew in clumps. Hallow had no idea if the grass was savory or not, but assuming it wasn't, he readied feed bags and got them on the animals while Allegria dismounted and moved over to talk to Deo.

Lord Israel's company, being on foot, moved more slowly than those who were mounted, and since Deo saw the wisdom of not outpacing the men guarding their backs, he and his companions busied themselves hobbling their mounts and taking what refreshment they could find in such a blighted land.

"The Askia are sure to be around," Allegria was saying when Hallow returned from relieving himself. "In fact, I'm surprised they haven't met us by now. Mayam and I saw them a short while after we arrived at the altar."

"Your men are just around the bend, Lord Israel," Hallow announced. He stopped next to where Allegria sat on a tree stump, one hand tangling itself in her wild curls. He loved those curls—their refusal to be tamed reminded him of her spirit. "Perhaps the Askia have gone off in search of more interlopers?"

She shook her head, leaning into him, her face tight with worry. "I don't think so. I can...I can almost feel them. I don't know how it is, but I feel that they are around. Hidden. Unseen by us, but aware that we are here."

Hallow didn't dispute that statement since he, too, had a feeling they were not alone. The very air prickled with static, making him feel itchy with the need to be doing something.

"They're here?" Deo looked up from listening to Idril. She had been speaking quietly, but with many short, abrupt gestures of her hands, mostly consisting of her poking Deo in the chest, Hallow noted with a little amusement. Deo bore the expression of a man being called upon to exercise patience, never one of his strong points. He turned now with a grateful look, and strode over to where Israel was consulting a small map he'd drawn from his pocket. "Excellent. Now we can proceed."

"Deo!" Idril said with a little stamp of her foot. "I am not done telling you to be careful! If you get captured again, leaving me alone for another year, I swear to you that I will marry every unmarried man I see!"

Deo paused to give her a pointed look, then turned to give orders to one of his father's newly arrived men about tending the animals.

"Kiriah will be fading in an hour or less," Allegria warned, casting a glance behind her, where the sky was already starting to turn peach above the line of broken and burned trees. Beyond the trees, a low range of rocky mountains curved to the south, as if confining the desolation that all but oozed up from the land to just this area. "Mayhap we should set up a camp here for the night, so that we can face Nezu with Kiriah's full blessing."

Deo, Idril, and Hallow all turned to look at her. The golden glow that emanated from her cast the light of approximately ten torches. *Bright* torches. "I think, my heart, we can take it for granted that you have Kiriah's full support," he said with only a minor twitch of his lips.

"You're lit up like a moonbug that's been dipped in arcany and rolled in crystal dust," Deo said at the same time, obviously dismissing her suggestion. "Come. I would have this over so that Idril has no further opportunities to lecture me on the proper way to fight a god."

He strode off. Lord Israel, ending a short consultation with two of the company leaders, nodded to Hallow.

"Are you ready?" Hallow said to his wife, hesitant to ask her to do something she was clearly uncomfortable doing.

"Aye," she said with a dramatic sigh. "But if we all end up dead and roaming around the spirit world, wringing our hands and wailing that we had made so many bad choices, do not come running to me for comfort! I'll be too busy writing up large signs that read, 'I told you not to do this!'"

Hallow laughed, and with an arm around her, followed Idril and Lord Israel.

"Do you think you can release me from my servitude after this?" Quinn asked. He, Ella, and Dexia fell into step behind the others, with Lord Israel's small army on their heels. "Not that I haven't enjoyed myself running all over Genora, being shot by Lyl's army, and blown to smithereens when Deo showed up at Deeptide—not to mention gutted by one of those Askia when I tried to protect Nether Dangles—but I think, I really think I'd like to go a few weeks without being killed in some horrible manner or other."

"You should be happy to die in the service of Lady Allegria," Ella told him in a sibilant whisper that was quite audible. "Look at all she's done for us!"

Quinn shot her a startled look.

"For the Shadowborn," she corrected herself quickly. "The family who took me in now has a life beyond that of slavery and pain. All of Eris does. And you complain about a little discomfort that comes when you die. Tch."

"It hurts!" Quinn protested. "Just because I don't remain dead doesn't mean I enjoy the process of dying. Besides, I picked up a device from Red Eva that she promises will bring many hours of enjoyment. It's a swing of some sort. You sit in it with your feet in little loops, and I—"

A call from Deo ended that conversation.

"You *did* get one of those swings, didn't you?" Allegria asked, running with Hallow over the crest of the hill after Israel and Idril. "Because it really sounds like something we'd—oh, blessed Kiriah, no! They're here."

The land sloped downward to a bowl-shaped dip in the landscape, in the center of which stood a large black slab of the strange glass-like rock Hallow had absently noted. Surrounding it were twelve women, the Askia he'd glimpsed fighting the dirgesingers. Just as one of the women brought a horn to her lips, Deo lifted his sword and started forward.

"No!" Hallow called, bolting after Deo and causing the latter to hesitate. To his surprise, the woman with the horn paused, as if she was waiting to see what they would do. Hallow took that as a sign from Bellias. "We have a big enough battle to come with Nezu. I'd rather we not drain ourselves fighting everyone else beforehand. Let us see if we can't reason with the Askia first."

"Reason with them?" Deo shook his head. "Allegria said they decimated half of Lyl's army. They clearly aren't willing to be reasonable."

"Not half, just a few dozen. Let us first try diplomacy," Hallow argued.

"About this, the arcanist is right," Lord Israel said. "Let us see if they will treat with us before we risk depleting what limited resources we have."

Deo grimaced, but gestured to Hallow. "You may try, but if they kill you, don't come crying to me."

Hallow couldn't help but smile. "Oddly enough, Allegria just told me the same thing."

"That's because you insist on not heeding me," the love of his life told him, watching the Askia warily.

"May the blessings of Bellias fall upon you, Askia of the All-Father." Hallow moved forward to the lip of the concave dip in the ground, his hands spread wide to show he held no weapon. He made his courtliest bow. "I am Hallow of Penhallow, once Master of Kelos, and now seeker of knowledge. My companions and I mean no harm to you or the one whom you serve."

The Askia stood still and silent for a minute. Then, with a quick glance to those nearest her, one of them stepped forward, a sword held in one hand, a small shield in the other. "I am Mist, banner maiden and weaver of fates. What business do you have at the Altar of Day and Night, mortal?"

"We are here to banish Nezu from this world," Deo said, moving up to stand next to Hallow.

The Ask examined him, her face placid, but her eyes glittered despite the fading of the sun. "You bear the stain of his sins. Why would you banish that which you must honor, Savior of the Fourth Age?"

For a moment, Deo appeared to be taken aback, but then his runes sparked, and he all but snarled, "I honor him not. He has destroyed Starborn and Fireborn alike. He wiped Eris clear of all but a small fraction of the Shadowborn native there. He has tortured, killed, and promised retribution to those I hold dear. He threatens all of Alba, and must be sent elsewhere. That is why we three are here."

"Three?" Mist raised one eyebrow, her gaze flickering behind Hallow. "I see many more than three."

"The others are here to aid us, but it is Hallow, Allegria, and I who have the responsibility of banishing Nezu," Deo answered.

Mist moved forward, her sword still held in her hand, but her expression was almost amused when she circled around, finally returning to take up her stand in front of them. "A lightweaver, an arcanist who reeks of both Eris and its master, and a servant of Nezu. What a very odd group you are."

"I am no man's servant," Deo growled. "Certainly not Nezu's. Did you not just hear me state that it falls to us to banish him?"

"I heard," she said with a little waggle of the sword. "I also heard what you did not say."

Deo frowned.

"Guilt," she said, leaning forward, touching his chest lightly with the tip of her sword. "It lies heavily upon you. While you..." She moved to the side, her head tipped a little as she examined Hallow.

He found himself suddenly nervous, as if his old master had caught him misusing the magic he'd been taught.

"You are filled with compassion, and the fear that it will leave you weak when you need to be strong." A little smile touched her lips. "You fear for naught, arcanist."

Her gaze shifted to Allegria, whom Hallow felt stiffen in response. He twined his fingers through hers, hoping to give her the comfort he suspected she needed. "What is your name, fleet-of-foot lightweaver?"

"Allegria." She gave Hallow a quick look, adding, "I am called Hopebringer, and what Hallow and Deo say is the truth. We mean no harm to you or the All-Father. When you chased me earlier, I didn't have time to explain that."

"You think to blame us for protecting the altar from you?" Mist gave a little shake of her head, her expression not giving away any emotion. "We saw you with the betrayer. We are the Askia, defenders of the All-Father, and we tolerate no trespassers."

"We would not be here if it was not necessary," Allegria said just as Deo muttered something rude under his breath. "But Nezu will come here again. He has an agreement with the Eidolon, and it is here he will come. Thus, we must also be here."

"The Eidolon?" Mist's nose wrinkled, as if she smelled something foul. "They have long been asleep, too cowed to show their faces after their defeat at the hands of the All-Father. Why do you believe Nezu will come here—"

A ripple in the air caught their attention, interrupting the Ask. Instinctively, Hallow gathered arcany while clamping down hard on the chaos that wanted to burst into immediate action. Allegria whipped her swords from her back, spinning to look. Behind them, Hallow heard Lord Israel take up what was no doubt a protective stance, probably similar to the one Deo had adopted.

But rather than the massive, terrible figure of Nezu emerging from the spirit world, a frail old man with spiky white hair and a small fat dog emerged. He glanced around him, blinking at all the people. "Eh?" he said, just as if someone had asked a question of him.

"Exodius?" Hallow released the arcany, grateful to feel the chaos ebb. He made a short bow in deference to the former Master of Kelos. "I am surprised to see you in the mortal world. You told me you had no intention of ever returning here."

"Eh?" the old man said again, then focused his eyes on Hallow, shambling over to him, the fat dog in tow. "Ah, it's the boy. Still have the large one and the priest with you, do you? Well, that's your own business, although I don't know what you're thinking, consorting with them. The woman'll just lead you astray, and the other will spell your doom."

"Hey!" Allegria said, tucking her hand into the crook of Hallow's arm. "I will not lead him astray! And besides, we're married. If he goes astray, I go with him."

"It's neither here nor there to me," Exodius told her.

"I must insist that you leave," Mist said loudly, giving Exodius a quick glare. "There is nothing here for you."

"Not yet, but there will be just as soon as we draw him from the spirit realm," Deo told the woman. "We have no fight with you, nor, as we have all assured you, are we interested in the All-Father. Your determination to keep us from this area is misplaced. Stay and help us fight, or leave and let us do our job."

"Deo, that is not how you talk to Askia," Allegria said with obvious exasperation.

"Boy, come here. That pesky Thorn told me what you are up to. You must not do this." Exodius took Hallow by the arm and tugged him forward a few yards, speaking as he did so. "Thorn is most distressed, and I agree with him that what you intend to do is folly, sheer folly. I did not leave you in charge of Kelos just so you could gallivant off picking fights with gods."

"I assure you, Master Exodius, we are not picking a fight with Nezu. I don't know why Thorn has abandoned us, but with or without him, we must do this."

"Thorn can't help you," Exodius mumbled, dropping his sharp gaze.

Hallow had a good sense of when someone was being untruthful, and he had a very strong feeling that Exodius had just done so.

"Why not?"Allegria asked, and Hallow allowed himself to be momentarily sidetracked by Exodius' odd behavior.

"He can't," Exodius repeated, still not meeting Hallow's eyes. "It's the way of things, you understand."

"We don't understand," Hallow said with patience that was fast running thin. He glanced over to Deo, but he—along with Lord Israel—was now arguing with Mist, trying to get her to back down so that they could use the area to confront Nezu. "Explain it to us, please."

"I have no time for this. I must return to my home. Eagle and I have many things underway, many important experiments with the inhabitants of our town. We have almost perfected a spell that will keep the wraiths from moving through walls to disturb one's rest. That alone will be invaluable."

"Did Thorn say something to you about Nezu?" Allegria asked, a little frown between her brows. "Did he say something about what he—Nezu—intends?"

"It's folly, all folly," Exodius answered her. "I told the boy that, but would he listen to me? He would not. Never was one to heed my advice. Took over as Master just as bold as you please, and left Eagle and me to rot. Or was that someone else?" Exodius frowned, then squinted at Hallow. "You still here? I thought I told you about the folly you were undertaking?"

Hallow took a deep, deep breath, holding firmly onto his temper. His short time with Exodius had taught him well the value of patience when dealing with the old man. "Yes, I'm still here. We all are. And we can't leave, not just yet. We must stop Nezu."

"Oh, you don't want anything to do with him. He lies, you know. Lied to everyone about the All-Father. Lied to the twin goddesses. Lied to their people, trying to turn the mortals against them." Exodius waved away the subject of Nezu. "If you try to get any sense out of him, he'll just lie to you, too."

"What did Nezu lie about?" Allegria asked, looking just as curious as Hallow felt.

Deo snapped a rude word at the Ask, who pulled the sword she had sheathed. Lord Israel looked put-upon. Quinn, Idril, and the others were huddled together, talking softly, but keeping their eyes on Deo and Israel. Hallow turned back to Exodius.

"The All-Father, don't you see?" Exodius grasped the front of Hallow's jerkin and shook it. "That's why Thorn is worried. He fears you will summon the All-Father."

"Why would we do that?" Hallow asked, trying to puzzle out the mystery that he sensed behind Exodius' words. "The All-Father tried to destroy Alba—it's why the twin goddesses imprisoned him in the Altar of Day and Night. He is more destructive than Nezu, hard as that is to believe, so we do not wish to summon him."

"No, no, those are the lies, boy, the lies! That's what *he* wants you to believe so that the All-Father will not return and punish him for what he's done."

"Are you saying that Kiriah and Bellias didn't banish the All-Father to the altar?" Allegria asked, clearly just as confused as Hallow.

There was a shout from the Askia when Deo pushed aside Mist, marched over to the massive stone that made up the altar, and leaped upon it, declaring, "I am not leaving here until I have banished Nezu, and nothing you can say will stop me!"

"Bellias' nipples," Hallow swore to himself. "He's determined to get us into a fight with them. My apologies, Exodius. What did you say about the All-Father and the altar?"

"He always was hard of hearing," the old man told Allegria. "I was forever repeating myself to him. Always had a mind of his own, too, and wouldn't take advice. THE ALL-FATHER, BOY! I SAID HE WASN'T BANISHED."

"You don't have to yell. Despite what you believe, I can hear perfectly well," Hallow told him. "I'm afraid I don't understand what you're saying, though. The All-Father is in the Altar of Day and Night, isn't he?"

"Yes, yes, I just said that." Exodius picked up his fat dog, saying to it, "I may not have made the wisest choice for my successor, Eagle."

"Are you saying he...what, went there willingly?" Allegria asked, glancing briefly at Deo when Idril and Lord Israel approached the base of the altar stone, entreating him to come down, while the Askia gathered around him, all shaking their weapons at him. At the same time, Mist stormed around waving her hands and calling for the goddesses to witness what she had to put up with when dealing with mortals.

"Of course he did. You don't think anyone has the power to defeat the All-Father, do you? Eagle, you are getting fat. I must cut back on your after-dinner treats." Exodius set the dog down again, absently patting his pocket until he turned up part of a heel of bread, which he gave to it.

"But the story we heard says that the twin goddesses and Nezu banished the All-Father after the Eidolon angered him, and in retaliation he wanted to wipe Alba clean of all life." Hallow spoke slowly, trying to poke through the lore to work out what didn't fit. "If he wasn't banished, does that mean he didn't intend to destroy everything?"

"Of course not," Exodius said with a sniff. "He was mourning the loss of the Life-Mother. Once he saw to the downfall of the Eidolon, and confined Nezu where he couldn't cause any more trouble, he retreated to the Altar. That is why you must not summon him."

"*He* confined Nezu?" Allegria asked, rubbing a hand over her forehead. Her glow was getting brighter now even as all around them night closed in. "Not the twin goddesses?"

"Not the goddesses. But Nezu couldn't bear the shame, so he lied, and conscripted the abjurors to do his bidding when the goddesses hid their essences. What are those people shouting about?"

"Deo," Hallow said, glancing over again to make sure the arguing hadn't gone past the point of no return. "What essences do you mean?"

"The essences, boy, the essences!" Exodius' eyebrows were made up of long white tufts that Hallow thought of as little tentacles. One of them waved at him now in aggravation. "When the goddesses joined the mortals, they had to leave their essences behind somewhere. Boy doesn't think, that's what it is," he told Allegria. "He just opens his mouth and lets the words come out without first considering what he's asking."

Allegria shook her head and turned to Hallow, clearly too taken aback to put words to her confusion.

"I know how you feel," he said, kissing the tip of her delightful nose. "But I think we've almost reached the heart of it. Exodius, we don't understand when you say things like the goddesses joined the mortal world. Are they here? Now? On Alba? In physical form?"

"Of course they're in physical form. How else could they learn what went so wrong with the Eidolon if they weren't here to see what their children were up to? Nezu saw to that, of course. He whispered in their ears that what happened to the Eidolon could happen to the Starborn and Fireborn, and the goddesses couldn't risk that. So they joined the mortals, leaving behind their essences, and that is why you must not summon the All-Father."

"I think I have it," Allegria said, taking his arm, her eyes narrowed in concentration. "The All-Father is the one who banished Nezu, which means that he can banish him again. Hallow, we have to summon him. Or rather, since I don't know how we'd do that, we have to let Nezu summon him."

"No, no, no!" Exodius' hair joined the eyebrow tentacles as they waggled with irritation. "That is just the opposite of what I said! If you summon him, you will destroy us all!"

"Wait, you just said that he *didn't* want to kill everyone—" she started to say, but Hallow interrupted her.

"The goddesses left their essences behind, out of reach of the mortal realm," he said slowly, his eyes on Exodius. "Does that mean that the All-Father did the same?"

"Yes, of course! He imbued it into Alba, into us, giving Lord Israel over there the Grace of Alba. It lets you wield arcany, lets the priestess shape Kiriah's light. It is imbued into us, into Alba itself, and if you summon the All-Father, it will return to him."

"Leaving us stripped of everything," Hallow said, feeling sick.

"It will mean the death of all mortal beings," Exodius said in a softer voice, glancing around him suspiciously. "Only those out of the reach of the physical realm will exist."

"That's why Nezu made the agreement with the Eidolon," Allegria said thoughtfully. "Because they would survive the summoning. Oh, Hallow, we have to stop him. We have to—"

A noise sounded behind Hallow, a metal sliding upon metal noise that made the hairs stand up on the back of his neck.

Allegria gasped in horror just as the low murmur of startled voices from Lord Israel's company washed over them.

Hallow turned slowly, his hand on his sword hilt as the thane strode toward him, a stream of Eidolon emerging from a tear that led to the spirit world.

The thane smiled. "Come to witness the end of everything, have you? As you wish. Lord Nezu? We are ready. You may commence the summoning."

Chapter 15

"It just figures he brought Nezu with him," I told Hallow at the same time I swung around to face the onslaught. But for the second time, the Askia surprised me—they stopped arguing with Deo, and at the thane's words, instantly ran toward him, their weapons drawn.

"Deo!" Hallow shouted, gesturing, but it was unnecessary, since Deo had seen Nezu come through the rift that led to the spirit domain.

Pandemonium broke out. Exodius, yelling to Hallow to make sure the All-Father was not summoned, disappeared, taking his dog with him. Hallow started drawing in arcany, which made the hairs on my arms stand on end as the air around us seemed to thicken. Deo snarled and leaped off the altar, heading for Nezu.

Lord Israel shouted orders to his men, who joined the Askia in their attack on the Eidolon, with Lord Israel stalking toward the thane himself.

"Hallow, the shards," I swung my sword when one of the Eidolon got through the line of Askia, lunging toward us. "The moonstone shards. If we each take a piece, perhaps it will give us strength, or at least focus."

"Blast Lyl to Bellias and back—I wish I had Thorn and the staff," Hallow said, digging around in the small pouch that hung from his belt. Sounds of the battle between the Eidolon, Askia, and Lord Israel's company filled the air, echoing back to us. He held the four pieces of moonstone in his hand for a second, looking curiously at them before meeting my eye. "No," he said.

"No? No what?" I pointed to where Nezu was stalking toward Deo, somewhat hindered by the battle that raged between them. "He's here. We don't have time to dither over what to do with the pieces of the stone."

"No, I don't think we should divide them up. I think instead, we should recharge them."

"Charge how?" I asked, slashing at another foolhardy spirit who was trying to lop off my head. This one was a bit more persistent, and it took my cutting off his spectral arms and Hallow punching several melon-sized holes in him before he lost his corporeal form. "By Bellias? It's barely nightfall. The moon won't rise for a few hours."

"Deo's boon," he answered, rushing past me and calling out, "Deo! Your boon! Give me your boon!"

Deo, like Nezu, had been hacking and fighting his way through the mass of bodies. He paused to glance back, his face filled with disbelief. "Have you finally gone irrevocably mad, Hallow? I need the boon to call on Bellias so that we can send the monstrosity back to his domain!"

"I don't want to keep it, I just need it for a few minutes," Hallow answered. I ran alongside him, summarily lopping off heads and arms, and beating back spirits when even more swarmed out of the rift.

As I did so, heat grew inside me, filling me with the joyful knowledge that once again, Kiriah was with me. I stopped briefly, staring at a spirit who lifted a massive sword, about to strike me down, and thrust my palm outward to send a burning stream of sunlight through the five nearest spirits. The looks of incredulity on their faces as their forms dispersed gave me much pleasure. "Blessed, blessed Kiriah," I murmured, leaping in front of Hallow to blast the nearest spirits back to their realm. He shot me a startled look for a moment, then grinned.

"I could get used to having my own personal one-woman army. We must get to Deo's side, my heart. I'd use arcany, but I'm pulling on that to control the chaos, and I hesitate to split my concentration."

His runes had lit up red, sending a chill down my overheated flesh. Hallow had told me how he had lost control of the magic when Lyl attacked, and I knew he dreaded doing so again. "It's far better you conserve your energy for charging the stone's shards, assuming that can be done. I will keep the spirits from reaching you."

"You are the best wife in all of Alba," he said, swinging me up against his chest for a kiss that was as hot as Kiriah's fire burning in my blood.

"Hallow!" Deo bellowed, his body half turned toward us, his usual scowl in place. "If you can stop engaging in carnal acts with your wife and attend to what is important, I'd be grateful."

I pulled myself away from Hallow and his enticing mouth, and spread my hands wide, sending a wave of Kiriah's heat flowing forth in an arc, melting the spirits in its way, and clearing a path to Deo. "There is nothing more important than Hallow kissing me, but since you are being so grumpy about it—"

"Grumpy!" Deo spun around to cleave in two one of the thane's captains, who had come up behind him. "I am not grumpy! I have never been grumpy! I have been a bit distracted by the fact that my mortal enemy is even now working his way over to do goddess knows what sort of heinous act, but that, priestling, is not grumpy. Here."

He pulled from inside his tunic a small, square, silk-covered object that I recognized from the year before, when I'd retrieved the boon for him.

I peered over Hallow's shoulder while he unwrapped the silk, revealing a small wooden box. Inside it lay a crescent moon cast in silver, with glittering pale blue stones, and tiny chains from which hung a scattering of minute crystal stars. "It's so pretty! Is it an amulet? There's a chain. Can it be worn?"

"Not by a Fireborn," Deo warned, pinning Hallow with a long look. "I wouldn't trust this to anyone else. I want it back in the same condition so that I can use it to call Bellias."

"Of course," Hallow said, glancing around, obviously looking for a relatively quiet spot. He took my hand and pulled me after him, scrambling down the rocky incline to the center of the altar.

"Go ahead," I told him, turning so that my back was to his. He laid both Deo's boon and the shards of the moonstone onto the altar, his hands glowing blue-white. I felt oddly triumphant, filled to the brim with confidence, sure that nothing could go wrong. I almost danced with the joy of it all. I wanted to throw back my head and sing to the skies. The same odd sense of rushing power flowing from my fingertips built inside me, my voice deepening and taking on a slightly different timbre when I spoke. "Nothing can defeat us now. We will defeat the thane and drive him back to his crypt. We will send the Askia flying before us in fear. We will right the wrongs that Nezu has done, and when we have chained him—"

"Then what?"

My mind boggled for a second just as my body fought the sudden constriction on my throat. One moment, Nezu was ten yards away, the next he was on me, holding me by my throat, his face with its red, oiled skin thrust into mine. His eyes glittered with a dull red glow deep in their onyx depths. Noises registered in my ears, sounds of shouting and a deep voice that I recognized calling my name, but all of that faded into insignificance as I faced the monster. Fear that was both my own and foreign gripped me, my breath stopped in my throat.

"Then what?" Nezu yelled, shaking me as if I was one of Dexia's rag dolls.

A blue-white explosion lit up the side of his face, but he shoved out a hand, sending a figure flying backward. Another explosion, this one a golden red, slammed into Nezu's back, rocking us forward, but still his fingers bit into my neck, his gaze holding mine, filling me with dread. Behind him, a curtain of shimmering red chaos magic formed a barrier around us, separating us from Hallow and Deo.

Slowly, one of Nezu's lips curled. "You do not speak, sister? I thought not. It was ever thus with you. Ah, I see by the fear dawning in your eyes that you did not know I recognized you. I will admit the stink of Bellias that is wrapped around you threw me off, but in the end, you gave yourself away."

With a noise that was filled with disgust and loathing, he tossed me onto the altar. I lay gasping for breath, my brain trying to make sense of his words, of the whole nightmare scene. Sister? Nezu thought I was his sister? What madness had beset him? I pushed myself up from the rock even as I drew in painful, rasping gulps of air.

"You're mad," I managed to choke out at last. With one shaking hand, I massaged my throat, aware of Deo and Hallow nearby, but held back by Nezu's power. The world seemed to shrink down to just us four. Nezu paced back and forth in front of the altar, scratching symbols into the glass stone, droning foreign words that I didn't recognize. "I am not your sister. I am Kiriah's priest, not Kiriah herself."

"You are one and the same," he spat out, causing me to reel back as he leaned over me, his long black hair slithering over my arms. "You hid well for all those centuries, but not well enough. I bided my time, knowing the day would come when you or the other would come to taunt me. And when I smelled the scent of her arcany all over you, I knew the time had come to do what the Eidolon failed to do. This time, Alba will be mine. It will be remade in *my* image." Little flecks of spittle gathered in the corners of his mouth as he loomed over me, causing me to scramble backward. "It will be peopled by my spawn, and when the All-Father sees what I have wrought, he will be destroyed."

I tried to make sense of it, unable to tear my gaze from his to catch Hallow's eye. I shook my head, saying again, "I am not Kiriah."

"The abjurors did their work too well," he said with a low, grating laugh, then grabbed my wrist in a painful grip, and held up my hand. "The truth burns out of you, but this time, you will not triumph. You are alone, and soon, you will be destroyed in the unmaking."

"Unmaking of...Alba?" I asked on a breath, my voice once again strange, holding a resonance that I felt to my toes. And for a moment, for the few seconds it takes the heart to beat, I was calm. "You think to unmake an entire world with a few spells and runes? The All-Father will not allow it. He will not allow himself to be summoned. He will not let you use him to destroy that which he gave his life for."

"He has no choice," Nezu said, releasing my hand to inscribe more runes into the rock, and with that, the fear and confusion was back inside me, driving me upright. I wanted to flee, to run to Hallow, to protect him and urge him away from there. I wanted to call down the light of Kiriah onto Nezu, sending him back to his place of exile. I looked beyond him, past the shimmering red wall of chaos that kept my love from me. Deo stood with his head bowed, his hands outstretched as he poured wave after wave of his Kiriah-touched chaos magic into the wall, while next to him, Hallow drew symbols over the broken pieces of crystal. He suddenly stood up straight, holding in his hand the shimmering moonstone, whole again.

"Everyone has a choice," I said softly, my eyes on Hallow.

He turned to Deo, handing him back the silver moon. Deo clutched it in both hands, his eyes lifted to the sky, his mouth working while beyond them both, black shadows danced in and out of the glow of the red wall of chaos. I could see Lord Israel's men, and Quinn, and Idril fighting with the Eidolon. Everyone I cared about was here, counting on us to stop the horror who stood before me. I looked back at Hallow. He doubled over, the moonstone held in his hand, his runes turning black. I knew he was dangerously close to losing control, and with the moonstone as a focus for it, this time he would not survive the explosion of chaos magic. None of us would. My gaze settled on Nezu, and I smiled. "I am not Kiriah Sunbringer," I said loudly, my voice carrying over the rush of power that flowed around me, over even the sounds of battle. "But if I was, I would die rather than see you destroy everything I made."

Nezu glanced up from his runes just as I leaped off the altar, my hands thrust forward, slamming every morsel of light I had gathered into the wall of chaos. And then Hallow was there, his arms wide, his head thrown back, a beacon in the darkness, as light poured out of him, thick, red waves crashing forward, covering the altar. Deo shouted something, and then he, too, let his control slip, thrusting the amulet toward Nezu. The peculiar golden red chaos caught the monster and sent him reeling to the side. My gaze on Hallow, I sent up a prayer to Kiriah to save my love, the man who was everything to me. I poured her light onto him, bathing him in the golden fire, protecting him from the black corruption that had started to eat its way up his legs.

"Bellias Starsong, I call due your boon!" Deo bellowed, his voice echoing in my bones. "Grant me your power that I may banish Nezu to the Altar of Day and Night."

A black shape flickered in and out of the broken trees, the fleeting shape of a bird catching the edges of my vision.

Thorn flashed over the top of Hallow, diving through the light I poured on him and disappearing into it. For a moment, the silhouette of a woman formed in the blackness beyond the burnt trees, her face in shadow, her voice as soft as the wind. "Only joined, Savior of the Fourth Age. What was put asunder, must again be joined."

And then she was gone.

A sob caught in my throat, tears burning my eyes. My hands and heart and soul were suddenly empty of Kiriah's light. Hallow fell to his knees, his body bowed. Thorn hopped on the ground next to him.

Deo looked as thunderstruck as I felt. I threw myself on Hallow, clutching his shoulders, wanting to protect him, and kiss him, and watch his eyes light with laughter. I knew then that we had failed, that we weren't strong enough to defeat Nezu, and just as surely as Kiriah's sun would rise in the morn, Nezu would destroy us.

Nezu snarled in his strange language, regaining his feet right at the moment that Deo's chaos ran dry. He spat an oath, then said in that horrible, grating voice, "Did you think it would be so easy? I am not such a fool—"

Tears fell from my eyes onto Hallow's bent head where he knelt doubled over, my vision blurring.

Nezu stopped speaking, an indescribable expression crawling over his face. Deo, panting, his shoulders sagging, had started toward him with his sword in hand but now stumbled and stopped, staring when the altar behind Nezu shifted, moving as if it was liquid so that it spread out under Nezu's feet.

"This cannot be! You are not of this plane!" He stared down at the blackness moving up his legs in incomprehension, then fury filled his face, causing a red corona to form around him that snapped out at us, tearing into my soul. I cried out and pulled Hallow to me even as he struggled against me, wrapping his arms around me and pulling me tight against his body, twisting so as to protect me.

Nezu's gaze caught mine, holding it with a power that made every part of my being scream in agony. "You will not—"

And then he was gone. The altar, which had sucked him into its inky depths, stood before us solid and immovable once again, with the light of the Eidolon's torches glinting off it.

Chapter 16

"Do we say 'By Allegria's nipples' now when we wish to exclaim about something?"

Quinn, his jerkin covered in blood, one arm hanging lower than the other, and his hair matted with dirt and sweat, staggered over to where I knelt next to Hallow, trying to peel his tunic off over his head so I could see the wounds in his back.

I paused in that act to glare at Quinn.

He dropped to his knees, grimacing in what I assumed was meant to be a smile.

"I am *not* Kiriah. Don't you think I'd know if I was a goddess? I'm her priest, that's all. Nezu clearly was in Eris too long and confused me with her because she sometimes favors me with her power. Hallow, stop struggling. I must check your wounds to see what sort of damage the chaos did to you. It was very clever of you to release it upon the altar, protecting the All-Father inside from Nezu, but I saw how much pain it caused you."

He said something that was too muffled to understand. I finally managed to pull the tunic off, exposing his glorious chest. I braced myself to find it scarred and bloody from the battle he'd had within himself, but to my surprise—and utmost pleasure—there was no damage. "It's just your chest," I said, looking up to catch his gaze. His eyes, his wonderful, dancing blue eyes, looked weary but triumphant, and so filled with love it made me feel as if Kiriah was blessing me anew.

"*Just* my chest?" He smiled, his eye crinkles making my insides flip flop with happiness. He sighed in mock regret. "And to think you used to write odes to my chest. How a year of marriage changes things."

"I have a nice chest," Quinn said, then toppled forward onto his face. "Many women have said so. Ow."

"Your chest fills my soul with joy, my heart with love, and my body with profound lust," I said, unable to keep from caressing the lovely planes of it as the soft golden curls tickled my fingers. "As you well know. What I meant was that I expected the chaos to harm you. It looked as if it was consuming you.

"It was," he said, pulling me forward into a kiss that steamed my lips and lit a fire in my blood. "I couldn't control it any longer. I hoped the moonstone would allow me to direct it, but that was all I could hope for. Until you saved me."

"Is there a healer about?" Quinn asked, moaning softly.

"*I* saved you?" I shook my head, remembering the need I'd felt to bathe Hallow in Kiriah's light. "Oh, that. I wasn't sure—it just seemed to me that if Kiriah's light brought life to Alba, then it must protect you."

"It did much more than protect me," he said, his eyes crinkling again as he kissed my fingers, then turned my hand over so my palm was up. He placed on it a curved metal object, dull gray that was singed black in spots.

"That's…that's your cuff. The one with the runes. Goddess, did I blow those off you like I did myself when I channeled Kiriah in Abet? But I didn't channel her this time. She just fed me her power." Horror filled me at the thought of the chaos running amok inside Hallow, uncontrolled by his cuffs. I got to my feet, saying quickly, "Don't move. Just stay quiet. I'll get Deo, and we'll make you another cuff so that the chaos won't harm you—"

"You could fetch a healer for me while you're at it," Quinn said, managing to roll himself over onto his back and wave a feeble hand in the air.

"My heart, my heart, for someone who apparently has a goddess living inside her, at times you are exceptionally unaware of what goes on around you." He got to his feet and put his hands on my shoulders before planting a kiss on my forehead. "You did more than just protect me with your light—you burned the chaos out of me. It was consuming me, but then your light destroyed it just as surely as it would have destroyed me. If you need any further proof that you are Kir—"

I clapped a hand over his mouth, furious, irritated, and so in love my eyes swam with tears of gratitude. "Don't say it!"

"Kiriah would find me a healer. She likes me," drifted up from our feet.

"I would know if I was a goddess!" I told Hallow, who just kissed my fingers where they lay across his lips. "Look at me! I'm not even glowing anymore. I'm just plain old me, a priestess and a lightweaver, born of a poor, ignorant, superstitious family. A goddess wouldn't pick someone

like me if she wished to hide from Nezu, not that I understand that. Why
would the goddesses feel the need to be mortal?"

"That is something I very much wish to know, and I suspect we will
find out. But first, Lord Israel is approaching, and he does not look happy."

"Of course I'm not happy. May Kiriah blast that thane and all his
horde—just as I was about to best him and drain him of the last of his
power, he retreated into the spirit realm again. How is one supposed to
fight a spirit if he keeps running away?"

"Are you, by chance, a healer?" Quinn asked softly when Ella squatted
next to him, tsking over the blood covering him.

"No, but I do know how to make you sing with happiness when I flex…
er…" She gave a soft cough, blushed, and busied herself dabbing at his wounds.

"You!" Deo stomped over from where he'd been allowing Idril to fuss
over the few scratches he'd endured during the fight with the Eidolon.
He limped slightly, but the anger in his eyes was reflected in his glowing
runes. "You are Kiriah Sunbringer! It was *your* sister who refused me aid
when I called upon her! What good is a boon if there is a condition upon
its use? I demand you make her explain herself!"

"I told him using the boon would do no good, but he heeds not my
counsel," Lord Israel said to no one in particular.

"I am going to say this just one more time, and then I expect everyone
to let it drop, because I'm already getting tired of this." I leaped onto the
altar and turned to face the people who were slowly recovering from the
fight. Torches bobbed as the Askia milled around in the background, hauling
the wounded and dead to one side, while the few who were mobile moved
forward to form a semicircle. Light flickered and moved with the breeze
from the shore, making shadows dance eerily. Despite that, I lifted my chin
and said in a near shout, "Nezu was wrong! I am not Kiriah Sunbringer!
I am her priestess, and a lightweaver, and yes, sometimes I am blessed in
her sight, but blessed does not a goddess make! Half the time I can't even
pull her power—she only seems to give it to me when it pleases her, which
again, is not something I would do if I had her abilities! And I swear, if
just one more person tells me I'm Kiriah, I will smite them!"

"You do know that only goddesses can smite others at will," Deo pointed
out, but some of the anger in his face eased.

I pointed at him. "You're going to be first if you keep that up!"

"Allegria!" he roared, outraged.

"Well, stop being so annoying," I snapped, taking Hallow's offered hand
and jumping down off the altar. "It's as much as a sane woman can bear."

"Ah, my heart," Hallow said, giving me a swift kiss before turning me and gently pushing me up the incline to the road. "I can see that you will ever keep me on my toes what with all the smiting, and chest odes, and swing usage there is in our future."

"There is much that remains to be done," Deo said an hour later as we headed north while several men with torches led the way. Those of us who were Fireborn disliked traveling at night, but no one wanted to remain at the altar, even if the Askia would have allowed it. As it was, they had hustled us out of there as quickly as they could manage, saying not one word about what had happened. "I have made a list."

"How very scholarly of you," I said. "The next thing we know, you will read a book."

"I read books all the time, priestling," he said with lofty disregard of the fact that he'd told me the year before that he never understood the attraction that 'dusty old tomes' held for Hallow. "Idril suggested I make a list, so that we might prioritize the many claims on my attention. First and foremost, I must reclaim Starfall for my mother. Lyl will not go unpunished for what he has done."

"No, the first thing on the list is returning to Aryia, so that I may take my father's place leading the tribe," Idril insisted, steering her horse close enough that she could smack him on the thigh.

"Then, of course, we must free my mother from whatever hold the water talkers have on her," he continued, absently rubbing his thigh.

"First the Tribe of Idril, then Starfall, then the queen," Idril corrected.

"What about the thane?" I asked, glancing at Hallow. He'd been silent for the last half hour, but he didn't look as if he was ailing. His back wounds had healed up—no doubt thanks to Kiriah's blessed light—and he said that he could no longer feel the chaos magic within him. "He could pop out of the spirit world at any time and attack again."

"For what purpose?" Deo asked.

I thought about that. "Well…he doesn't like us. Revenge?"

"It's possible, but not very probable," Deo allowed. "In any case, the Eidolon are the arcanist's problem. As Master of Kelos, he should have the ability to deal with them."

"Yes, well, until Lyl gives him back Thorn's staff and relinquishes that title, the point is moot," I said, nudging Hallow's calf with the toe of my boot. Buttercup didn't appreciate my riding her so close to Penn in order to do so, and tried to nip the horse on the shoulder.

"Hmm?" Hallow looked over to me, frowning at Buttercup's bared teeth. "No," he told her, moving Penn to the side a smidgen. "He has done nothing wrong, and you may not take out your bad temper on him."

Penn nodded his head in agreement.

"The Eidolon?" I asked Hallow.

"What about them?"

"Are they going to attack again?" I searched his eyes, but there was no shadow of pain in them, no sign of anything worrying him. Perhaps he was tired, or just introspective after the confrontation with Nezu.

He thought about that question. "That's hard to say. They have no reason to now that Nezu is out of their reach. But the Eidolon are not noted for their willingness to let slights to their honor merely fade away, so they might wish to seek revenge."

"Add the Eidolon to your list," I told Deo.

"No. They are your problem, not mine," he answered, stubborn as ever. "Last on the list is to return to Eris and destroy any Harborym who remain there."

It seemed to me that there was much more to be done, but my mind was too tired to pull together my own list of tasks.

It was morning, and Kiriah—the real one, not me—sent the sun to warm the lands and the hearts of her people just as we arrived back at Nether Wallop. I was exhausted, but oddly contented at the same time when I stood in the main room of Red Eva's house, watching Hallow negotiate a bedchamber for us. Idril and Quinn—whose natural healing abilities had healed up the worst of his injuries—were arguing over whose turn it was for the room with the two ceiling hooks when Lord Israel entered the room, glancing around it.

He stopped next to me, his eyes shadowed. I'd never felt comfortable with him, not since he'd first tried to have me imprisoned and beheaded, then later succeeded in having me banished from my own temple.

"She fought like the warrior she truly was," he said softly, his eyes watching Deo when the latter took Idril's hand and hauled her, still protesting that Quinn didn't deserve the two-hook room, into the nearest bedchamber.

I looked at Israel in confusion for a moment, wondering if he was talking about Kiriah. Then my eyes burned. I blinked rapidly a few times. "She was a remarkable woman. I owe her much."

"You do. We all do. Alba has been diminished with her leaving it. I would not have you think that her death was senseless, however. Her actions protected many lives."

I said nothing, just folded my hands and sent a prayer to Kiriah that would she let her beloved priestess Sandorillan know how many lives she'd touched.

Lord Israel turned his head to consider me, his dark amber eyes examining my face with an impersonal, almost detached air. "You deny that Kiriah Sunbringer lives within you. And yet, you have done more than even her most favored supplicants. Sandor told me when she took you in that you were a special child, one whose praises I would some day sing. She said there was much about you that most people would never see."

I blinked again, pained at the thought of Sandor. "I had no idea she felt that way. She gave me no idea of that—all I ever seemed to do was give her grief," I said, rubbing away an errant tear with one knuckle. "I tried her patience endlessly. She was forever lecturing me about the proper way a priestess conducted herself, and she denied me the right to train so that I could fight the Harborym. I've always felt I was a failure in her eyes, her troublesome priest who ran off to be a soldier."

He was silent for a moment, then awkwardly patted my hand. "She loved you greatly, and took much pride in you. If you carry that certainty in your heart, you will never shame her."

My throat ached with the knot of tears that wanted to form. Unable to speak for a moment, I simply nodded and moved over to join Hallow, who was collecting some food and a skin of wine from one of Eva's man minxes.

"Red Eva says we may have the room as long as we wish to remain here," Hallow said, handing me bread, cheese, a couple of apples, and a huge bunch of grapes. He gathered up our bags, and the wine, and gestured toward the room we'd had before. I followed him, pausing at the door to look back at Lord Israel.

He stood alone in the middle of the room, his expression bleak.

"The queen—" I stopped, unsure of what I wanted to say.

He raised an eyebrow in question.

I hesitated for a few seconds, then gave a little mental shake of my head. "We will not let her remain bespelled."

He said nothing, but gave a little nod of his head, then turned on his heel and strode out of the house.

Have you read all the books in the Born Prophecy series by Katie MacAlister?

Fireborn

TWO REALMS AT WAR

Thousands of years ago, the twin gods Kiriah and Bellias made a wager as to who could raise the best civilization. Kiriah created the Fireborn, the children of light, who would wield the power of the sun and the blessings of nature. Bellias nurtured the Starborn, the children of the heavens, who would harness the arcane power that rippled across the night sky and flowed through all living things. And so the battle began . . .

THREE FATES ENTWINED

As the war between the Fireborn and Starborn enters the Fourth Age, three unlikely heroes emerge. Allegria is a young priestess who longs to honor the goddess of the sun with her battle skills rather than her prayers. Hallow is an apprentice without a master, eager to explore his power over the stars. And Deo is the chosen one, a child of both worlds who could be the key to bringing peace across the land—or the ultimate weapon in the war to end all wars . . .

ONE PROPHECY FULFILLED

The time has come for these three companions to choose sides—and seal their fates—in the thrilling first novel of the epic Born Prophecy saga by bestselling author Katie MacAlister.

Starborn

THE ILLUSION OF PEACE

The battle for sovereignty among the seven lands of Alba has ended. The prophecy of Peace appears to have come true. But appearances can be deceptive. A new battle is brewing. Its outcome is dependent on the retrieval of a sacred triad of artifacts. . .

THE REALITY OF CHAOS

The hunt for the three precious moonstones begins. For Allegria, Fireborn lightweaver, and her Starborn lover Hallow, it means saving more than worlds. It means rescuing their friend Deo, prisoner in the shadowlands of Eris, where the secrets of the moonstones are buried. Steering Allegria and Hallow in their ocean quest is a mysterious lifebound captain. And he's setting sail with a warning: no mere mortal has ever survived the journey to Eris, let alone come back alive . . .

THE MYSTERY OF SHADOWS

As the bonds of friendship are threatened and the courage of three heroes challenged, the fate of two kingdoms will be at risk as bestselling author Katie MacAlister's breathtaking Born Prophecy saga continues.

CPSIA information can be obtained
at www.ICGtesting.com
Printed in the USA
BVHW081538050321
601818BV00001B/184